Watson Heston

Old Testament stories comically illustrated

Watson Heston

Old Testament stories comically illustrated

ISBN/EAN: 9783741191657

Manufactured in Europe, USA, Canada, Australia, Japa

Cover: Foto ©Andreas Hilbeck / pixelio.de

Manufactured and distributed by brebook publishing software
(www.brebook.com)

Watson Heston

Old Testament stories comically illustrated

OLD TESTAMENT STORIES

COMICALLY ILLUSTRATED

— BY —

WATSON HESTON

———

THE STORIES BEING HUMOROUSLY TOLD, AND HARD FACTS GIVEN CONCERNING
THE ORIGIN AND AUTHENTICITY OF THE OLD TESTAMENT.

———

New York
THE TRUTH SEEKER COMPANY
28 Lafayette Place

CONTENTS:

OLD-TESTAMENT STORIES COMICALLY ILLUSTRATED.

CHAPTER I.

ADVENTURES OF ADAM.

"And the Lord God formed man of the dust of the ground, and breathed into his nostrils the breath of life, and man became a living soul" (Genesis ii, 17).

That is the way the Christians tell us, that the human race happens to exist. The Bible says it, and, say they, it must be so. But it is needless to observe that it is not so at all. The idea is borrowed from preceding religions, and is no more original than true. According to Grecian mythology, the God Prometheus created man, in the image of gods, out of clay; and the God Hephaistos was commanded by Zeus to mold of clay the figure of a maiden, into which Athene, the dawn-goddess, "breathed the breath of life." The Peruvians, Collas, Caribees, and North American Indians believed that the human race originated from the soil. In fact, the

North American Indians' theology is very similar to Christianity, but the Indians could never have heard of Jesus Christ. The same belief was prevalent in Egypt, China, India, and Mexico. The Chaldeans asserted that man was made by mixing of the blood of Belus with the dust of the ground. This belief was current with these people long before Genesis is known to have been written, and could not have been inspired by a knowledge of the Bible legend.

But strange as is the origin of man, in this tale, the first woman was formed still more strangely. When God made the beasts he made two sexes, but when he manufactured Adam he seems to have forgotten the most important part of the family. He had used up his material, and with the finishing of the universe his power to make something from nothing ceased. So he "caused a deep sleep to fall upon Adam, and he took one of his ribs, and closed up the flesh instead thereof. And the rib which the Lord God had taken from man, made he a woman, and

And the Lord God formed man of the dust of the ground, and breathed into his nostrils the breath of life, and man became a living soul.—Gen. ii. 17.

brought her unto the man." The meeting of this uniquely made pair is thus described by an inspired writer: "It is Sunday, January 8, 4004 B.C. Morn has just rolled up the curtain of the night and opened the front door. A man walks in a garden admiring the beauties of nature. It is Adam. He does not know that since he went to sleep last night he has been deribbed and provided with a helpmeet. He has not as yet counted his ribs this morning and is insensible of his loss. He is about to be enlightened. At a short distance he perceives a creature who is his exact counterpart except in a few unimportant items. He approaches and it recedes. Adam murmurs, 'This is one too many for me, but I suspect it is my intended.' Counting his ribs, he discovers that one is missing, and is convinced. 'If so,' he continues, 'she will approach. Ah! she comes!' He is quite right. She comes, holding in her hand the large fifty-cent bouquet shown in the engraving which accompanies this sketch. 'I presume,' he says, turning toward her, and lifting his hat with one hand, while speaking with the other, 'I presume that I have the pleasure of addressing Eve, the mother of our race. I trust that you will par-

don my unshaved face. It is the Sabbath, and all barber-shops are closed out of respect for the sacred character of the day. Madam, I'm Adam. May I trouble you to marry me?' Eve, for it was she, jumped at this her first offer, landing lightly on both feet. It was in the gloaming that the wedding took place; and as Adam approached the bride to place upon her willing hand the marriage-ring, he said. 'My dear, can you tell me why I resemble the departing day?' 'I can,' she replied; 'it is because you are drawing near Eve.' Thus was committed the original sin."

The superstitious ignorance of the early Christians is noway better shown than by the fact that they believed that man has one rib less than a woman. The first heretic was the gentleman who counted his wife's ribs.

The world is greatly indebted to this rib, however. Had Adam not succumbed to its winning charms, the world would still be peopled with naked idiots. Without this rib, as has been well said, we should have had no knowledge, no reason, no experience, no choice, no progression; but instead, a childlike simplicity, a trusting confidence, an unquestioning credulity,

And the rib, which the Lord God had taken from man, made he a woman, and brought her unto the man.   Gen. ii. 22.

would have pervaded the whole human family. It was this way: "And out of the ground made the Lord God to grow every tree that is pleasant to the sight, and good for food; the tree of life also in the midst of the garden, and the tree of knowledge of good and evil. And the Lord God took the man and put him into the garden of Eden, to dress it, and to keep it. And the Lord God commanded the man, saying: Of every tree of the garden thou mayest freely eat; but of the tree of knowledge of good and evil thou shalt not eat of it; for in the day thou eatest thereof thou shalt surely die." This was before Eve was born, and Adam, like a Sunday-school boy who dies young, obeyed the command and was content to be a fool. However, he must have had a streak of good material in him, for when Eve appeared the submission to authority and respect for vested rights ceased. The same inspired writer before quoted describes the beginning of the rebellion. "One day when apples were ripe Eve came to her husband with the following interesting story: During her innocent rambles within the confines of the garden she had fallen in with a gentleman of polite address, who entered into discourse with her. He called her attention to the superior quality of the fruit on the tree of knowledge, and assured her that the city ordinance forbidding her to eat of it had some years since fallen into a desuetude that was quite innocuous. He gave her further instructions as to family life in the suburbs. The gentleman called himself a parson, and did business as a serpent under the name of Satan. Adam grew quite interested, and the account says that 'she gave also to her husband with her, and he did eat.' Thenceforward the tree of knowledge was always full of clubs. It became, in the course of time, Adam's favorite fruit, and he made up his mind as soon as the spring opened to set scions from it in every tree in the orchard. How certain other events interfered with his plan we shall soon see."

The certain other events were as follows: "Adam let nature take its course, and had nearly ceased to think of his disobedience of orders, when one evening as he and his amiable consort were promenading the garden in the cool of the day, and had just hooked another hatful of apples, they saw what they afterward found out was a voice, walking down the path

And they heard the voice of the Lord God walking in the Garden in the cool of the day; and Adam and his wife hid themselves from the presence of the Lord God amongst the trees of the Garden.—Gen. iii, 8.

toward them. Adam remarked that a fellow always sees queer game when he has forgotten to take his gun along. He also deemed it prudent to conceal himself and await developments. Presently the voice cleared itself and inquired, grammatically. 'Adam, where art thou?' Adam said, 'Present.' 'Come out of that,' continued the voice. 'Excuse me,' replied our heroic but dignified first parent, 'I am not appareled for dress parade. Neither was Eve expecting company. Call some other time; this is my busy day.' The voice receded, with the observation that it was about time to turn the dog loose."

At this time Adam and Eve were appareled only in aprons of fig-leaves, and the voice, being of gentlemanly instincts, did not intrude, but instead retired and started a tailor shop, making them coats of skins of the fashion as shown herewith. The monkey, it will be observed, was even at that time of an imitative disposition, and seems to have kept pace with the times. The origin of the "Grecian bend," a style of ladies' dress which became old some time in the seventies of the nineteenth century, is here clearly traced to our first mother. Adam, however, did not wear trousers; they were introduced at

a much later period by Dr. Mary Walker, a subscriber to THE TRUTH SEEKER.

The farther adventures of Adam are thus graphically described by our inspired writer: "'Therefore the Lord God sent him forth from the Garden of Eden to till the ground from whence he was taken.' In these words does the writer of Genesis describe the primitive agricultural operations of our early ancestors. With the picture on page 17 in mind, we can better understand that 'no man who putteth his hand to the plow and turneth back is fit for the kingdom of God.' A man capable of such a feat with the appurtenances before us would do better in conjunction with a circus. Exactly how the eviction of our first parents was effected, it is not permitted us to know, but it is supposed that Adam heard a voice speaking in the night, saying unto him, 'Git,' and he got. This might also have been supplemented by a large dog with a disagreeable disposition running loose among the parterres. The long steps which Adam and Eve appear to be taking (see page 19) indicate that they are in haste. The gentleman with wings standing at the corner of the wall is a cherubim. The object which he holds in his

Unto Adam also and to his wife did the Lord God make coats of skins, and clothed them.—Gen. iii, 21.

haud is not a windmill. nor yet a steamboat pro-
peller. It is a sword which looketh four ways
for Sunday, as described in Genesis third chapter and twenty-fourth verse. But Adam did not
always remain a farmer. At the age of nine
hundred years he wrote a book on "How to
Live a Million Years and Grow Old Gracefully."
This work he sold about the country until in the
year 3074 B.C. a law was passed making a book
agent punishable by death. Then one day as
he rang the door-bell of a fashionable up-town
residence and asked to show the lady of the
house his little work on 'How to Live a Million
Years and Grow Old Gracefully,' somebody
threw a brick. The account simply says, 'And
all the days of Adam were nine hundred and
thirty years: and he died.' The next day's
papers turned their column rules, and chroni-
cled the death of the oldest inhabitant, but
there is sufficient reason to believe that little or
no inquiry was instituted into the mysterious
circumstances attending his demise.

"The funeral of Adam, which was largely attended, took place under the auspices of the
Ancient Order of Hibernians, the officiating
clergyman dwelling touchingly and at length
upon the virtues of the deceased; his long residence in the community; his great labors in
natural history, particularly in the nomenclature
of species; his public spirit as a citizen: his
work as author of a remarkable treatise on
'How to Live a Million Years and Grow Old
Gracefully,' and above all his exemplary piety
as a Christian. The clergyman likewise bespoke
the sympathy of all for the bereaved relict,
promising to call upon her often himself and
administer to her the consolations of religion—a
promise which he fulfilled in such good earnest
that his attentions to Eve did not fail to become
the subject of scandal. He hath many imitators
at this day.

"The following touching verse on the demise
of Adam and the disposition of his personal
effects is attributed to Thothmes Obeliskus, a
contemporary, translated from the original
Greek at the same time as was the New Testament:

"Soth putt awaye ye spyketak guy, the whf' dyd Adome weare,
And eke putt hye ye trowsern hi—they were hys favouryte
    peare,
His waystcote ahold to herthen enld anoon be carryed
Y wole hys hatts bee gin to Put too weare vpon hys bed.

Therefore the Lord God sent him from the Garden of Eden, to till the ground from whence he was taken.—Gen. iii. 23.

Sayute Patryk e caye, on ye hiwaye, whence that tyme comen
    round,
Be yck, a bryck both longe and thycke mite in that sayme be
    found,
Hee shall yt pawe at kirk for femmen, en, on or offe, wee hope,
Whate'er that Pat hathe in hys hatte belongeth too ye pope."

In closing these adventures of Adam, we will discuss the story seriously just enough to remark that it is now recognized by all intelligent people to be only a legend and of no importance except as the babyish ideas of a people having no scientific knowledge. It is one of the nursery tales of the race. "Man has existed on this planet, ruder in form and character the farther we go back, for hundreds of thousands of years. Long before events alleged to have occurred in the garden of Eden, there were millions of civilized men in Egypt and India and probably in Assyria and China; and long before that in the obscurity of prehistoric ages, the earth was peopled by barbarians. These, also, were preceded by savages who, in their turn, had succeeded the ape-like progenitors of mankind." But "the rejection of the Bible account of the peopling of the world involves also the rejection of the entire scheme of Christianity. According to the orthodox rendering of both New and Old Testament teaching, all men are involved in the curse which followed Adam's sin. But if the account of the fall be mythical, not historical; if Adam and Eve—supposing them to have ever existed—were preceded on the earth by many nations and empires, what becomes of the doctrine that Jesus came to redeem mankind from a sin committed by one who was not the common father of all humanity? Reject Adam, and you cannot accept Jesus. Refuse to believe Genesis, and you cannot give credence to Matthew, Mark, Luke, John, and Paul. The Old and New Testaments are so connected together that to dissolve the union is to destroy the system. The account of the creation and fall of man is the foundation-stone of the Christian church. If this stone be rotten, the superstructure cannot be stable. It is therefore most important that those who profess a faith in Christianity should consider facts which so vitally and materially affect the creed they hold."

So he drove out the man: and he placed at the east of the Garden of Eden cherubims, and a flaming sword which turned every way, to keep the way of the tree of life.—Gen. iii, 24.

CHAPTER II.

THE ORIGIN OF THE YOUNG MEN'S CHRISTIAN ASSOCIATION.

Sacrifice, the Bible dictionaries tell us, is "one of the most important elements of divine worship common to all nations of antiquity, and therefore traced by some to a primeval revelation. The best and first fruits of the soil, the finest and most immaculate animals of the flock, are offered to the gods." It is said that the animals the skins of which were used to make coats for Adam and Eve, were sacrificed to Jehovah; but by whom, unless it was the Lord himself, no one can tell. But sacrificial rite was certainly the cause of the first murder recorded in the Old Testament.

The Lord God, our God, has always been fond of sacrifices—at least his priests have, for the reason that the sacrifices or offerings of the people always fell to them. Therefore it is natural that the rite should be perpetuated. In former days the priests asked for food offerings. The Most High, as Voltaire says, "kept a very sumptuous table; men, children, oxen, sheep, and the firstlings of the flock were served up to him," or to his priests, which is the same thing. And we see the survival of this in the donation parties of the present day, when the people bring to the minister the best potatoes and turnips and the straightest sticks of cordwood that they possess. But since the clergy have been generally placed on salary, money is the most acceptable offering to the Lord.

That the priests of the Lord were not formerly vegetarians is clearly shown in the story of Cain and Abel, and to impress upon the people the desirability of bringing fat lambs for their tables they invented the tragedy of Cain and Abel as recorded in holy writ. But that's another story. The present tale, dealing with the only known origin of the cabalistic letters Y. M. C. A., is as follows, according to a certain inspired writer of our own, who, we can only regret, has not explained more of the divine mysteries:

"1. Abel was a keeper of sheep, but Cain was the tiller of a canal-boat.

"2. And in process of time it came to pass that there was a donation party in the house of the high priest.

And Cain talked with Abel his brother: and it came to pass, when they were in the field, that Cain rose up against his brother and slew him.—Gen. iv, 8.

"3. And upon the day thereof Cain went forth into his garden and yanked from the soil the handsomest bunch of onions that he had

"4. Likewise did Cain jerk from the vines an homer and a half homer of cucumbers; also green corn from the cornstalk.

"5. And these things did Cain superimpose upon an ark which is known in this day as a wheelbarrow; and upon the top thereof was a pumpkin: the same had scooped the first prize at the agricultural fair at Pumpkinville.

"6. And Cain brought them unto the house of the high priest, walking between the handles of the ark; and laid them upon the altar; and he said, Behold now shall my name appear in the county paper.

"7. Now Abel's offering was a spring lamb of great fatness, and when the high priest saw it,

"8. Behold he caused it to be roasted; and great was the roast thereof.

"9. But it came to pass that he ate of the cucumbers which Cain had brought; and

"10. They doubled him up, and he scorned the offering of Cain, and chucked the whole business out of the window.

"11. Then was Cain wroth, and he waxed angry because the high priest had respect unto the offering of Abel and had not shown a proper appreciation unto the pumpkin.

"12. And Cain rose up and stretched forth his hand and laid hold on a biscuit which a virgin had made;

"13. And he threw the biscuit at the high priest; but the priest being wary betook himself beneath the altar, and the biscuit passed by.

"14. And it was so that Abel, standing behind the high priest, received the biscuit in his vitals.

"15. And he said, Behold there is something in my bowels which I have not swallowed; and he yielded up the ghost."

After this sad occurrence the Lord exiled Cain, who went to the land of Nod, which was the Canada of those times. The mark was put upon him to prevent the populace of Nod from slaying him, as the members of the Y. M. C. A. nowadays label themselves to prevent the fool-killer from doing his duty. Cain was the first member of the association, and his successors have nobly upheld his reputation, though instead of being slayers of men they are now noted as "lady-killers." This is only one of thousands of instances where evolution has modified species.

And the Lord set a mark upon Cain, lest any finding him should kill him.—Gen. iv, 15.

CHAPTER III.
SUSTAINING A THEORY.

Enoch was, so the ministers say, transported into heaven without the experience of death. How this was accomplished no one has until now attempted to tell. But the manner illustrated by our artist is undoubtedly the one used, as is proved by the following syllogism:

1. God made man in his own image, consequently God is a man. 2. When a man lifts a boy who is wearing his first pair of trousers he chooses as a grasping-place that part offering the largest spare surface. 3. God being a man and Enoch in comparison a small boy, God therefore took hold of Enoch's clothes in the place corresponding to the broadest surface of a small boy's garment.

Any theologian who disputes the accuracy of our picture is hereby challenged to disprove it, and to prove his denial. If he denies it, what will he give us in its place? Everything goes to show that it is so. The position of Enoch proves it; the hand reaching down is corroborative evidence; the upward gazing of the two spectators reveals it; the apparent solicitude of the simian lest Enoch falls is conclusive testimony; and if these are insufficient, the fact that God took him irrefragably demonstrates the correctness of the artist's theory. It is the crucial test, for where else could he have taken hold of him to such good advantage? In short, the claim of this theory is stronger than that of any other, which is easily shown by a reference to a few palpable facts. 1. The size of the hand. It is neither so small as to be contemptible nor so large as to render such grasp impracticable. 2. The simplicity of the theory. It is natural, free from pedantry, without affectation. 3. It is candid; there is no ingenious attempt to make a plain matter difficult to show the learning of the author. 4. It is infinitely suggestive. There never was a man who could say, I do not understand it. 5. It is exhaustive. It stops all criticism at once by explaining just how it could be done; and no man can say it was *not* done so. 6. It is reasonable and practicable. It shows humility, patience, contentment, forbearance, peaceableness, gentleness—in short, the precepts of the twelfth chapter of Romans are all illustrated by it. Therefore it must be believed, or something given in its place.

And Enoch walked with God; and he was not; for God took him.—Gen. v, 24.

CHAPTER IV.

SOME GIANTS.

MARRYING and begetting children was a favorite pastime of the old patriarchs whose histories are set forth in holy writ, but they had the example of the sons of God, who saw the daughters of men, that they were fair, and took them for wives, with the result that there were giants in the earth in those days, who thought no more of elevating an ordinary mortal by the ear than the Brobdignagians would have thought of lifting a Lilliputian. Naturally those not so elevated would flee to escape the closer acquaintance of the giants. We must believe of course that God had sons, and that these sons married the daughters of men, for it is in the Bible. But the sons are not be censured. If they had not wanted the daughters of men they should have been exiled to Wyoming, where a heavy tax on bachelors is proposed. Who these sons were, however, and where they came from, the account does not state: but it is presumed that they came down from heaven, and were angels, who have always been favorites with godly women. It may be that it was these sons who visited Sarah, Rebecca, Rachel, Manoah's wife, Hannah, and Elisha's Shunamite woman, none of whom bore children until God or an angel had visited her. Elizabeth and Mary also may have seen these sons, though it is not stated in history that John the Baptist and Jesus were giants.

The truth is, this story is just a story. Every nation, as one commentator writes, has similar legends of "mighty men which were of old, men of renown." They are conspicuous in the mythologies of Greece, India, China, and Scandinavia, and we find them also in the mythologies of America.

We should fail in our duty, however, should we neglect to draw attention to the great similarity between the sons of God in ancient days and the ministers of God in the present day, as regards their attentions to the fair sex. So great indeed is this similarity, that some irreverent persons in picturing God's sons have clothed them in clerical garb.

There were giants in the earth in those days.—Gen vi, 4.

CHAPTER V.

THE ADVENTURES AND WORK OF NOAH.

> There's a harmless and innocent game
> Whereof the description is poker;
> But mighty uncertain the same
> When a monkey sits in as a joker.
> —*D. Boyle.*

1. Now the sons of men dwelt in tents, and Jared dwelt over against Enos, and over against Enos dwelt Jared.

2. And Enos sat at his tent door upon a keg, which anon he smote, and the sound thereof was hollow, and the wind made music in the bunghole.

3. And Enos lifted up his voice and wept because the keg was empty.

4. Then Jared journeyed across the plain bringing a flagon: the same was the applejack of Lebanon.

5. He brought also tokens which were called cards, and the colors thereof were as the colors of the rainbow.

6. And he gave to Enos to drink, and taught him the uses of the tokens, for he was learned in all the wisdom of the faros. And the stakes wherefor they played were shekels of gold and pieces of silver.

7. And it came to pass that Enos parted the tokens and took privily unto himself a club, the king thereof; a spade, the king thereof; a heart, the king thereof, and a diamond likewise the king thereof.

8. And he said, Behold he that is diligent in business shall stand by four kings. And he stood.

9. Now Jared held three aces. But he put forth his hand secretly and took yet another ace from the hand of his servant.

10. Then did Enos say, Behold my hand is worth to seven shekels. And Jared said, I will go you seven better.

11. So Enos said, And yet seven more; and Jared said again, And yet seven more.

12. And it came to pass that Enos pledged all his shekels, and his wife, and his ox, and his household goods, and his maid-servant; yea, even his boots, and all that he had. And Jared did the like unto him.

13. Then Enos said, Show me, I pray thee, what thou holdest in thy hand: and Jared

And God saw that the wickedness of man was great in the earth, and that every imagination of the thoughts of his heart was only evil continually.—Gen. vi, 5.

showed him. So that all the possessions which were the possessions of Enos became the possessions of Jared; and he possessed them.

That the wickedness of Jared, Enos, and the other gentlemen who ornamented the earth in those days consisted especially in gambling, we do not find in holy writ. Our artist had to illustrate some form of wickedness, and chose that. In our description of the gambling scene we drew upon our imagination, and as that is a thing which Bible writers never do, we think it but fair to confess, and so obviate all possibility of our fanciful relations becoming confounded with their strictly true ones. The Bible does scarcely anything toward specifying the crimes of the time. Gen. vi. 4, 5, says that "there were giants." Also, "after that, when the sons of God came in unto the daughters of men, and they bare children to them, the same became mighty men which were of old, men of renown" —as we recounted in a previous chapter. We see no harm in being a giant. Giants in intellect, it is true, are obnoxious to God and his priests nowadays, but we can discern no ground for reprobating giants in stature. Perhaps they

were ugly customers when under the influence of excessive bibulation, and made trouble for the police. As to the "sons of God," we shall say that their father ought to have kept them at home. Another hopeless mystery is why exception was taken to the children of said "sons" and the daughters of men, who became "men of renown." The clergy are always jealous of all renown that is not their own; perhaps they calumniated these men to their heavenly patron. At any rate, certain it is that "the wickedness of man was great in the earth, and that every imagination of the thoughts of his heart was only evil continually."

But "Noah was a just man and perfect in his generations, and walked with God" (Gen. vi. 9). He may have been perfect when compared with the turbulent giants and licentious sons of God and the rest of "his generations," but perfect in our generation he would not be called, for his only recorded acts besides those in connection with the ark were the two shameful ones of getting beastly drunk and committing indecent exposure.

God's remedy for the failure of his attempt to make a workable article in the way of mankind,

Noah was a just man and perfect in his generations, and Noah walked with God.—Gen. vi, 8.

is thus described in dialogue between a Christian and a skeptic in Ingersoll's "Talmagian Catechism:"

"*Answer.* He made up his mind that he would drown them. You see they were all totally depraved—in every joint and sinew of their bodies, in every drop of their blood, and in every thought of their brains.

"*Question.* Did he drown them all? *Answer.* No; he saved eight to start with again.

"*Question.* Were these eight persons totally depraved? *Answer.* Yes.

"*Question.* Why did he not kill them, and start over again with a perfect pair? Would it not have been better to have had his flood at first, before he made anybody, and drowned the snake? *Answer.* 'God's ways are not our ways;' and besides, you must remember that 'a thousand years are as one day' with God.

"*Question.* How did God destroy the people? *Answer.* By water; it rained forty days and forty nights, and 'the fountains of the great deep were broken up.'

"*Question.* How deep was the water? *Answer.* About five miles.

"*Question.* How much did it rain each day?

Answer. About eight hundred feet; though the better opinion now is, that it was a local flood. Infidels have raised objections and pressed them to that degree that most orthodox people admit that the flood was rather local.

"*Question.* If it was a local flood, why did they put birds of the air into the ark? Certainly birds of the air could have avoided a local flood? *Answer.* If you take this away from us, what do you propose to give us in its place? Some of the best people of the world have believed this story. Kind husbands, loving mothers, and earnest patriots have believed it, and that is sufficient.

"*Question.* At the time God made these people, did he know that he would have to drown them all? *Answer.* Of course he did.

"*Question.* Did he know when he made them that they would all be failures? *Answer.* Of course.

"*Question.* Why, then, did he make them? *Answer.* He made them for his own glory, and no man should disgrace his parents by denying it."

We must cease this Ingersollian dialogue to relate that God directed to preserve "of every living thing of all flesh, two of every sort"

And of every living thing of all flesh, two of every sort shalt thou bring into the ark to keep them alive with thee: they shall be male and female.—Gen. vi. 19.

(Gen. vi, 19). Hereupon ensued troublous scenes like that of our picture on page 35.

Noah was to take into the ark "two of every sort" (Gen. vi, 20). But hold, how's this, ha, hum, heh?—when chapter vi has ended with the taking in of all beasts and the finishing of that job, they being taken by *twos*, chapter vii goes back to the beginning and has the ordering and the execution all done again, and this time only the unclean creatures are taken by twos while all clean ones go by *sevens* (vii, 2, 3). In viii, 20, we learn that when the voyage was over Noah "took of every clean beast, and of every clean fowl, and offered burnt offerings on the altar." If he had taken only twos into the ark he would by these sacrifices have destroyed his entire stock of clean creatures.

The truth of the matter is that, in the words of Professors Oort and Hooykaas, "in the creation story and all the legends of which we have so far spoken, we have discovered the work of two writers, the first of whom speaks of the Supreme Being under the name of 'God,' and gave us the first account of the creation, and the family register of Adam down to Noah, while the second uses the name Yahweh (though translators have rendered both alike), and gave us the story of paradise and the account of the Cainites. It is natural to ask, therefore, from which of these writers the story of the flood is derived ; but it is not easy to answer the question. In the three chapters which contain this story there are two documents mixed up together, and though we can sometimes distinguish the style and the peculiar ideas of the former writers, it is at other times very hard to say whether we have either of the two before us, rather than some third writer. For the most part they quite agree with each other, and consequently the story is not free from repetitions, but here and there the accounts are unmistakably contradictory."

On page 37 we view the victualing of Captain Noah's craft for the huge multitudes of passengers (Gen. vi, 21)—all done, the scripture says, in the impossible space of one week.

Amongst almost all ancient peoples we find a tradition that, when the world was buried in sins, a great flood destroyed it, with the exception of some few persons who escaped. The Chaldees, for example, told of a certain Xisuthros, the tenth and last ruler before the flood.

Of fowls after their kind, and of cattle after their kind: of every creeping thing of the earth after his kind; two of every sort shall come unto thee, to keep them alive. - Gen. vi, 20.

to whom the highest god foretold that the beginning of the judgment would fall upon the fifteenth day of the month Daesius. On this he buried the written archives of ancient times in Sapharraim, the city of the sun, embarked with his relations and friends in a great ship, into which he took every kind of quadruped and of flying and creeping thing, together with the necessary food, and then sailed for Armenia. By letting birds fly out of the vessel he frequently tested the state of the earth. When these birds came back a second time they had mud on their feet, and when they flew out a third time they did not come back at all. Upon this Xisuthros, with his wife and the steersman, left the ship; but, in reward for their piety, they were suddenly carried up to the dwelling of the gods, and Xisuthros was only able to cry out from the air, to those who were left behind, that they must go back to Babylon and restore the books which he had buried, to mankind; which accordingly they did. A similar story is found among the Phrygians, who even mention Enoch's preaching and ascension in connection with it. The Syrians Phoenicians, and Persians, all had stories of the flood, which agreed in

some points with those of the Israelites, and differed from them in others. In the same way we find them among the European nations, too. In the Greek story it is Deucalion and Pyrrha who are spared on account of their piety; with the Celts and Germans the persons saved have other names; but everywhere we find some story of the sort. This fact, with others like it, points with the greatest likelihood to a common fatherland, the cradle of these nations, from which they all came, taking these traditions with them.

The observation of shells, corals, and other remains of aquatic animals, in places above the level of the sea, and even on high mountains, may have given rise to legends of a great flood. Fossils found imbedded in high ground have been appealed to both in ancient and modern times, both by savage and civilized man, as evidence in support of their traditions of a flood; and, moreover, the argument, apparently unconnected with any tradition, is to be found, that because there are marine fossils in places away from the sea, therefore the sea must once have been there. It is only quite recently that the presence of fossil shells, etc., on high mountains,

And take thou unto them of all food that is eaten, and thou shalt gather it to thee; and it shall be for food for thee, and for them. —Gen. vi. 21.

has been abandoned as evidence of the Noachic flood.

We will add the Hindoo legend: "Many ages after the creation of the world, Brahma resolved to destroy it with a deluge, on account of the wickedness of the people. There lived at that time a pious man named *Satyavrata*, and as the lord of the universe loved this pious man, and wished to preserve him from the sea of destruction which was to appear on account of the depravity of the age, he appeared before him in the form of *Vishnu* (the Preserver) and said: In seven days from the present time . . . the worlds will be plunged in an ocean of death, but in the midst of the destroying waves, a large vessel, sent by me for thy use, shall stand before thee. Thou shalt take all medicinal herbs, all the variety of seeds, and accompanied by seven saints, encircled by *pairs* of all brute animals, thou shalt enter the spacious ark, and continue in it, secure from the flood, on one immense ocean without light, except the radiance of thy holy companions. When the ship shall be agitated by an impetuous wind, thou shall fasten it with a large sea-serpent on my horn; for I will be near thee (in the form of a fish), drawing the vessel, with thee and thy companions. I will remain on the ocean, O chief of men, until a night of *Brahma* shall be completely ended. Thou shalt then know my true greatness, rightly named the Supreme Godhead; by my favor, all thy questions shall be answered, and thy mind abundantly instructed." Which plan was carried out as proposed.

Perhaps our readers would be pleased if the foregoing serious considerations of a very unserious and ludicrous legend were relieved with a humorous one, which we have lit upon in an old periodical:

"There is a fable believed by certain persons in New Jersey, and by the less intelligent elsewhere, that at a remote period in the history of our race a flood of water occurred which drowned all but one family of the residents. By some it is held that this flood was universal; by others that it was local. In the newer light of biblical research, it is now known to be neither. The tale is an allegory, and points a temperance moral. Not a universal flood nor a local flood, but universal inebriety and local option were the sources of this pleasing legend. One of the young ladies of the Women's Temperance Union,

And Noah went in, and his sons, and his wife, and his sons' wives with him, into the ark.—Gen. vii. 7.

who lived at that time, in a recent address before a west-side congregation, pointed out that at the period of the flood the residents of the earth had been stimulating rather freely with tanglefoot. As a consequence, *delirium tremens* became epidemic. Christian reader, you no doubt have had the Jas. Jams; and if so you will know that Noah's menagerie sinks to a procession of one flea and a bedbug compared with the colossal aggregation of animated nature which marches before your vision at such a time. This same zoological collection appeared to the eyes of the antediluvians, and gave rise to the myth of Noah's menagerie. Through the efforts of the W. T. U. a local option act passed the legislature, and 'the waters prevailed,' i.e., water was consumed as a beverage; hence the myth of a deluge. Some of the people called it a drouth, but that part of the story is among the Lost and Hostile Gospels.

"The warning given to Noah to prepare for the flood instructed him to lay in a stock of wet goods, which he did, and was thus enabled to attain that comfortable degree of fulness described in Gen. ix, 21."

On page 43 is a scene which surpasses all that any of us ever saw when, in our younger days before we had been baffled and aged by the Bible and the other impenetrable difficulties of life, we attended the railroad station to see the circus come in. "And Noah went forth, and his sons, and his sons' wives with him; every beast, every creeping thing and every fowl, and whatsoever creepeth upon the earth, after their kinds, went forth out of the ark" (Gen. viii, 18, 19). How, asks Ingersoll, "did the animals get back to their respective countries? Some had to creep back about six thousand miles, and they could only go a few feet a day. Some of the creeping things must have started for the ark just as soon as they were made, and kept up a steady jog for sixteen hundred years. Think of a couple of the slowest snails leaving a point opposite the ark and starting for the plains of Shinar, a distance of twelve thousand miles. Going at the rate of a mile a month, it would take them a thousand years. How did they get there? Polar bears must have gone several thousand miles, and so sudden a change in climate must have been exceedingly trying upon their health. How did they know the way to go? Of course, all the polar bears did not go.

And the waters prevailed and were increased greatly upon the earth; and the ark went forth upon the face of the waters.—Gen. vii, 18.

Only two were required. Who selected these? Two sloths had to make the journey from South America. These creatures cannot travel to exceed three rods a day. At this rate they would make a mile in about a hundred days. They must have gone about six thousand five hundred miles to reach the ark. Supposing them to have traveled by a reasonably direct route, in order to complete the journey before Noah hauled in the plank, they must have started several years before the world was created. We must also consider that these sloths had to board themselves on the way, and that most of their time had to be taken up getting food and water. It is exceedingly doubtful whether a sloth could travel six thousand miles and board himself in less than three thousand years."

The Lord proclaimed to Noah in Gen. ix, 3: "Every moving thing that liveth shall be meat for you."

Many of the notions of the later Jews on eating were queer. If they did not include in their diet things that they should not have eaten, they at least superstitiously excluded many that they had no sound reasons for rejecting. Horses we know to be proper meat enough, but the Jewish

religious law forbade their utilization for the purpose. The origin of the distinction between clean and unclean animals in Israel is not known with certainty. The rule given out by the priests was that no quadrupeds might be eaten except those that had a properly cloven hoof and chewed the cud; and only those fishes that had fins and scales, which would exclude the lamprey and the ell, for example, as well as oysters and all shell fish; while certain kinds of birds mentioned by name and all creeping things (among which the weasel, the mouse, the tortoise, the hedgehog, the crocodile, the toad, and the mole were reckoned) were unclean. There are certain differences in the law in the two versions in which it appears. For instance, the locust is said in Leviticus to be clean, but in Deuteronomy to be unclean. The law of Deuteronomy is the earliest, and dates, as has been said, from the last century before the captivity. All attempts to find definite reasons for which the Israelites pronounced some kinds of animals clean and others unclean, have been unsuccessful. It was all, like everything else then, a matter of superstition and chance.

Along with the dietary instructions the Lord

And Noah went forth, and his sons, and his sons' wives with him; every beast, every creeping thing, and every fowl, and whatsoever creepeth upon the earth, after their kinds, went forth out of the ark. —Gen. viii, 18, 19.

favored his protégées with divers others, one of which reads: "And the fear of you and the dread of you shall be upon every beast" (Gen. ix. 2). With the above contract in his pocket Noah and his family journeyed down the mountain side and located a ranch on the plains of Shinar. Confident that the animal kingdom had been broken to harness, as it were, Noah contemplated the stocking of his place without misgiving, and he therefore one day sent forth Japhet and the dog to drive in a few stray animals which were feeding on the adjacent slope. The quadrupeds that Japhet succeeded in corraling with the assistance of the pup were a goat, a mule, and a lop-horned cow of unpleasant cast of countenance. Noah read the riot act to these, and they listened so submissively that members of the family were moved to make friendly advances toward their four-footed servants. Then was presented a harrowing spectacle. The cow of unpleasant cast of countenance chased the old lady into the house, and at the same moment the mule lifted up his heels and knocked Shem galley-west, while simultaneously the goat slammed Ham against the side of the building,

44

and, to employ a nautical phrase, hammered seven bells out of his dusky stomach. The dog caught the enthusiasm of the occasion, and made it so lively for Noah that our revered ancestor was fain to sacrifice a portion of his mantle as he went over the fence flying. Having cleared the field, the stock went quietly to grazing as they had previously done, and the dismembered human family gathered itself together. A short time after this, Ham chanced to pick up the family Bible, and read aloud the misleading verse, to wit, "An' de fear ob you, an' de dread ob you, shall be upon ebery beast ob de yairth, an' upon ebery fowl ob de air, an' upon all dat moobeth upon de yairth." This, delivered in a sarcastic tone of voice, so angered Noah that he cursed Ham, and some of Noah's descendants have displayed a decided aversion to ham from that day to this.

The account of Noah's drunkenness and indecent exposure of the person is more fit to remain in Gen. ix, 21-23, than to appear here. Scarcely more decent, to one with a respect for truth, is the statement in ix, 29, that he died aged nine hundred and fifty years.

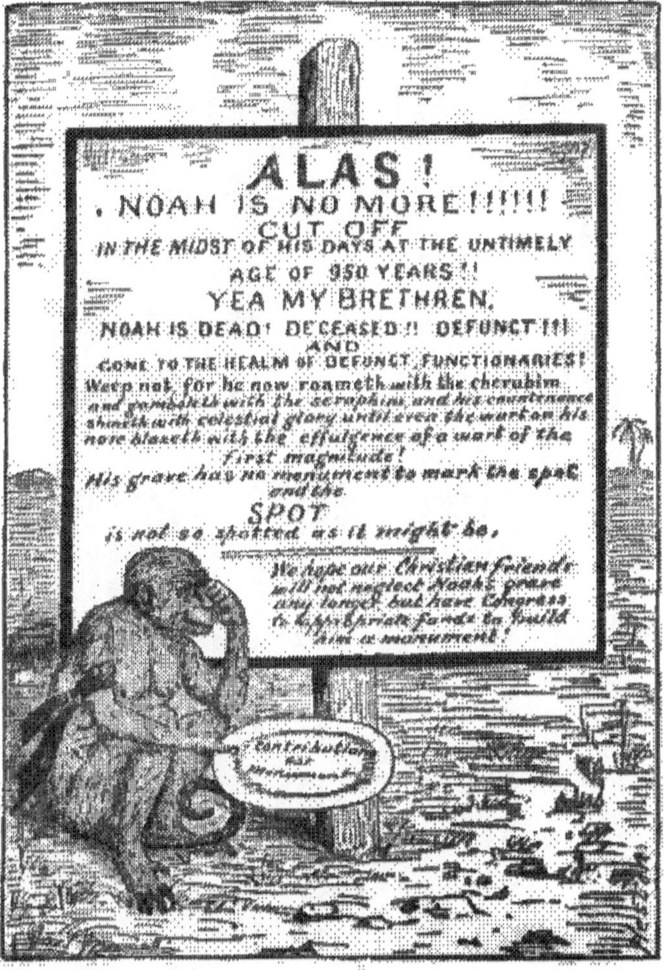

And all the days of Noah were nine hundred and fifty years and he died.—Gen. ix, 29.

CHAPTER VI.

A HUNTING ANECDOTE.

"HE was a mighty hunter before the Lord: wherefore it is said, even as Nimrod, the mighty hunter before the Lord" (Gen. x, 9). Here is a verse in which some valuable piece of knowledge might have been conveyed to us, used instead to communicate a triviality of no connection with the surrounding narrative and of no use to a person in the world.

As if enough time had not been wasted in the inditing, printing, and perusing of such a piece of inanity, shoals of commentators have racked their heads and taken up their own and their readers' time with conjectures of an obscure meaning in it. Some suppose that Nimrod did good with his hunting, served his country by ridding it of the wild beasts which infested it, and so insinuated himself into the affections of his neighbors and got to be their prince. Other commentators sagely infer that under pretense of hunting he gathered men under his command and by their help established a tyrannical and absolute power. Carrying this line of conjecture farther, other exegetical noodles say that calling him a mighty hunter signifies that he was a violent invader of his neighbors' rights and properties and a persecutor of innocent men, carrying all before him and endeavoring to make all his own by force and violence.

"The prophets," we are told, "sometimes express war under the name of hunting." And as the war and turbulence on the part of God and his people were so abundant, we find mentions of their *hunting* one another thick enough. Ezekiel complains (xiii, 17–23) of false prophetesses who *hunt* the souls of the people; we might complain now of all the prophetesses and prophets too who hunt our dollars. Micah informs us (vii, 2) that among his nation "there is none upright," but "they *hunt* every man his brother with a net;" this state of God's chosen people is paralleled by that which we now see among those nations closest under the Lord's guidance. Saul receives so little virtue from the holy anointing that David is driven to exclaim to him, "Thou *huntest* my soul to take it." So much for *hunting.*

He was a mighty hunter before the Lord: wherefore it is said, Even as Nimrod, the mighty hunter before the Lord. Gen. x. 9.

CHAPTER VII.

ABRAHAM, CHRIST'S GREAT ANCESTOR.

ABRAHAM is of interest not only in himself, but also as the father of the chosen stock of Israel set apart for the generation of Christ. Of course it is nothing that Christ's alleged father was related to no person on earth, and that his mother's genealogy is unknown. He was of the "house of David," just the same.

We once read of a Brooklyn girl who stole shoes to wear to Sunday-school. The notion that it is right to ride rough-shod over the laws of man when on the service of God, is too common. This course is well exemplified in the father of Israel. In the beginning God proposes to him a favoritism at direct odds with impartial justice. He says: "I will bless them that bless thee, and curse him that curseth thee." The normal laws of morals were to be unheeded and people were to be punished or rewarded as they disliked or liked the Jews, whether they were right in so doing or not.

Abraham was graced with the special title of

the Friend of God (2 Chron. xx, 7; Isa. xli, 8; James ii, 23). All friends of God should be specially distinguished as such, that we might readily tell them from those quite opposite characters, the friends of man.

We purpose to treat the scriptural Abraham as a real personage, but we may mention parenthetically that some critics doubt that he ever existed. And other scholars believe him to have been not the founder of the Jewish nation at all, but a leader of the Arabs or some other Eastern people. The Arabs insist that he was one of their illustrious chiefs. They make his name Ibrahim. They say that he founded Mecca, and that they are descended from him through Ismael, whom the Jews call Ishmael. Mohammed in his Koran says: "Abraham was neither Jew nor Christian; he was an orthodox Mussulman." He was not, adds Mohammed, in allusion to the Christian notion of the threefold nature of the deity, "of those who imagine that God has colleagues." Abraham is also claimed as him whom the Greeks called Zoroaster. He is likewise said, with less probability, to be the Brama of the Indians. The name of Abram or

And Abram took Sarai his wife, and Lot his brother's son, and all their substance that they had gathered, and the souls that they had gotten in Haran; and they went forth to go into the land of Canaan; and into the land of Canaan they came.—Gen. xii, 5.

Bram was famous through Persia as well as Judea. The Jews are not, as Christian teachers were once able to make people believe, an ancient nation, but are very modern; they were wandering barbarians when surrounding peoples had flourishing civilizations; and it is to be supposed that they, like all other tribes similarly situated, took their legends from their superiors. And they began at a late date, it is thought, to call themselves descendants of Abraham, to conciliate the peoples of Asia by whom that personage was so highly venerated.

Father Abraham "dwelt in old time on the other side of the flood" (Josh. xxiv, 2, 3). Where that was can best be solved by some commentator "half seas over." From this locality he went into Canaan, which the Lord promised to give to him and his heirs for an abiding-place forever. But either he had already had some experience of the tricky ways of his promise-breaking patron, or he set his judgment as to the best land for him above that of the creator of the heaven and earth, for he seems to have shown no intention of staying there. Indeed, pretty soon his protector sent a grievous famine into the land, and he incontinently betook himself off into Egypt. Here he found a nation that, we must judge from the way in which it is spoken of, and from the profusion of the presents that he afterward received, was a populous and civilized one. But to make the country inhabitable and to build towns must have cost immense labor. It was necessary to construct canals for draining the Nile. It was also necessary to raise the towns at least twenty feet above these canals. Works so considerable would seem to have required hundreds of ages. Yet there were only about four hundred years between the deluge and Abraham's arrival in Egypt. The Egyptians must have been miraculous in propagation and industry, since in so short a time they invented the arts and sciences and changed the face of the country. But this is only one of the wonderful things that in the Bible we see.

The old preacher whose Bible had had two pages stuck together by bad boys, read at the bottom of one page, "When Noah was one hundred and forty he took unto himself a wife, who was (turning the leaf) one hundred and forty

Behold, now, I know thou art a fair woman to look upon.   Gen. xii, 11.

cubits long, forty cubits wide, built of gopher wood, covered with pitch inside and out." After some staring he said, "My friends, this is the first time I ever met this in the Bible, but I accept it as an evidence of the assertion that we are fearfully and wonderfully made." It would require the faith of this preacher to accept the statement that at this time in our story, when Sarai was over sixty years of age, Abraham said to her, "Behold, now, I know thou art a fair woman to look upon," and feared that she would enamor the princes of Egypt. And that, in addition, these princes actually did become at once charmed by her beauty. And that twenty-five years afterward she similarly bewitched the king of Gerar. But passing over, or dodging around, or in some way getting at a distance from this difficulty, we will view the method by which this Friend of God proposed to evade any trouble that might follow the arousing of the passions of the Egyptian princes. He directed Sarai: "It shall come to pass, when the Egyptians shall see thee, that they shall say, This is his wife: and they will kill me, but they will save thee alive. Say, I pray thee, thou art my

sister: that it may be well with me for thy sake; and my soul shall live because of thee." Thus this "perfect" (Gen. xvii, 1) individual, rather than stay away from Egypt, or defend his wife like a man, begs her to sacrifice herself to the lusts of whomsoever covets her that he may save his own skin. To get the best idea of how such conduct should be rated, we should imagine how it would seem to us if adopted among ourselves here now. What would be the effect on general morals if each person whose wife is coveted by a stronger man should weakly surrender her thus? And what must be the inference as to the propriety of lying of any boy or girl who reads this story? "Why, if so good a man as Abraham was justified in lying, then we may take the same liberty whenever it will help us out of a tight spot." Not a good lesson for school-children.

One of the motives—perhaps the only one—of Abraham in thus letting out his wife for immoral purposes begins to appear. Abraham received at the court of Pharaoh presents of many "sheep, and oxen, and he-asses, and menservants, and maid-servants, and she-asses, and

And the Lord plagued Pharaoh and his house with great plagues.—Gen. xii. 17.

camels " (Gen. xii, 16). He became " very rich in cattle, in silver, and in gold " (Gen. xiii, 2). Thus the riches that supported him in his position as patriarch of God's people seem to have had as their source the hire of his wife.

This lucrative business of Abraham was interrupted by the action of the Lord, who found himself unable longer to refrain from one of his dearest practical jokes, viz., punishing the innocent for the guilty. Pharaoh, who had supposed Sarai to be really Abraham's sister, was plagued " with great plagues." His household were likewise afflicted, though they were still farther removed from guilt than their master. In Gen. xx we find that when Abimelech, king of Gerar, had been deceived by Abraham and had taken Sarai in the same manner as Pharaoh, it was the king that received the punishment while Abraham went free. It availed not for Abimelech to plead: "Said he not unto me, She is my sister.   And she, even she herself said, He is my brother: in the integrity of my heart and innocency of my hands have I done this." This mattered not, and the Lord "fast closed up all the wombs of the house of Abimelech, because

of Sarah Abraham's wife." This innocent king was recommended to beg the services of the man who had deceived him to ask pardon of God for himself, the king, having suffered by the crime of the deceiver: "For he is a prophet, and he shall pray for thee, and thou shalt live . . . So Abraham prayed unto God : and God healed Abimelech, and his wife."

It would appear that Pharaoh was finally told of the cheat that had been practiced upon him by the wily stranger, for he "called Abram, and said: What is this that thou hast done unto me? Why didst thou not tell me that she was thy wife? Why saidst thou, She is my sister?" Pharaoh could not have come at his knowledge merely by means of the plagues. We do not know that he recognized them as from Jehovah, and if he had he had no means of knowing which of all his actions, right and wrong, had offended that cantankerous and whimsical individual. So we may suppose that he learned the facts by some incidents which are left in oblivion by our model history. The injured king naturally packed the father of Israel and letter-out of his wife off out of Egypt as soon as pos-

And when Abram heard that his brother was taken captive, he armed his trained servants, born in his own house, three hundred and eighteen, and pursued them unto Dan.—Gen. xiv. 14.   [N.B.—The monkey in these pictures is for ornament, not for use.]

sible. He went with him "his wife, and all that he had." If Abraham had possessed a spark of honor he would have left the riches that he had obtained in barter for his wife's honor, but he failed to do so. His conduct was similar in the case of Abimelech king of Gerar, mentioned on a preceding page. That king gave the friend of God "sheep, and oxen, and men-servants, and women-servants, . . . and . . . a thousand pieces of silver." All these gifts the perfect man in God's eyes cheerfully accepted, and kept. This was his meed for having deceived Abimelech. Such are the rewards of those who do wrong to man with the countenance of God. It is on this principle that popes take their dupes' money for deluding them, inquisitors confiscate their victims' estates in return for torturing them, and preachers appropriate our money to pay their taxes as compensation for denying us our civil rights and despotising over our holidays.

Our reverend friend when his profitable transactions with Pharaoh were ended, journeyed to a land between Beth el and Hai, where he settled with his kinsman Lot. One of these worthies being a friend of God and what God called a perfect man, and the other being at least a friend of God and therefore presumably of a character pleasing to that deity, they found it impossible to dwell together without quarreling, and were forced to part. Some years after, however, when Lot got into trouble with enemies, his relative forgave him sufficiently to come to his rescue. Hereupon was fought a battle without parallel in profane history. Abraham with three hundred and eighteen servants routed a king of Persia, a king of Pontus, the king of Babylon, and the king of nations. This exploit is approached only by two other feats of those times when the Lord's arm was not shortened, viz., the defeat of an army by Gideon with three hundred men and of a thousand Philistines by Samson.

To grace the final victory in this contest, the king of Sodom, who had been killed in one of the early encounters (Gen. xiv, 10), now came to life and met Abraham as though nothing had happened to him, to congratulate him on his conquest (Gen. xiv, 10-12). Such, at least, is the plain reading of the scripture; if it be sug-

And Sarai, Abram's wife, took Hagar her maid, the Egyptian, and gave her to her husband Abram to be his wife.—Gen. xvi, 3, gested that perhaps the king of the latter text was a newly installed one, the remark is called for that such gaps of narrative as this would indicate must upset the whole conception of the Bible as an understandable and a safe guide. If there are omissions and liabilities to confusions like this throughout the Bible, we cannot depend upon any part of it.

The Bible contains only a part of the legends regarding ancient characters and events. There are many Jewish, Arabian, and other tales about Abraham that did not chance to get a carrying vote in the wonderful councils that decided which one should be passed off as inspired. Some of the omitted Jewish legends have it that Abraham was deserted by his servants but attacked the opposing armies single-handed and beat them by daybreak.

Abraham, evidently appreciating by this time the unprincipled character of his heavenly ruler, became uneasy as the years passed and no sign appeared of the numerous family which had been promised him. But " when the sun was going down, a deep sleep fell upon Abram ; and lo, a horror of great darkness fell upon him." This

was a preparation for communion to be vouchsafed him with the Lord. It is usually in times of darkness that supernatural communications take place. The light, either physical or mental, is rarely made a condition of revelation from God. Often Freethinkers who have absentmindedly strayed into churches feel " a horror of great darkness " fall upon them. However, they never get any farther in the process of revelation.

Abraham's friend defended himself against the reproaches of his protegée, and declared on his honor that this promise was one that could be depended on. Accordingly, Sarai proposed to her husband: " Behold now, the Lord hath restrained me from bearing : I pray thee go in unto my maid." Abraham adopted the counsel. As the Lord had taken the matter of Abraham's children under his special direction, we are to regard this arrangement as emanating directly from him. And Abraham was " perfect " anyway. What is a boy or girl to think who reads of this event in the Bible which Christians are so desirous of having in our schools ? Will not he or she think that if this perfect man, evi-

And when Sarai dealt hardly with Hagar, she fled from her face.—Gen. xvi, 6.

dently under God's control, made no scruple to adopt his servant-maid as his concubine, a man nowadays may do the same?

When Hagar the maid " saw that she had conceived, her mistress was despised in her eyes." Indeed, her mistress may, we should say, properly enough have been despised in her eyes before this. Sarai had lent herself to Abraham's money-making scheme of hiring her out to Pharaoh without any objection or shame. Indeed, to how many more well-paying princes she had, with her husband's assistance, submitted herself, we cannot tell, but we may suspect many, as Abraham says, later on : " When God caused me to wander from my father's house, . . . I said unto her, This is thy kindness which thou shalt show unto me ; at *every place* whither we shall come, say of me, He is my brother." Perhaps when Hagar reflected on such conduct she awarded her mistress a rather poor opinion. And when she came to conceive by her master, probably she thought that if he could so easily part with Sarai for goods and chattels he could as well part with her or diminish her station for the sake of the woman

who could bear him a child. Abram, however, had an eye solely to monetary benefit and to his own well-being. To obtain these two things he had willingly prostrated his wife to a prince, but as no such ends could be served here he concluded to resent these indignities upon her though he had not resisted the others. Instead of endeavoring to regulate or smooth the circumstances in which he had involved his maid, he delivered her over to the mercies of a jealous wife. " Abram said to Sarai, Behold thy maid is in thy hand ; do to her as it pleaseth thee." It pleased Sarai to do to her so violently that " she fled from her face."

Hagar when she fled from the troubles that had been brought upon her by God's friend and his wife wandered into the wilderness. Here she was found by an angel of the Lord, one of those beings who were around so thick in those days and whose striking absence in these times forces us into all the desperate struggles that we have with republics, empires, Socialism, and all our other contrivances for governing ourselves. This individual said to her, " Return to thy mistress, and submit thyself under her hands."

And Hagar bare Abram a son; and Abram called his son's name, which Hagar bare, Ishmael.   And Abram was fourscore and six —Gen. xvi, 16, 16.

As she was only a slave, it did not matter what barbarities she suffered. As the angel, of course, spoke by God's order, we see the opinion of the Lord upon a runaway slave case. Next said the angel to Hagar: "I will multiply thy seed exceedingly, that it shall not be numbered for multitude. . . . Thou art with child, and shalt bear a son, . . . and he will be a wild man; his hand will be against every man, and every man's hand against him; and he shall dwell in the presence of all his brethren." Here are two promises—one seemingly favorable, to make her seed numerous, and the other manifestly unfavorable, to make her son a wild man, abusing and abused by all mankind. Nothing can be made out of this contradiction. No one can tell what God meant, or what his intentions were by her. Here, as in many other places in the Bible, all is without aim, consistency, comprehensibility, or common sense.

"And Hagar bare Abram a son; and Abram called his son's name, which Hagar bare, Ishmael. And Abram was four score and six" (Gen. xvi, 15, 16). It is not customary for men to beget children at the age of eighty-six. But let it go.

The Lord appeared again to Abraham, and, referring to Sarai, said, "I will bless her, and give thee a son also of her." Abraham, we are told, at this "fell upon his face, and laughed, and said in his heart, Shall a child be born unto him that is an hundred years old? and shall Sarah, that is ninety years old, bear?" We cannot tell whether Abraham's laughter arose from a supposition that the Lord was joking or a rash determination to show just what he thought of the promises of his untruthful friend. If the latter, the proceeding was certainly Lazardous. In either case, he was mistaken, for Sarai soon blessed him with a bouncing lad whom they called Isaac. Jewish tradition relates that at this august birth many barren women brought forth, the blind saw, the dumb spoke, the deaf heard, the lame walked, crazy people became sane, and the sun shone forty-eight times as bright as usual. On the weaning of this youngster a great feast was made. Ishmael, very naturally, failed to see why a feast

And Abraham rose up early in the morning, and took bread and a bottle of water, and gave it unto Hagar (putting it on her shoulder) and the child, and sent her away: and she departed, and wandered in the wilderness of Beer-sheba.—Gen. xxi, 14.

should be given the son of the woman of many husbands and not to him the son of a woman who had had but one man and had remained faithful and true. The youth was espied by Sarai mocking, and that godly lady thereupon solicited that Hagar and her son be cast forth into the wilderness again. "The thing was very grievous in Abraham's sight, because of his son." He does not seem to have cared for Hagar's sake, she being only a bondwoman. God, however, appeared on the scene, and allayed his uneasiness by informing him: "In Isaac shall thy seed be called. And also of the son of the bondwoman will I make a nation, because he is thy seed." This reassured Abraham's egotistic desire to be made mighty in his male line. It is to be noted that Ishmael was looked after by the Lord, not on any general principle of justice and humanity, but because he was the son of his friend. So Jehovah's favorite gave Hagar and Ishmael bread and a bottle of water and thrust them forth to shift as they could. And they "wandered in the wilderness of Beer-sheba."

"Does God take the papers?" asked a little girl. "No, my child; why do you ask?" "Oh, I

thought he didn't, it takes our minister so long to tell him about things." There are more things than one calculated to produce a belief that God's knowledge is very limited. According to the doctrine that he is all-knowing, he would have been aware that Abraham was sufficiently implicit in obedience to offer up his son as a sacrifice at command, yet he had to try an experiment upon that patriarch to determine the matter. So he directed Abraham to take forth his son Isaac and sacrifice him.

In the language of the Bible, "God did tempt Abraham." To be sure, James i, 13, avers, quite to the contrary, that God tempts no man. Yet the example of hosts of Christians proves to us that there need be no difficulty in believing two contradictory statements at the same time. That is, in case that they are in the holy scripture. With self-contradictions in unholy scriptures, or the bibles of other religions, of course it is quite another matter. There they are proofs of falsity.

The crony of God did not pass through the preparatory stages of the sacrifice without ornamenting them with a few of the little lies which

And Abraham rose up early in the morning, and saddled his ass, and took two of his young men with him, and Isaac his son, and clave the wood for the burnt offering, and rose up, and went unto the place of which God had told him.—Gen. xxii, 3.

we find so plentifully in the records of his class.
He said to his young men, "Abide ye here with
the ass; and I and the lad will go yonder and
worship, and come again to you." Yet he did
not expect the lad to return with him. When
Isaac asked, "Where is the lamb for a burnt-
offering?" his father replied, "My son, God will
provide himself a lamb for a burnt-offering."
Will not the young who read these fibs of a
"perfect" man think it right enough in themselves to perpetrate the like?

Long is the roll of cruel murders for which
this story of Abraham and Isaac is responsible.
Many are the fanatics who after poring over the
Bible till half crazed, have been inspired by this
example to prove their devotion to God by sacrifice of an innocent child or wife or husband.
In the last notable case, that of the murder by
Freeman, of Pocasset, Mass., of his child, his
wife wrote to a friend : "He was willing to bear
the test of Abraham's faith. . . . When, after
getting no rest, he told the Lord he would have
the faith of Abraham, this brought him relief,
. . . came that terrible requirement, 'They
that have the faith of Abraham shall be blest
with Abraham." He [Abraham] was blest by
God. It was counted to him for righteousness.
Had it not been for him, we could have had no
Christ."

Along with this story of Abraham's sacrifice
go a number of others which have helped raise
the bloody designs in such fanatics as the above.
"You venture to affirm," thunders Voltaire to
the Jews, "that you have never immolated human victims to the Lord. What then was the
murder of Jephtha's daughter, who was really
immolated, as we have already shown from
your own books? How will you explain the
anathema of the thirty-two virgins, that were
the tribute of the Lord, when you took thirty-
two thousand Midianitish virgins and sixty-one
thousand asses? I will not here tell you, that
according to this account there were not two
asses for each virgin ; but I will ask you, what
was this tribute for the Lord? According to
your book of Numbers, there were sixteen thousand girls for your soldiers, sixteen thousand
for your priests: and on the soldiers' share
there was levied a tribute of thirty-two virgins
for the Lord. What became of them? You had

And Abraham stretched forth his hand, and took the knife to slay his son. And the angel of the Lord called unto him out of heaven, and said, Abraham, Abraham.—Gen. xxii, 10, 11.

no nuns. What was the Lord's share in all your wars, if it was not blood?"

The heartless old rogue, regardless, like all thorough pietists, of all feeling for mere humanity when it conflicts with devotion to the God who can so richly reward one's selfish desires, was about to consummate the devilish sacrifice when the curious God, having informed his ignorance of that which he had wished to learn, called out through his angel, "Now I know that thou fearest God, seeing thou hast not withheld thy son." Then, as the bloodthirsty customs of Jehovah and his people could not omit a sacrifice altogether, a ram was offered. A Jewish tradition which our infallible Bible-selecters did not happen to vote in, relates that this ram was brought from Eden, where it had long fed under the tree of life, and that the trumpets of the judgment day will be made from its wonderful horns.

Abraham's forwardness to commit a heinous crime at God's bidding is accounted a crowning proof of his merit. The Lord therefor heaped upon him blessings. Paul praises the act (Heb. xi, 17). James says that thus his faith was made perfect, and that "it was imputed unto him for righteousness: and he was called the Friend of God." But any honest man, if commanded by a god to do a heinous deed, would cry, Away with you, that would have me do this! Supernatural you may be, but tried by the immutable standard of right I find you no good god, but a devil, and such I worship not!

"I was directly inspired by the deity to remove President Garfield. Inspiration and retribution are the watchwords for God's army. The deity charged me with a duty. He inspired me to remove the president of the United States, and as God's man I did what I was bid. Guiteau, the inspired, is all right. I am satisfied that God inspired me to do the act for which I am to suffer. Father, thou knowest me, but the world hath no known me. I have very little confidence in the flesh, but a vast deal in the power and purpose of God. The favor of God is vastly more important, in my view, in the pursuit of an object, than anything else" (Guiteau).

"And Sarah died in Kirjath-arba." Sarah, as is remarked by the authoress of "The Godly Women of the Bible," as the wife of Abraham is

And Abram went and took the ram, and offered him up for a burnt offering in the stead of his son.—Gen. xxii, 13.

held in high estimation, but as the mother of Christ yet to be, she is regarded with little less veneration than his immediate mother, the Virgin Mary; for as there must be a Messiah, so-called, he must have a human ancestry, therefore Bible-makers and creed-mongers early set themselves at work to manufacture a parentage for this distinguished individual. Hence we find constructions to that effect as early as Abraham's time, placed upon declarations said to have been made by God to Abraham, thus, "I will make of thee a great nation; and in thee shall all families of the earth be blessed." Sarah, therefore, becomes an important personage in the great drama of human salvation. To study her character and criticise her life as the mother of the Hebrew nation and the future redeemer of the world, is our duty. And her character is well shown in the fact that this noble woman, along with the worthy patriarch rich in flocks and herds and this world's goods, and who had three hundred and eighteen trained servants born in his own house, made no provision for his child—then fourteen or fifteen years of age—and his mother other than taking bread

and a bottle of water, putting it on her shoulder and sending her away into the wilderness. And Abraham twice asked Sarah or commanded her to tell a lie, and twice did her lie, indorsing his, inflict trouble on the innocent, though they escaped without even a reproof. And this subjection to husbands, lie and all, is commended in Sarah by Paul as worthy of imitation. And such a lie! True, virtuous wives of to-day, how would you like the subjection of wives to husbands to the extent of being an active party in such indecent and criminal deception? Deny his wife and ask her to aid him in the falsehood, the coward! Disown her, the miserable poltroon; and she, abject woman, consent to it; Paul commend her for it (1 Pet. iii, 5, 6); and the clergy of the present day indorse the pretty tale and relate it as if it was a recommendation to him, to her, and to Christianity instead of a disgrace! "I would prefer," cries the lady who writes the forementioned book, "to be the maltreated cast-off slave, the bondwoman, rather than the rich, proud, haughty, hard-hearted, jealous, unjust mistress, with her coward husband and lies; the mother in whose seed all nations should be

And Sarah died in Kirjath-arba; the same is Hebron in the land of Canaan; and Abraham came to mourn for Sarah, and to weep for her.—Gen. xxiii, 2.

blessed in a Messiah; the holy, godly woman who is to-day idolized as a pattern of probity and excellence and for whom thousands of Christian mothers have named and christened their darling little daughter-babies Sarah."

"Then again Abraham took a wife and her name was Keturah" (Gen. xxv, 1). In verse 2 we learn that this wife bore him six sons. This was as late as when Isaac had grown to manhood and taken a wife. Abraham's age at this time is fixed by Christian commentators at about one hundred and thirty-seven or one hundred and forty. At the age of one hundred he had been obliged to have a miracle performed in order to beget Isaac, but now he begets six children and there is no mention whatever of a miracle. Rev. Dr. Giles surmises that Abraham was, like Jacob, David, and Solomon, a polygamist, and had had these children by Keturah while Sarah was living. Dr. Giles thinks that the scripture writer "ranges in successive dates events which really were contemporaneous."

Notwithstanding these six sons by a wife, the son Ishmael by Hagar, and the many altogether illegitimate sons, Isaac is frequently styled Abraham's only begotten son, as, for instance, in Heb. xi, 17: "By faith Abraham, when he was tried, offered up Isaac; and he that had received the promises offered up his only begotten son." Such are some of the "harmonies of the divine word." It has been conjectured by some that Abraham admitted a male partner to the bed of Keturah who did the begetting of the six sons. Certainly this act would be in keeping with the character of the man who had hired out his previous wife so freely. Yet the text reads plainly: "She bare *him* [Abraham] Zimran and the other sons." The language supposed to tell that Mary bore Jesus, or that any event at all happened, is no plainer, so if we admit this passage to have a different meaning than its face conveys, we must admit that the others may have a different meaning than their face conveys, and we cannot feel certainty as to Mary's bearing Jesus or as to any event at all.

Gen. xxv, 6, informs us that "unto the sons of the concubines which Abraham had, Abraham gave gifts." Concubines of the perfect man, the Friend of God, spoken of by the chronicler

Then again Abraham took a wife, and her name was Keturah.—Gen. xxv, 1.

without a shadow of reprobation and evidently without a suspicion of any wrongfulness, in the book which lies on the pupils' desks in our public schools!

Abraham, being born when his father was seventy, grew so slowly that when his father had reached the good old age of two hundred and five years Abraham had only arrived at seventy-five years, having apparently lost no less than sixty years' growth during his father's lifetime (Gen. xi, 27, 32; xii, 4) St. Augustine and St. Jerome gave this up as a difficulty inexplicable. Calmet endeavors to explain it and makes it worse. Next into the melée of exegesis rushes our own Charles Bradlaugh and lays about with these lusty strokes: "But what real difficulty is there? Do you mean, dear reader, that it is impossible Abraham could have lived one hundred and thirty-five years and yet be only seventy-five years of age? Is this your objection? It is a sensible one, I admit, but it is an Infidel one. Eschew sense, and, retaining only religion, ever remember that with God all things are possible. Indeed, I have read myself that gin given to young children stunts their

growth; and who shall say what influence of the spirit prevented the full development of Abraham's years? It is a question whether Abraham and his two brothers were not born the same year; if this be so, he might have been a small child, and not grown as quickly as he would otherwise have done." There is, indeed, no epoch in those ancient times which has not produced a multitude of different opinions. According to Moreri, there were in his day seventy systems of chronology founded on the history dictated by God himself. There have since appeared many more new methods of reconciling the texts of scripture. Thus there are more disputes about Abraham than the number of his years (according to the text) when he left Haran. So when we read that the patriarch died at the age of a hundred three score and fifteen years we are able to tell little more about his actual length of life than before.

The Lord, in keeping with his usual custom, fulfilled neither the promise to Abraham that he and his seed should *forever* possess those great countries described in Gen. xiii, 14, 15, and xv, 18, nor the promise that his seed should

And these are the days of the years of Abraham's life, which he lived, a hundred threescore and fifteen years. Then Abraham gave up the ghost, and died in a good old age, an old man, and full of years; and was gathered to his people.—Gen. xxv, 7, 8.

be as numerous as the dust of the earth (Gen. xiii, 16).

The father of the faithful is reputed to have left several books behind him. Origen, Athanasius, and the rabbis mention them. Probably the ascription of these books to him has as little truth in it as the attribution of the books of the Bible to their reputed authors, and to-day as he blandly sits on the edge of a cloud and hears them accounted to him no doubt convulsions of laughter agitate him until he has got a great hole kicked in the cloud.

Abraham in heaven is no improvement upon Abraham on earth, for when a man who had committed no greater crime than dressing and faring sumptuously (a thing which all ecclesiastics do to the extent of their power) was suffering in hell and implored the Friend of God for a drop of water, the reply was, "Son, remember that in thy lifetime thou receivedst thy good things, and now thou art tormented" (Luke xvi, 25). This decision has as little relation to justice as those of Abraham on earth, or those of the other saints of scripture, or those of Jehovah himself.

Our artist depicts God's boon companion engaged in one of his favorite earthly pursuits. How a right-thinking woman would view the residence in Abraham's bosom which is so often held forth as a rich reward, is seen in the sentiments of the authoress of "The Godly Women of the Bible," as follows:

"Hold not out the inducement of heaven to me, by promising that I shall lie in Abraham's bosom! Abraham's bosom indeed, the coward! Would I lie in such a man's bosom on earth, then why in heaven? His arms must already be full, and if not, there is no place there for me! Sarah might be jealous and thrust me out, as she did Hagar; thrust me out of her lord's bosom, and out of heaven; and God, as in the Hebrew story, might tell me to submit."

"AT REST IN ABRAHAM'S BOSOM."

CHAPTER VIII.

A QUEER FAMILY.

HEAVEN, like the Dime Museum, is full of wonders. As one is happy in the possession of a triple-headed calf, so the other enjoys a triple-headed God. That interesting being (the God, not the calf) one evening favored Abraham with a materialization of himself in the amusing and allusive form of three men (Gen. xviii, 2). This Godly trio, or tripersonal God, after washing its six feet, in response to its host's invitation, and seating itself in a triangle under a tree, partook of bread and cakes of fine meal, and "a calf tender and good." This triple form perhaps had been assumed with a view to multiplying the enjoyment of the repast, on the principle of the Dutchman who desired the neck of an ostrich in view of the pleasure of his beer tasting good all the way down. After some conversation with Sarah in which It grew a little miffed at being laughed at by that elderly but lovely creature (Gen. xviii. 12-15), the complicated visitor set off for Sodom. As it, or they, did not know the road, "Abraham went with them to bring them on the way." The Lord—viz, "they"—though infinite in knowledge and needing no deliberation, and though having foreordained all so that he could not change it, nevertheless fell to considering the question, "Shall I hide from Abraham that thing which I do?" Finally concluding to speak, he informed Abraham that he had heard scandals of Sodom and Gomorrah. "I will go down now," he said, "and see whether they have done altogether according to the cry of it, which is come unto me." The infinite knowledge which we supposed this deity to possess we should think would have comprised intelligence as to these cities, so that he would not have needed to travel thither. Indeed, being omnipresent, he must have actually been at those towns at the time; thus he was taking a journey to a place where he already was. Never mind. At a threat to destroy the cities his friend remonstrated, urging the old gentleman to preserve his honor with the words, "Shall not the judge of all the earth do right?" and persuaded him to spare the places if he found therein fifty righteous, and then, Jew-like,

A RIGHTEOUS CITIZEN ESCAPES.

beat him down to forty-five, forty, and finally ten. Of course, the Lord knew all the time the number of righteous there and that it was under ten, so the promises signified nothing to him. But Abraham did not see the trick, and allowed himself to be satisfied. Which proves that many (three) heads are better than one.

"There came two angels to Sodom at even." Lot, recognizing at once those visitors so familiar in days of old, prayed their acceptance of his hospitality. This they at first modestly declined, thereby showing their acquaintance with the "Handbook of Heavenly Etiquette," chapter "Angels." Finally accepting, they got themselves entangled in a string of adventures with a mob of men of a character quite common under Jehovah's government of old, but very rare now under human rule. In the morning the angels led Lot and his family forth from the cities, upon which the Lord, who had secured one of General Dyrenforth's rain-making apparatuses and adjusted it to fire and brimstone, forthwith let fall a deluge of destruction.

In the illustration on page 79 we see Lot and his two daughters and his wife engaged in making their escape. The angels of the

Lord are also depicted in the engraving, one on each side of Lot, leading him by his hands. They are represented in a state which is frequent with them, that is, as invisible. We ask of our readers no extra fee for engravings by this unusual and difficult process.

Mrs. Lot, however, we discover to have ceased escaping just at this moment and to be standing in a deplorable condition of fixity. This occurred thus: The angels of the Lord had commanded, "Look not behind thee." But Lot's wife "looked back from behind him, and she became a pillar of salt." Perhaps a sister clad in the latest mode from Paris passed and she had to have a view of it behind.

The origin of the fairy story which we have been relating would seem to be as follows: In southeast Palestine there is a sea, about forty miles by nine, of remarkable saltness. Asphalt or bitumen often floats on its surface and gives it a leaden, ghastly look. The plains by it are covered with saltpeter. The surrounding country is barren and thinly inhabited. Tradition has ever dwelt about this dismal region and magnified its wonders. Ancient writers, Israelite and other as well, say that several

But his wife looked back from behind him, and she became a pillar of salt. —Gen. xix, 26.

cities, two of them named Sodom and Gomorrah, once occupied the site of the lake, then a fruitful plain, when there came a devastation of this region by earthquakes and subterranean fire. The great quantity of bitumen that is found there, largely composed of petroleum, makes the occurrence of these terrible phenomena quite credible. It seems, therefore, that the tradition is true. The recollection of such a devastation would not easily be blotted out from this region that had suffered so much at the hands of nature. The gloomy spectacle furnished by the sea, as it lay between its salt-bound shores, was constantly calling the havoc of a by-gone age to mind, and, to those ancient spectators who saw the hand of an avenging deity in all the destructive agencies of nature, it told of wrath and chastisement. Here was food enough for the imagination! That little city Zoar, on the southeast coast, appeared to have been spared through special favor. What was the reason of this? If we make the inquiry in a scientific spirit we see that the strip of land on which it lay was higher than the rest of the plain, so that when the plain became a prey to fire, and the water of the sea overflowed

into it, this piece of land very naturally remained above water. But in ancient times they never thought of this explanation, and saw a sign of God's favor in the fact that the city had escaped. Grotesque pillars of salt were to be found in abundance by the Hill of Sodom, and imagination often traced the petrified human form in them.

Lot and his daughters left Zoar and took up quarters in a cave in a mountain. "And the first born said unto the younger, Our father is old, and there is not a man in the earth to come in unto us after the manner of all the earth. Come, let us make our father drink wine, and we will lie with him, that we may preserve seed of our father." Of course there were a plenty of men on the earth, distant but a few miles on every side of them. Their excuse is of the same consistency as that of every person desirous to commit a crime and catching at any shadow of a subterfuge to justify it.

The infallible historian now furnishes the reader with one of the most important and sacred miracles on record—nothing less than these two godly daughters each becoming the mother of a boy by her father.

LOT AND HIS DAUGHTERS FIND REFUGE FROM A WICKED WORLD.

CHAPTER IX.

ISAAC AND HIS "SISTER"

At the tinkling of the bell Isaac steppeth forth upon the stage of holy drama—in which drama, contrary to the custom in plays written by uninspired men, it is the evil man that triumphs over the good and receives all the praise. As Isaac sat in the door of his tent of evenings, we may suppose, after having thrashed a few of his male slaves, dealt with sundry bond-women after the manner of his line, and in general having conducted himself in the ways which had obtained the favor of God, he often gave ear to the stories of his father's deeds and escapades, and thereby imbibed much instruction for the guidance of his own career. The tale that pleased him about the best of all was that of the tricks which his father had played off on Pharaoh and Abimelech. "Ha, ha!" he used to laugh when this was told, "*he* knew too much to fight for her. Get himself in trouble, not he! Just said the old lady was his sister and let 'em take her. Well, that *was* a keen one!" "Sarai," the story-teller would continue, "bow-

ing herself unto the will of her lord, and in all things consenting——" "Well, I'd like to see a wife that wouldn't, if she was mine," interrupted Ike; "if she didn't I'd——" and he concluded with a vicious wag of his head, for quite a vein of brutality ran through his disposition —though this needs not mentioning, as we know that such a strain was present in the whole race of barbarians. "And the sheep," resumed the chronicler, "and the oxen, and the men-servants, and the women-servants, and the silver, these did Abraham keep——" "Yes," broke in Isaac, "you may bet he did. Keep 'em? *Of course.* When a man once gets a thing in his hands, if he *is* a man he's going to hang on to it. That's what *I* say." And Ike stroked his beard and sent for another skinful of wine, while his eye twinkled with mingled admiration and emulation as he contemplated the like dodges that he himself was scheming to carry out. The dutiful son soon had an opportunity to fulfill his designs. His father, who was not dead yet, but was keeping up an establishment separate from Isaac's, sent him on a journey for a wife. The stale, flat, and unprofitable details of his courtship occupy Gen. xxiv. Notwithstanding

And Isaac dwelt in Gerar. And the men of the place asked him of his wife, and he said, She is my sister, for he feared to say, She is my wife, lest, said he, the men of the place should kill me for Rebekah, because she was fair to look upon.—Gen. xxvi, 6, 7.

our strong proclivity to search the scriptures, for in them ye have eternal life (laughter lengthens life), we will pass over this. We may notice by the way that the wife was "a virgin, neither had she known man," a proof that she had never served as bondwoman or handmaid in the tents of any of the godly fathers of Israel. Isaac entered Gerer; the men asked him of his wife, and he lyingly answered, "She is my sister" (Gen. xxvi, 7).

Rebekah was still a fair damsel of only sixty summers. Abimelech, king of the Philistines, was immediately infatuated with her, and sought to excite her tender affections toward himself. Looking out of a window, to his amazement, Abimelech beheld Isaac "sporting with Rebekah," and, being a 'cute monarch, he reasoned within himself in the following strain: "That cannot be his (Isaac's) sister: if it were, he never would sport about with her in that fashion. Now, if it were his country cousin, or his young wife, I could understand such conduct; but to say it is his sister will not do at all." So Abimelech called to Isaac, and made him acknowledge the falseness of his statement. He also very properly censured him for

exposing Rebekah and the amorous young men of the city to such strong temptations. As for the Lord, Mr. Moss observes, he had no word of blame for Saint Isaac, but blessed and prospered him in all his undertakings.

Whether Isaac gave up his wife through fear, or through desire of presents such as his father had received in a similar case, is not known. We find no mention of presents, but as the infallible history is full of omissions of things that we have to guess at, and as we find Isaac wealthy quickly thereafter, we think it not unlikely that the crafty fellow contrived to make the transaction a paying one. In case that his motive was fear instead of avarice, he is equally to be reprobated. Not the humblest man or even youth in these days for an instant dreams of abandoning a female to dishonor when it is threatened by a wayside tramp or by any other ravisher. Every creature, even of the lowest class, that wears the human male form in these days stands by such a charge at the sacrifice of his life if necessary. But the elect of God made it a habitual course basely to yield their wives to everyone who demanded them. How long will it be thought that our youth are

And behold, Isaac was sporting with Rebekah his wife.—Gen. xxvi, 8.

elevated in morals by incitement to imitation of courses an incalculable distance beneath their own?

Dr. Kitto's Biblical Cyclopedia, speaking of the accounts of Abraham and Isaac surrendering their wives, says: "We think that the simplicity and naturalness which pervade . . . them will explode the notion that fiction has had anything to do in bringing the narrative into its present shape." Certainly *morality* has had nothing to do with bringing it into shape.

And the two subjects of these tales, we are to bear in mind, carried into all their dealings the same ill principles which they evinced in their wife-surrenderings. Slavery, it is to be borne in mind, flourished during all these times. These men of God while communing with their divine guardian received from him no condemnation of the practice. That which is not rightful enough for us in these times was good enough for God and his favorites then. When we read that "the Lord blessed" so and so with increase we are to understand this as meaning that God prospered the specified saint's efforts in depriving his fellow-men of their liberty and bringing them under the bitterest yoke in the conception of man. When we are informed that some saint's possessions were greatly multiplied, we must conceive of abundant harvests gathered in to be sure, but of harvests watered by the sweat and blood of heart-broken bondmen. When it is said that some favorite's flocks and herds were added to exceedingly, it is to remembered that an additional number of unfortunate human beings were brought under thrall to serve as keepers. And indeed, there are farther facts that we are not to lose sight of in all these cases, which are, that the bondmen and bondwomen, and wine and meal, and flocks and herds, were quite as often got by rapine and conquest as by other methods. Where is the wonder that with an omnipotent friend favoring all his projects in these rude but ready ways of acquiring pelf, Isaac "waxed great, and went forward, and grew until he became very great" (Gen. xxvi, 13)?

Add to the methods of gathering riches just mentioned, the custom of forcing their women to perform the most laborious of all their work, and we have a very good conception of the means by which the successful robbers and tyrants among the ancient Jews,

And the man waxed great, and went forward, and grew until he became very great.—Gen. xxvi, 13.

the patriarchs, grew to their greatness. Women were employed in those tasks which because of their severity were otherwise given only to slaves and captives. Grinding corn is one of these. Indeed, the situation of women was in all its circumstances oppressed and unhappy. The husband was addressed as lord by his wife, and the very term for husband, *baal*, is the same as that for lord and master. Women, in default of having sons, were inherited by their husbands' brothers. Marriage was commonly by capture or purchase. "They that have wives should be as though they had none," wrote godly St. Paul afterward; and truly these ancient Jews when they had wives were as though they had none, as far as affection and consideration were concerned. "Man," adds Paul, "is the image and glory of God; but woman is the glory of man;" the women of Abraham and Isaac and all the pious patriarchs certainly were the glory of their husbands, the means by which they grew until they became very great. "Neither was the man created for the woman, but the woman for the man," continues

our expresser of those Jewish views on women of which his patriarchal ancestors had been the practioers. In the view of those patriarchs, not only were women created for them, but so too were the surrounding tribes, and the goods of the surrounding tribes, and in short everything which they could lay their hands on. "Did yer hear thet preacher?" excitedly queried one cowboy of another, in a wild Western town, as they emerged from a shanty in which an exhorter had been holding forth; "did yer hear that he didn't talk about nothin' but lost sheep? Fix yer pistol an' let's wait till he comes out and give him a chance to explain what he meant by them personal remarks." If a divine had come among God's friends in time of old and began talking about lost sheep he probably would have struck the greatest trouble of his life. Such were the holy patriarchs who were honored living, and mourned dead, as was Isaac when he " gave up the ghost, and died, and was gathered unto his people, being old and full of days, and his sons Esau and Jacob buried him" (Gen. xxxv, 29).

And Isaac gave up the ghost, and died, **and was gathered unto his** people, being old **and** full of days, **and his** sons Esau and Jacob buried him.—Gen. xxxv, 29.

CHAPTER X.

ONE OF TWINS.

Enter Esau. The means and manner of his entrance are after this fashion: "Isaac entreated the Lord for his wife because she was barren;" the Lord kindly changed his immutable purposes, and Rebekah conceived. This good lady was informed by God that of the twins within her womb "the elder shall serve the younger," whereby the divine speaker showed his partiality for social inequality. He does not say that he will give a fair field to the two and that one may serve the other if they so agree and as long as they agree, but instead has decreed beforehand that the elder *shall* serve the younger. The slaveholder's determination, one race *shall* serve the other, was a match. These twins were born in a ridiculous and fantastic style, the details of which we may as well omit in these days when we know more about delicacy and morality than did the Lord in those early times wherein he was so unfortunate as to live. Esau was born, and continued, "red, all over like a hairy garment." From feelings of modesty rejecting tempting offers from the Great Egyptian Dime Museum, he devoted most of his time to the field, where he became "a cunning hunter." His brother Jacob lived as "a plain man, dwelling in tents." Soon the family became divided by an unhappy partiality. The father had an especial sweet tooth for venison, and grew unduly fond of Esau for keeping him well filled with this savory meat. But Rebekah loved Jacob. And thus a very pretty train of jealousy and intrigue took its start. Presently Esau offended by taking "to wife Judith the daughter of Beeri the Hittite, and Bashemath the daughter of Elon the Hittite." Naturally the parents were displeased at such wrong-doing as taking two wives at once, I hear the reader exclaim. But, bless your simple heart, kind reader, which is so unsophisticated in the ways of the wicked world, and the wicked world's governor and his protégées—the offense was not at all the taking of two wives. That was a thing never condemned in the God-governed era. The wrong lay in the fact that the marriage was into a people with whom the parents were at loggerheads.

And Esau was forty years old when he took to wife Judith the daughter of Beeri the Hittite, and Bashemath the daughter of Elon the Hittite. Which were a grief of mind unto Isaac and to Rebekah.—Gen. xxvi, 34, 35.

CHAPTER XI.

JACOB AND ESAU.

Esau, being the elder brother, possessed the birthright. Jacob envied him, and coveted his right. Now, to anticipate whether or not Jacob would attempt unfair means to obtain his brother's claim, and to learn his character generally, we must consult Rom. ix. 13. Here we find that God had said, "Jacob have I loved, but Esau have I hated." It being beyond challenge that God throughout his intercourse with men regularly selected the rogues for his favorites and disliked the manly and honest, we are at once satisfied by this text that Esau is a good fellow, and Jacob a scoundrel from whom we are to expect scurvy tricks. This expectation begins to be fulfilled as we reach Gen. xxv. 29-34, where we find Jacob in a contemptible and unbrotherly way taking advantage of a suffering moment of Esau's, when, coming in from hunting, he was faint and "at the point to die," to force him to give up his birthright for a mess of pottage to preserve his life.

Having maneuvered Esau out of his birthright, Jacob of course lent willing ear to a scheme which his mother proposed for swindling his brother out of the only thing remaining to him, his father's blessing. Isaac, nearing his end, longed for a last bit of the venison which had so tickled his belly and swayed his affections, and sent Esau for it. "And Rebekah spake unto Jacob her son, saying, Behold, I heard thy father speak unto Esau thy brother, saying, bring me venison, and make me savory meat, that I may eat, and bless thee before the Lord before my death. Now, therefore, my son, obey my voice according to that which I command thee. Go now to the flock, and fetch me from thence two good kids of the goats; and I will make them savory meat for thy father, such as he loveth. And thou shalt bring it to thy father that he may eat, and that he may bless thee before his death. And Jacob said to Rebekah his mother, behold, Esau my brother is a hairy man, and I am a smooth man: My father peradventure will feel me [Isaac was blind], and I shall seem to him as a deceiver: and I shall bring a curse upon me, and not a

REBEKAH PERSUADETH JACOB TO SWINDLE ESAU.—Gen. xxvii, 6-11.

blessing. And his mother said unto him, Upon me be thy curse, my son: only obey my voice, and go fetch me them. And he went, and fetched, and brought them to his mother: and his mother made savory meat, such as his father loved. And Rebekah took goodly raiment of her eldest son Esau, which were with her in the house, and put them upon Jacob her younger son: And she put the skins of the kids of the goats upon his hands, and upon the smooth of his neck: And she gave the savory meat and the bread, which she had prepared, into the hand of her son Jacob."

Jacob the "plain man"—plain like the heathen Chinee with his oily tricks that are peculiar—said to his father, "I am Esau thy first-born." Isaac queried, "How is it that thou hast found it [the venison] so quickly?" The cheating son replied, "Because the Lord thy God brought it to me," adorning his vile deeds with canting phrases in the style which all pious rogues of to-day so notoriously follow. "The voice is Jacob's voice," said Isaac, "but the hands are the hands of Esau . . . Art thou my very son Esau?" Jacob again solemnly

asseverated in a Wanamakerish snuffle, "I am." So the old man finally became convinced, and gave his blessing to the infamous villain.

Pleaded the colored prisoner: "Last time yer had me here I was a good Meffodist and got sent up for borrowing a couple of chickens, while yer let a fellow off who had killed his mudder 'cause he war a somnambulist. I'se changed my creed and when I stole dat pig I war a regular howling somnambulist." Judge: "Three months for the prisoner." Prisoner: "Yo' don't mean ter say dat somnambulists has gone out ob style already. I might jest as well er stayed a Meffodist." Here is the expectation plainly shown that sin against man will be condoned because of loyalty to God, and we will ask the reader if such a way of looking at things is to be wondered at after centuries of instruction in the long string of scriptural history wherein criminals like Jacob are blessed and prospered for devotion to God notwithstanding all their abuses of men like Esau who are honest but not on the Lord's side.

Esau after a while arrived with the real venison. The poor old man "trembled very exceed-

And Jacob said unto his father, I am Esau thy firstborn; I have done according as thou badest me: arise, I pray thee, sit and eat of my venison, that thy soul may bless me. And Isaac said unto his son, How is it that thou hast found it so quickly, my son? And he said, Because the Lord thy God brought it to me.—Gen. xxvii, 19, 20.

ingly," and cried, "Who? Where is he that hath taken venison and brought it me, and . . . I have blessed him?" At the revelation of the infernal deception the unhappy Esau "cried with a great and an exceeding bitter cry." Melancholy scene! All his pleas, "Bless me, even me also, O my father!" were bootless. The old man acted as queerly as most of the strange characters which meet us in these narratives, by refusing to transfer his blessing, and decreeing, "Thou shalt serve thy brother." Esau swore vengeance, and Jacob, being as cowardly as dishonest, fell into a fright. The old lady became frightened for fear she should lose her favorite son, and resorted to lying again to screen her motives and cover her purposes. When she heard that Esau would kill Jacob, she ordered the latter to obey her voice and flee to Laban, her brother, in Haran, and thou went to the old man with a lie in her mouth as usual, pretending, as an excuse why she sent Jacob away, "I am weary of my life because of the daughters of Heth; if Jacob take a wife of the daughters of Heth, such as these

which are of the daughters of the land, what good shall my life do me?"

"What a lying hypocrite!" exclaims the author of "The Godly Women of the Bible." "Did she, this godly woman, fear that Jacob could find any worse wife, any greater liar, a more unfeeling and inhuman woman and mother, than his father Isaac found in Rebekah, his mother. O Rebekah, Rebekah! you were a bad egg, and in these modern times would not answer for a first-rate deacon's wife; but Bible-makers could not dispense with you, as you were one of the great-great-grandmothers of the second person in the trinity, the immaculate savior of mankind."

This remarkably godly woman and holy mother in Israel is not again mentioned in the Old Testament, though referred to in the New as one of the mothers of the Hebrew nation (Rom. ix, 10).

Jacob went to his uncle Laban's and his career will be pursued in connection with Laban's godly daughters—his future wives, the amiable Rachel and her exquisite sister Leah—without

ESAU FINDS THAT JACOB HAS LIED HIM OUT OF HIS RIGHTS.—Gen. xxvii. 32-33.

whom the deity could not have incarnated himself in the person of Jesus Christ.

Critic: "What does that fashionably attired young man with wings represent?" Cartoonist: "The angel of style." Critic: "Who ever saw an angel wear a silk hat and a suit of clothes?" Cartoonist: "Who ever saw one that didn't?" The would-be funny man who wrote the above simply made a fool of himself, for it is here in Gen. xxviii as plain as print can make it that Jacob saw a lot of angels. While on a journey for a wife he one night lay down to sleep and placed some stones under his head for a pillow. We know that this is so, for the Arabs show Jacob's stone pillow at Jerusalem to this day. As if this were not enough, the stone pillow is also in Westminster Abbey, London. Pious men in old times carried it to Scone, Scotland, and it was used at the Scottish king's consecration, and afterward conveyed to the Abbey. Jacob—as was not surprising in view of his pillow—dreamed, and "behold a ladder set up on the earth, and the top of it reached to heaven; and behold the angels of God ascending and descending on it." What on earth—or in

heaven—these creatures wanted a ladder for when they had wings. is one of those things that no fellow can find out, you know. It has been suggested that they were moulting. The Lord, in the language of one paraphrast, comported himself gracefully upon the topmost rung, holding on tight, we suppose, with "his feet like unto fine brass" (Rev. i. 15). While his angels were acrobatically disporting themselves, Jehovah, from time to time encouraging them with a paternal grin, halloed down to Jake that he would do no end of good things for him.

"Mother," asked the youngster. "is Dod everywhere?" "Certainly, my son." "In me, mother?" "Yes, my child. Why do you ask?" "Oh, I was only thinking that you musin't spank me any more." "And why not?" "Because, mother, when you spank me you spank Dod." This doctrine of the present day that God is everywhere, which after all its affirmations by wise councils it would be presumption in us to doubt, was strangely unknown to the patriarchs in the days when Jehovah was most familiar with men and they should have known best all about him. For we continually meet among

And he dreamed, and behold a ladder set up on the earth, and the top of it reached to heaven; and, behold, the angels of God ascending and descending on it.—Gen. xxviii. 12.

them views like that implied in Jacob's remark on awaking, "Surely the Lord is in this place; and I know it not." He was surprised to find the Jewish deity in that strange land, seeming to believe that he confined himself to one limited locality.

When Jake came to consider what the Lord had said, he was sharp enough to see that all of Jehovah's fair words, though fine-sounding enough, were nothing more than the same old promises that he had made Abraham, and never fulfilled. And to tell the truth and shame the devil—no, we mean the other fellow—the promises have not been fulfilled to this day. So Jake, with his national cunning, made his offer with these conditions: "If God will be with me, and will keep me in this way that I go, and will give me bread to eat, and raiment to put on, so that I come again to my father's house in peace, then shall the Lord be my God, . . . and of all that thou shalt give me I will surely give the tenth unto thee." Reasonable enough. If a God is not willing to do anything on his side of the bargain, he cannot expect to draw trade. Let him step aside and

leave counter-room for his betters. Live and let live. If that God would not furnish a fair article at a living price, perhaps some of the other gods of those regions would. This is just the reason that we personally have never given any of our custom to God. He has never been willing to do anything for us on his part of the engagement. We have to work about sixteen hours a day for all of our commodities or go without.

We now enliven and sweeten our romantic tale by the introduction of two of the fair sex—Rachel and Leah. Rachel appears first. Scene, a charming rustic spot, canvas now painted in pink-and-blue-and-green; music plays a tender air; enter Rachel as Little Bo Peep. "And while he yet spake, . . . Rachel came with her father's sheep, for she kept them."

"And Jacob kissed Rachel, and lifted up his voice, and wept" (Gen. xxix, 11). Those moments in a good man's life when some chord of emotion is irresistibly struck and tender feeling wins a momentary indulgence, are creditable to the man, and revered and loved by us. But we must remain as cold to the tears of

And while he yet spake with them, Rachel came with her father's sheep; for she kept them.—Gen. xxix, 9.

this self-seeking fellow, defrauder of his brother and continual wrong-doer, as we should to the like in any miserable rascal of to-day in jail or out. Laban had another daughter, Leah, who was the elder; but "Leah was tender-eyed [i. e., had some defect of the eyes], while Rachel, the younger, was beautiful and well favored," and as young Jacob had fallen in love with her at first sight at the well he told Laban, when he bargained with him for wages, that he would serve him seven years for Rachel, and the daughter-seller accepted the proposal for wife-flesh with alacrity. But Uncle Laban was not quite so fair in the trade as his nephew had supposed. Knowing that "tender-eyed" Leah would not be salable property in the matrimonial market, he conceived the idea of substituting Leah for Rachel, and may be supposed to have reasoned thus: "Now, if I let Jacob take beautiful Rachel what am I ever to do with her homely elder sister, Leah? Shall I not always have her, an old maid, on my hands? Jacob loves Rachel so well that he will serve another seven years for her if I put Leah in her sister's place. Besides, I shall secure

fourteen years' wages. I'll do it!" So he deluded Jacob in some way, likely enough by getting him blind drunk with the wine which the saints consumed so freely, and on his bridal morn the son-in-law awoke to find that he had gone in unto Leah. Mortified at finding himself, whom he had supposed unrivaled in saintly swindles, so egregiously overreached, he upbraided Laban, who after making a paltry excuse offered Rachel for another seven years' work. Jacob worked a week of this second term, at the end of which week Laban had promised that he could have Rachel, and then in happy Mormonistic possession of two wives finished his seven years.

On the foregoing getting of wives a lady writer remarks: "It does not appear that these girls had one word to say in this matter, but were bargained off by their father like cattle without consultation or consent; and whatever may have been Rachel's feelings when her father supplanted her with Leah, was of no manner of consequence; her affections were not to be taken into consideration, neither were Leah's—thus to be bartered off like a lame ani-

And Jacob kissed Rachel and lifted up his voice, and wept.—Gen. xxix, 11.

mal, deceiving the purchaser, who would not have bought had he known the value of the stock. And yet our Christian friends have the audacity to inform us that woman owes her present elevation and privileges to the Bible and religious influences arising from its teachings. I deny the assumption, and will prove from and by the book that its whole tendency is to degrade woman and give her an inferior position, ranking her even among the cattle, as in the tenth commandment."

To add to this, concubinage comes on the heels of polygamy. Rachel and Leah were jealous of their husband and envious of each other. Rachel, failing to bear children as Leah had done, gave Jacob Bilhah her maid, by whom he had two sons. Leah, feeling herself able to see her sister and go her one better, contributed Zilpah her maid, and more offspring gladdened the saintly hearth. Mr. Foote says: "Rachel appears to have owned Jacob and farmed him out. Leah's eldest son found some mandrakes in the field and brought them home. 'Give me some,' said Rachel to Leah, 'and Jacob shall sleep with you to-night. The

bargain was struck, and Leah posted off to meet Jacob. 'Thou must come in unto me,' she said, 'for surely I have hired thee with my son's mandrakes.' Holy scripture adds that 'he lay with her that night.' This is a very pretty story for parents to put in the hands of their daughters! Surely the word of an all-wise God might teach something more useful and decent."

And through all this polygamy and concubinage the Lord was superintendent, condemning nothing but ordering all, that the seed of Abraham should flourish and that the line of Israel should flow on to the end of the production of Jesus Christ.

An urchin who had pounded his finger related: "I came near saving devil, but then I remembered papa has told us we must not take the name of the Lord our God in vain." Do not appearances indicate that it was the devil whom the Bible patriarchs had for the Lord their God? Was not the conduct in them which their Lord sanctioned, and often commanded, of a nature which would be most acceptable to the devil?

THE CURTAIN DROPS.—(Read your Bibles at Gen. xxix and xxx.)

Jacob, having got Laban to agree that the speckled and spotted cattle should belong to the son-in-law and the rest to the uncle, placed before the animals who were about bringing forth young, rods covered with speckles and streaks, that the offspring might have the same markings. This is, in Mr. Foote's words, a brilliant specimen of Bible biology!

Youatt, who is a high authority on breeding, attributes this result to "the power of the imagination in the mother, carried to an extent *the like of which is certainly not seen in the present day*," or to "some superior over-ruling agency." St. Jerome, St. Augustine, and St. Isidore, who probably knew as much about sheep and cattle as about the Copernican astronomy, held that Jacob's method of breeding was perfectly natural; but St. Chrysostom, Theodoret, and others, who were equally learned on the subject, held that it was "something above nature." "It is scarcely necessary," remarks G. W. Foote, "to say that modern farmers are not in the habit of following Jacob's methods. Those were Bible days, and Bible sheep and cattle."

Finally, having got about all of Laban's belongings—daughters, sheep, cattle, and goats— Jacob sneaked off while his wife's father was out sheep-steal—we mean sheep-shearing. As a crowning misdeed, Rachel took along Laban's gods (*teraphim*, household gods, images of gods). Atheists of to-day who likewise have not a god to worship may imagine the poor old fellow's feelings. He pursued the guilty couple, resolved to inflict upon Jacob the terrors of the law against abducting daughters, and of the law against stealing gods, if there was such a one. His meeting with his godly wronger is portrayed by our artist. Farther on his journey Jacob met Esau and received the forgiveness of that generous-hearted brother.

The most remarkable part of this narrative is the account of the extraordinary wrestling match between God and Jacob during the night (Gen. xxxii, 24-32). Jacob rose in the night and sent his two wives, his two concubines, and his eleven children and all his treasures, over the ford of Jabbok, and he was left alone, and God came in and wrestled with him till the break of day. The Bible does not state whether this match was made up on a wager or

And Jacob was wroth and chode with Laban, etc.—Gen. xxxi, 36.

whether the two wrestled all night simply for sport.

Jacob must have been one of the most powerful athletes ever known, to hold an even contest with God so vigorously for several hours. It may easily be supposed that any of the most noted gymnasts or prize-fighters that ever lived would be unable to hold God an even contest for hours, if God did his best. If he would consent to meet the ablest of them in a contest of this kind, had we money to risk on the result we should bet on God every time.

Still God seems to have gained nothing until he took an unfair advantage and put Jacob's hip out of joint. By modern rules such conduct would be called "foul," and would forfeit the game and the stakes. But God doubtless considered it fair, as daylight had come and it was important he should be off. He had asked Jacob to let him go, but Jacob had refused, unless God would comply with his demands, so the

putting out of his hip perhaps was, after all, justifiable.

We recollect that in our boyhood days wrestling was tabooed by the strictest teachers of morality as being of an immoral and objectionable tendency, but if God engaged in it, and gave lessons to one that he was so partial to as he was to Jacob, we cannot see upon what grounds the exercise can be pronounced immoral. What was done by God and Jacob would seem good enough for anybody. Though God saw fit to put Jacob's hip out of joint, he did not leave him in that unpleasant predicament without doing something for him in return. Before this time he had simply been called Jacob; but God now gave him the name of "Israel." Jacob may have considered this full compensation for the injury inflicted, but for our own part, we would not have our hip put out of joint for a dozen new names.

And Jacob was left alone; and there wrestled a man with him until the breaking of the day.— Gen. xxxii. 24.

CHAPTER XII.

JOSEPH THE MAN OF DREAMS.

ISRAEL, or Jacob, we are informed, had one son whom he loved better than any of the others. The reason for this preference was not, of course, any excess of merit in Joseph, but one purely fanciful and arbitrary, or perhaps selfish. It was that Joseph "was the son of his old age." Wherefore Jacob invested his favorite in "a coat of many colors." The artist, we see, supposes this garment to have been a crazy-quilt picked up somewhere by old Jacob, which we think likely enough. American Indians used to seize upon the queerest pieces of gay-colored apparel which they could get from the whites, and, ludicrously arrayed in tattered chamber-gowns or fiery red flannel shirts, strut about in the belief that they were enrobed in majesty unapproachable. If the artist wishes to conjecture that Jacob while prowling about the outskirts of some of the civilizations which environed the Jewish barbarians lit upon a discarded crazy-quilt and found it good in his eyes, why, our pictorial illustrator has as good a

right to his opinion as any commentator.

Joseph's brothers all hated him. Perhaps the hate arose from a very natural fear of their father's partial and unjust preference for Joseph resulting prejudicially to themselves. Or perhaps it sprang from that dissensious disposition for which the ancient Jews were notorious. We do not accuse their present generations; civilization has ameliorated the savage natures of all races: but it is undeniable that the Jewish people of Bible times were of an exceptionally envious and bickering temper. To this quality their nation owes its fall and dispersion.

Whatever may have been the origin of the dislike of Joseph by his brothers, it at least soon received just ground for continuance and growth, in a conceited and arrogant recital by that individual of two dreams in which they were represented as prostrating themselves to him. Drs. Oort and Hooykaas say: "It would hardly be worth while to stay to inquire expressly whether Joseph's conduct will bear testing, had not his character often been described as noble, and even as one of the most exalted to be found in the Old Testament. But since our moral perception may easily suffer from

Now Israel loved **Joseph more** than all his children, because he **was the son** of his old **age, and** he made him a coat of many colors.—Gen. xxxvii, 3.

such perverted judgments, we must enter an emphatic protest against this excessive praise of him. Joseph as a boy, repeating a dream in which his own exaltation is foretold, twice over, and telling his father tales about his brothers, is surely no one's ideal; but the brutal chastisement inflicted on him by his brothers seems at least to have had the effect of taking down his conceit."

The brutal chastisement of which the foregoing extract speaks consisted in casting the young boaster into a pit. About this incident, as about all others in the lives of the patriarchs, there are numerous legends. And besides the many books in existence, we are told of others that have been lost. The particular legend which happens to be foisted on us in our collection of "inspired books" says that "the pit was empty, there was no water in it." But an oriental tradition says that there was water, and Joseph stood on a stone. And the rabbis relate that it was dry, but full of scorpions and adders.

The story as it usually goes in our Sabbath-schools and churches runs that Joseph's brothers, with the pecuniary alertness of their race,

did not let slip the possibility of making money, but sold their captive. Josephus makes the number of pieces of silver which they received twenty; the Hebrew version gives it as twenty; the Vulgate, thirty; the Septuagint, twenty pieces, but of gold. Now, as each of these legends has just as good authentication as the one in Genesis, we may believe whichever tickles our fancy and agrees with our constitution, and remain guiltless—except in the eyes of our parson.

But it is when we strike the next event that we must recoil in failure and vexation. "Eh, mon," said the Scotch divine to a son of Erin who had strayed into his congregation; "eh, mon, but treating that text was vara deeficult!" "Be jabers," cried the Hibernian, "Oi wish it had been impossible." That it had been impossible to write the account of Joseph, is our feeling wish when we attempt to disentangle its complications. For here we are met by a contradiction, not between the biblical narrative and a non-biblical, but between one part of the biblical and another part. Now, in the language of the stage, may herring help us, for other aid is cut off] Gen. xxxvii. 25-28, reads: "A com-

And they took him, and cast him into a pit: and the pit was empty, there was no water in it.—Gen. xxxvii. 24.

pany of Ishmaelites came from Gilead with their camels, . . . And Judah said unto his brethren, Come, and let us sell him to the Ishmaelites, . . . and his brethren were content. Then there passed by Midianites, merchant men; and they drew and lifted up Joseph out of the pit, and sold Joseph to the Ishmaelites for twenty pieces of silver: and they brought Joseph into Egypt." Who can make head or tail of this? *Who* drew up Joseph? *Who* sold him?

It is on such confused passages as this that millions of men have believed their salvation to depend, and they have accordingly squandered on their elucidation untold time and labor, and shed over differences in their understanding seas of blood. For it is not merely the historical portions of the Bible that lie in such strange jumble, but likewise those passages of supposed fearful import to the everlasting beatitude or perdition of man.

The remarks of Drs. Oort, Hooykaas, and Kuenen upon this fearfully and wonderfully made narrative are of value. Dr. Oort is professor of Oriental languages, etc., at Amsterdam; Dr. Hooykaas, pastor at Rotterdam; Dr. Kuenen,

professor of Theology at Leiden. These men have led in the movement which has brought to light the true origin of the scriptures, and are shunned as too radical by some, but the greater part of the Christian world is involuntarily attracted by their scholarship and ability. They say: "If we read this story straight through it runs pretty smoothly, and we should hardly guess that, like most of the legends of the patriarchs, it is put together from two accounts. So it is, however. Here and there slight contradictions and repetitions betray the joints and fastenings, and show us that the work is not all of one piece. In many points the two traditions differ considerably from each other. According to one, for example, Joseph is sold to some Ishmaelites by his brothers, while the other relates that he was thrown into the well by his brothers, and was found there by some Midianites who were passing by, so that he was really stolen, as he tells the chief butler in prison, from the land of Canaan, which is here described, somewhat prematurely, as the land of the Hebrews. According to one tradition he is imprisoned on the accusation of Potiphar's wife; the other knows nothing of this circum-

Then there passed by Midianites, merchant-men; and they drew and lifted up Joseph out of the pit, and sold Joseph to the Ishmeelites for twenty pieces of silver; and they brought Joseph into Egypt.—Gen. xxxvii, 28.

stance, and brings Joseph to the prison not as accused of any crime, but simply as the slave of Potiphar who had charge of the prisoners. If we could separate the two stories accurately we should have mentioned each of them separately. But as that is at present impossible, we have given the narrative as it lies before us in Genesis." At the close of the tale of Joseph these doctors indulge in a retrospect of the book of Genesis, and remark : "The first point that excites our attention is the extraordinary manner in which the book of Genesis is put together. We cannot help asking, 'How could sensible men by any possibility write such a book?' For what is it that we have observed? That this book is made up of portions of at least three works. . . . No doubt my readers have sometimes become quite perplexed in listening to these legends so strangely fused together and worked up into a single whole, and now and then the scholars who are trying to separate the whole into its parts feel just the same confusion. Since the middle of the last century, when a French physician published a book to show that Genesis is made up of different fragments, many Biblical scholars have

devoted their powers to this question, and though great progress has been made already, we are not at the end of our labors yet."

This being, like all novels which aspire to popularity, "A Tale of Love and Passion" as well as of Adventure and Intrigue, it is time for woman, lovely woman, to glide upon the scene. She now proceeds to glide in the person of Potiphar's wife. Who Potiphar was the devil only knows. The Lord doesn't, for in the legends which he has transmitted to us through his sacred people, the Jews, Potiphar is said to be sometimes one thing and sometimes the other. Genesis calls him "an officer of Pharaoh, captain of the guard." So the usual rendering of the original, but Dr. Kitto translates it "chief of the royal police ;" and Dr. Taylor, "chief of the executioners." Josephus and the *Testaments* are shabby enough to give Potiphar no higher office than that of chief cook. However all that may be, he had a wife who became desperately enamored of Joseph. Well she might be, if there is truth in the Oriental traditions that Joseph was so beautiful as to be styled the Moon of Canaan, or in the rabbinical legends that his face shone like the sun and all females

And it came to pass after these things, that his master's wife, etc. But he refused, etc. Read Gen. xxxix.

ran out on their terraces to see the light, while the wealthy ladies of Heliopolis sent their husbands or other relatives to purchase him. Mrs. Potiphar, if we follow the Bible account, solicited him to acts of license, and finally caught hold of his garment, when he fled and left it in her hand. She, mortified, represented to her husband that Joseph had attempted her virtue by force, and exhibited the garment as proof. Josephus, the rabbis, and the *Testaments* give many details not in Genesis. The Mohammedans also have in their Koran an account, one of the circumstances of which is that Joseph " would have resolved to enjoy her, had he not seen an evident demonstration of his Lord." To this statement Sale in his translation of the Koran appends a foot-note: " Some . . . suppose that the words mean some miraculous voice or apparition, sent by God to divert Joseph from executing the criminal thoughts which began to possess him. For they say that he was so far tempted with his mistress's beauty and enticing behavior that he sat in her lap, and even began to undress himself, when a voice called to him, and bade him beware of her; but he taking no notice of this admonition, though it

was repeated three times, at length the angel Gabriel, or, as others will have it, the figure of his master, appeared to him; but the more general opinion is that it was the apparition of his father Jacob, who bit his fingers' ends, or, as some write, struck him on the breast, whereupon his lubricity passed out at the ends of his fingers."

The Koran adds an ingenious little story, in which Potiphar's wife's cousin, then a baby in the cradle, plays a miraculous part. This infant cried to Potiphar, " If his garment be rent before, she [Potiphar's wife] speaketh truth, and he [Joseph] is a liar; but if his garment be rent behind, she lieth, and he is a speaker of the truth." And when " her husband saw that his garment was torn behind, he said, . . . O woman, ask pardon for thy crime, for thou art a guilty person. And certain women said publicly in the city, The nobleman's wife asked her servant to lie with her: he hath inflamed her breast with his love; and we perceive her to be in a manifest error. And when she heard of their subtle behavior, she sent unto them, and prepared a banquet for them, and she gave to each of them a knife; and she said unto

And he left his garment in her hand, and fled, and got him out.—Gen. xxxix, 12.

Joseph, Come forth unto them. And when they
saw him they praised him greatly; and they
cut their own hands, and said, O God! this is
not a mortal; he is no other than an angel, de-
serving the highest respect. And his mistress
said, This is he for whose sake ye blame me:
I asked him to lie with me, but he hath constantly refused. But if he do not perform that
which I command him, he shall surely be cast
into prison, and he shall be made one of the contemptible. Joseph's . . . LORD heard him, and
turned aside their snares from him; for he both
heareth and knoweth. And it seemed good
unto them, even after they had seen the signs of
his innocency, to imprison him for a time." By
the " them " who continued to imprison him,
Potiphar and his friends are meant. The motive of their detaining Joseph in prison is said
to be, either that they suspected him to be
guilty, notwithstanding the proofs which had
been given of his innocence, or else that Zolei-
kah (so the Koran calls Potiphar's wife) desired
it, feigning, to deceive her husband, that she
wanted to have Joseph removed from her sight
till she could conquer her passion by time;

though her real design was to force him to
compliance.

Dreams and their interpretations, with which
Joseph began his career, now pour upon us
thicker and thicker. The chief butler and the
chief baker were imprisoned with our hero. The
former had a dream one night, and Joseph
interpreted it to signify that the dreamer would
be reinstated in three days. The latter produced a dream likewise, but Joseph could find
for it no better import than that the baker
would be executed in three days. Both dreams
came true. The whole story hinges upon
dreams. Joseph dreams; the butler and the
baker dream; and Pharaoh dreams. And it is
clear that very great importance is attached to
these visions, for they all come out true, and are
evidently looked upon as communications from
God. This seems strange to us, who use the
word dream as the symbol of all that is vain
and unreal, but it was not by any means so in
ancient times. It was the common belief of all
nations that dreams were sent by the gods, and
of course, as a necessary consequence, that the
art of interpreting them was a science. It is

And Joseph's master took him, and put him into the prison, a place where the king's prisoners were bound: and he was there in the prison. —Gen. xxxix, 20.

easy to see how this belief came to be held. The dread of everything incomprehensible played an important part in the formation of the religious representations and ideas of the ancients, and it need not surprise us therefore if the mysterious phenomena of dreams, the clearness with which one sometimes sees all kinds of things in one's sleep, the misery or delight one experiences on these occasions, the recollection, sometimes so clear and sometimes so confused, that is left behind—it need not surprise us, we say, if all this made a deep impression upon people's minds, and was ascribed to the action of a deity. There is a characteristic passage in the celebrated Roman author Cicero, which helps us to understand the views of the ancients in the last century before Christ, in a time, that is, when people were beginning to give themselves some account of their beliefs. Cicero attaches great importance to dreams, and says that "what happens to a seer or soothsayer in his waking hours is experienced by ordinary people when asleep. For then, while the body is prostrate and almost dead, the soul is awake, and is free from the influence of the senses, and from all

distracting care. Since the soul has existed from all eternity and has held intercourse with countless numbers of other souls, it sees everything that lies in the nature of things, if only it is not too much disturbed by excess of eating and drinking to be able to keep awake while the body is asleep. Thus it is that the dreamer has power to read the future. The power of interpreting what the dreamer sees is no natural gift, but an artificially acquired power. . . . . Inasmuch as there is a great deal that is obscure and ambiguous in dreams, oracles, and predictions, we have recourse to the explanation of interpreters." Such was the argument of a philosopher from whose mind simple unreasoning faith had long vanished. In early times no such arguments as these were used, but people believed—without ever for a moment doubting their belief—in the first place that it was often God's will to reveal the future to man, and in the next place that dreams were amongst the means by which he did so. And thus in Israel the dream, together with the vision of the prophet and the oracle of the priest, was looked upon as a very common means by which Jehovah revealed his will ; and

And he made him to ride in the second chariot which he had: and they cried before him, Bow the knee: and he made him ruler over all the land of Egypt.—Gen. xli. 43.

the "dreamers" are mentioned by the side of the prophets and the priests. Although this age does not believe in the supernormal significance of dreams, it largely believes in this story of Joseph which is based on them, and so we will continue the narrative. Pharaoh had a dream in which seven lean kine devoured seven fat ones, and another dream in which seven thin ears of corn consumed seven full ears. On the butler's suggestion Joseph was sent for; he interpreted the dreams to mean seven years of famine following, and consuming the produce of, seven years of plenty. Whereupon Pharaoh, very strangely it seems to us, without waiting for verification, made Joseph prime minister, and "made him to ride in the second chariot which he had" (Gen. xli, 43).

We now come to the most infamous action of this Bible hero, and can do no better than copy the words of the English writer, G. W. Foote, concerning it. "Pharaoh's grand vizier began to save corn against the famine. According to the Bible, Joseph 'gathered corn as the sand of the sea,' and laid it up in granaries. The Jewish historian adds that he 'took the corn of the husbandmen, allotting as much to everyone

as would be sufficient for seed and for food, but without discovering to anyone the reason why he did so.' This virtuous Joseph was therefore a regrator, or, as the Yankees say, 'a coruerer.' He monopolized grain to sell at famine prices. Yet his action is approved and praised by men who ask for laws against the same thing being done now. In fact, the Yankees have passed a law against it, though Joseph is still treated as a perfect saint in all the churches and chapels in the United States. When the famine came 'the dearth was in all lands;' but we suspect it was like the darkness at the crucifixion, which covered the whole earth, yet was invisible at a distance. The Egyptians were obliged to buy corn of Joseph, or else starve. At first he sold for money, but he soon had all their cash. Next he took their horses and cattle. Then he took all their land, and when the transaction was finished he said ' Behold, I have bought you this day and your lands for Pharaoh' (Gen. xlvii, 23). *You* and your *lands!* They had lost all their possessions, and had become slaves to boot. Wishing to put a good face on this affair, Josephus says that he 'gave them back their land entirely,' but Whiston is obliged

And Joseph's ten brethren went down to buy corn in Egypt.—Gen. xlii, 3.

to differ from his author. 'It seems to me,' he writes, 'that the land was now considered Pharaoh's land, and this fifth part as its rent, to be paid to him, as he was their landlord, and they his tenants; and the lands were not properly restored, and this fifth part reserved as tribute only till the days of Sesostris.' Dr. Taylor says that Joseph 'also gave them back their cattle,' but he draws on his fancy for the statement, as there is not a suggestion of it in the scripture. Had the people been properly warned of the approaching drought, and provision made in the public granaries, they might have maintained themselves during the famine. It is infamous to trade on a natural calamity. What would be thought of a mercenary wretch who took advantage of the public starvation to reduce his fellows into a state of perpetual slavery or dependence? Yet that is what Joseph did, if there is any truth in the story. He was as cunning and unscrupulous a minion as ever basked in the smiles of a king. Joseph dealt with the people he had 'bought' in a high-handed manner. He 'removed them to cities from one end of the borders of Egypt even to the other end thereof.' 'This has

been supposed an arbitrary measure, in order to break the ties of attachment, in the former possessors, to their native farms.' Let it be observed that Joseph did not buy up the land of the priests, who were the highest caste, and in whom 'one-third of the whole land of the country was inalienably vested.' They were all supported gratis during the famine. The fact is, the priests were the real rulers of Egypt."

The land of Joseph's brethren becoming famine-stricken, ten of them "went down to buy corn in Egypt" (Gen. xlii, 3).

The brothers of this great grain-cornerer and friend of God (probably God is a friend of our present monopolists) made application to him for corn. They failed to recognize him. His proceedings thereupon are detailed in Gen. xlii to xlv. His conduct toward his brothers is anything but generous, and shows that he took an unfeeling and spiteful pleasure in annoying them. He conceals the fact that he recognizes them at once, and knowingly and purposely brings a false accusation against them; he puts them in prison three days—keeps Simeon back—compels his brother Benjamin, whom he is said to have loved tenderly, to un-

And Joseph saw his brethren, and he knew them, but made himself strange unto them, and spake roughly unto them; and he said unto them, Whence come ye? And they said, From the land of Canaan, to buy food.—Gen. xlii, 7.

dertake a journey which his father fears may be fatal to him—disturbs and alarms his brothers on two occasions by means of the money which they flu t mysteriously returned into their sacks —relieves them from their anxiety by his friendly reception only to make them still more uneasy about the cup that is found in Benjamin's sack of corn—and, most inexcusable of all, entirely overlooks the great and bitter sorrow that his conduct inflicts upon his gray-headed father. In the story it all turns out well, but, supposing it to be true, "more by good luck than good conduct." Though the writers intended their Joseph for a sketch of a model son and brother, they have not been successful. Joseph certainly seems very tender-hearted, and weeps, when he sees his brothers on the first occasion, and again when he meets Benjamin afterward; but for all that he is hard-hearted enough systematically in cold blood to punish them for the suffering they inflicted on him.

No thoughtful person can long remain in doubt as to the historical or unhistorical character of the story of Joseph. For we cannot possibly look upon a story as historical when sundry dreams, regarded as divine revelations,

appear in it, and its development hinges to a large extent upon those dreams and their fulfillment But we have spoken of this already. Now let us examine the credibility of the latter portion of the narrative. The representation here given is impossibility itself.

Only think for a moment of these points.

The famine was foretold seven years before it began, and during the whole interval the king did everything that could be done to lighten the misery that was to come. Yet no one else in Egypt or elsewhere appears to have taken any precautions, though there was nothing to prevent everyone's knowing all about it. Moreover, the whole world suffers from the famine, and is obliged to go to Egypt for corn. This is necessarily involved in the story; for why else should Jacob's sons have chosen Egypt for their second as well as their first purchase of corn? Is such a state of things credible in real life? Again, Jacob sends ten of his sons, each with his own ass, to buy corn. One cannot help asking why he did not send one son at the head of a caravan. What little provision was laid in in this way, however, cannot have gone far toward supporting the whole family, especially

And they laded their asses with the corn, and departed thence. —Gen. xlii. 26.

if, as we are told, part of it had to be used as fodder for the beasts on the way. Then, in Egypt things are managed after a somewhat homely fashion. Joseph sells corn to all the world in person. This is almost impossible to imagine, but it is distinctly the meaning of the story. It would appear from the story that there were no merchants in Egypt, and that no creature could carry corn to Canaan without buying it from the viceroy in person. Finally, the representation of Benjamin as a boy whose life would be in danger if he were separated from his father, hardly agrees with another piece of information according to which he was at this very time the father of ten sons.

Joseph now "went up to meet Israel his father, to Goshen, and presented himself unto him, and wept on his neck a good while" (Gen. xlvi. 29). Like many persons who treat the outside world villainously, he had that egotistic partiality for his own inner household, because it was *his*, which is but a modified selfishness.

Finally "Joseph died being a hundred and ten years." In his age we see an example of the gradual reduction of longevity that runs down the line of scriptural characters. The fabling priests who made up the stories placed their greatest wonders in the remotest periods, where they would be most easily believed. As they approached the present ages about which their hearers and readers would know more and therefore be more critical, they approximated nearer the truth. No one of information in this age believes that the ancient Jews lived to any of the inordinate periods with which the Bible credits them, and many of which we have copied into this book. Every evidence of science is to the effect that human longevity has been increasing steadily from a time about three or four centuries ago. All inference is against any measurable variation for eons before that date.

In closing the history of Joseph we may remark that he is, preëminently above his fellow-saints of scripture, the character of Dreams. And how shameful is it that our children in Sunday-schools have so much of their time engrossed with this Man of Dreams and his visions, to the exclusion of knowledge of any practical use. Study of dreams belongs not to the men and women of this age, not even to the children, but to a savage race and time. To savages, then, among others those thorough savages the ancient Jews, let dreams be left.

And Joseph made ready his chariot, and went up to meet Israel his father, to Goshen, and presented himself unto him; and he fell on his neck, and wept on his neck a good while.—Gen. xlvi, 29.

CHAPTER XIII.

HOLY MOSES.

By Egypt's banks, contiguous to the Nile,
King Pharaoh's daughter went to bathe in style;
She shed her duds and had a pleasant swim,
Then ran along the shore to dry her skin
(For towels in them days were not invented,
And with an annual bath were folks contented).
Disporting 'mong the rushes, thick and thin,
She found the basket which the child lay in.
She drawed the ark and child out from the water—
Inspection showed the kid was not a daughter—
Then to her maids she said in accents mild,
"Which of yez ladies is it owns the child?
'Tis none of yourn, ye all are quick to say:
I doubt your word; I've knowed yez many a day.
But since he have a nose like Hebrew noses,
Bedad, he shall be christened Holy Moses!"
—(Parochial Hymn).

AT this point the reader should be informed
that in the light of modern investigation that
part of the account of the Jewish nation which
we have so far given is discovered to be wholly
without historical ground. That such persons
as Abraham, Isaac, Jacob, etc., ever lived we
have no more reason to suppose than we have
to believe in the existence of Jack the Giant-
killer. And the story of Joseph seems to have
been added to the preceding to account for the
location of the Hebrews in Egypt. His highly
improbable rise to office, his bringing of his
family into that land, etc., were all devised to
that end. The fact with which authentic
history opens is that there were in Egypt an
alien and oppressed race, who left or were
ejected, and from them descended our modern
Jews. What comes before in the scripture is
all fable. What comes after is in part true, but
intermingled with impossible relations with
which Jewish writers have from age to age
essayed to adorn it. Here, then, history begins.
The author of "The Religion of Israel" says:
"The history of the religion of Israel must
start from the sojourn of the Israelites in Egypt.
Formerly it was usual to take a much earlier
starting-point, and to begin with a religious dis-
cussion of the religious ideas of the Patriarchs.
And this was perfectly right, so long as the accounts of Abraham, Isaac and Jacob were considered historical. But now that a strict investigation has shown us that all these stories
are entirely unhistorical, of course we have to
begin the history later on." Dunlap says:

And the daughter of Pharaoh came down to wash herself at the river; and her maidens walked along by the river's side; and when she saw the ark among the flags, she sent her maid to fetch it. And when she had opened it, she saw the child: and, behold, the babe wept. And she had compassion on him, and said, This is one of the Hebrews' children. — Ex. ii, 5, 6.

"The Hebrews came out of Egypt, and settled among the Canaanites. They need not be traced beyond the Exodus. That is their historical beginning." Professor Goldzhier says: "The residence of the Hebrews in Egypt, and their exodus thence under the guidance and training of an enthusiast for the freedom of his tribe, form a series of strictly historical facts which find confirmation even in the documents of ancient Egypt. But the traditional narratives of these events [were] elaborated by the Hebrew people." Count de Volney observes: "What Exodus says of their [the Israelites'] servitude under the king of Heliopolis, and of the oppression of their hosts, the Egyptians, is extremely probable. It is here their history begins. All that precedes . . . is nothing but mythology and cosmogony."

It may have seemed somewhat heartless in us to leave the tender young Moses all this time in the unpleasant fix in which our last illustration revealed him; but the fact is, his getting into that pickle came about through conditions affecting the whole of his race in Egypt, and we must come to him through first attending to those conditions. The king under whom Joseph

had acted as viceroy with such favor was dead, and the succeeding Pharaoh reduced that regent's kinsmen to bondage. Through fear of their increasing numbers he ordered the midwives of Egypt, Siphrah and Puah (only two to that great nation!), to destroy all male Hebrew infants on birth. Siphrah and Puah contrived by subterfuges not to execute this mandate. Therefore the Lord "dealt well with the midwives, . . . and made them houses" (Ex. i, 20, 21). This is among the most curious of the handicrafts at one time and another taken up by the Lord. What sort of houses they were that this Jack-at-all-trades built—with what architecture, fixtures, plumbing, sanitary arrangements, etc.—we are left without knowing. That these notable edifices were not preserved is equally a wonder and a pity. But like as not the Bible does not mean real houses at all. It rarely means what it is supposed to. Pharaoh's next resort was to order Egyptians to slay all Hebrew male children by throwing them into the Nile. The infant Moses was committed by his mother to a basket on that river, in hope that he might in some way be saved. He was found by Pharaoh's daughter while she was

And he looked this way and that way, and, when he saw that there was no man, he slew the Egyptian, and hid him in the sand.—Ex. ii. 12

bathing, and spared and reared. Moses's history falls into three periods—first, from infancy to the age of forty; second, from the age of forty to that of eighty, while he was a shepherd in Midian; third, from eighty to one hundred and twenty, during which time he led the children of Israel in their wanderings. His first period has no further events recorded of it, till its close by means of a pious murder committed by him. An Egyptian had struck a Hebrew. Moses "looked this way and that way, and when he saw that there was no man, he slew the Egyptian, and hid him in the sand" (Ex. ii, 12). "He who commits such a deed," wrote Goethe, "approves himself a thorough barbarian." Milman himself is constrained to admit that Moses was "guilty of a crime, by the Egyptian law, of the most enormous magnitude." He had incurred "the unpardonable guilt of bloodshed." Subsequently, in dealing with the first plague, Milman allows that the Egyptians viewed murder with the greatest abhorrence, and that "to shed, or even to behold blood, was repugnant to all their feelings and prejudices."

After setting this example of disregard of law

and indulgence of rage to all our present-day Bible-believers whom we are trying to get to go by law and restrain rage, the man of God fled to Midian and became a shepherd. Forty years passed, when one day while rounding up his sheep in a mountain called Horeb he observed the unusual phenomenon of smoke proceeding from a bush without the bush being consumed. Remarking that "where there was so much smoke there must be some fire," he approached. As he did so a voice from the foliage inquired, "Moses, is that you?" Being taken unawares, he told the truth and replied in the affirmative. The voice continued, "Take off your shoes and put yourself in a receptive frame of mind. This is a séance." The fugitive murderer was instructed to return to Egypt and deliver the Lord's people. Upon said assassin's doubting that Pharaoh would heed his request to let the people go, Jehovah reached behind to a bag of eye-deceiving contrivances for performing tricks of legerdemain which he had obtained of Hermann and Kellar, and whipped out an imitation snake with springs for wriggling and gunpowder for hissing and spitting. Upon Moses throwing his staff on the ground Jehovah deftly cast his

And the Lord said unto him, What is that in thy hand? And he said, A rod. And he said, Cast it on the ground. And he cast it on the ground, and it became a serpent; and Moses fled from before it.—Ex. iv. 2, 3.

snake upon it so that the serpent appeared to have sprung from transformation of the stick. He then gave Moses the apparatus for this and several other tricks with which to scare Pharaoh into compliance, and pompously closed the séance. Moses, proceeding to embark in his new conjuring business, "took his wife and his sons, and set them upon an ass, and returned to the land of Egypt."

Our artist has taken another view of these snaky transactions, and asks, "Did Mose have the D. T.'s?" Considering the proverbial fury and rancor into which debates between biblical commentators have always fallen, we shall dignifiedly refuse argument.

In regard to this snake-producing miracle, and similar ones which, we shall soon see, Moses and others afterward performed, we shall introduce remarks by Kelso. Some of their details refer to events which the course of our Gallery of Historical Pictures has not yet reached; but our recital is not half so mixed up as the scripture itself, and besides, our irregularity is done with a purpose, and we don't think that the exegesists could discover what purpose on earth the Bible was written for in a century of the perpetual Sunday which the God-in-the-Constitution party is trying to bring about.

Colonel Kelso writes: "If, without losing its identity, a serpent could thus exist a portion of the time as a wooden rod, could not a man do the same? Is there anything incredible, then, in the Arabian tales which have men change into dogs, horses, stones, etc.? Did not this tale, like nearly all other similar tales, originate in Arabia? When Moses changed his rod into a serpent, Pharaoh, for whose benefit the trick was performed, did not appear to be in the least surprised. He seemed to be well acquainted with the trick, and to show Moses that it was nothing new, and that it did not indicate, on the part of the performer, the possession of any supernatural powers, he instantly called in his magicians, who did not claim any such powers, and had them perform the same trick. They seemed to fully understand the trick, and, when required to do so, promptly proceeded to perform it. If, then, you still insist upon the truth of this monstrous snake story, you are bound to admit that, by their own powers or enchantments, mere men

And Moses took his wife and his sons, and set them upon an ass, and he returned to the land of Egypt. And Moses took the rod of God in his hand.—Ex. iv, 39.

could, and did, and consequently can yet perform the genuine and truly astonishing miracle of changing dry wooden rods into living serpents as perfect, in all their parts, as are those produced by nature. How, then, do you know that, on the occasion in question, Moses was aided by divine power? May he not also have been merely a skillful magician, performing his feats by means of *his own enchantments?* If, on account of the comparatively trivial miracles said to have been performed by him, you claim that Jesus was certainly a divine personage of a very high order, are you not compelled to admit that the far greater miracles performed by them prove that the magicians of Egypt were divine personages of a much higher order? The first miracle said to have been performed by Jesus was that of changing a few casks of water into wine. This transformation he performed upon water to which he had direct access. He performed it, too, in the presence of none but a crowd of drunken revelers who were totally unfitted to determine the means by which the transformation was made. Indeed, the performing of this feat, by jugglers and by chemists, is so common at the present time that it

no longer excites wonder in those who witness it. The party who would now claim this feat to be a miracle, performed by the power of God, would be regarded as a blasphemer, and would be hissed out of countenance by every intelligent audience. Not so, however, of the stupendous feat of instantly changing the great Nile, and all the other waters of Egypt, into blood. This prodigious transformation was performed upon immense bodies of water to which the operators had no access, the waters in some instances being a hundred miles distant. If, then, because he performed the quite common feat of changing a small quantity of water into wine, you are justifiable in regarding Jesus as a God, am I not justifiable in regarding as gods the magicians who performed the incomparably greater miracle of changing all the waters of Egypt into blood?"

As Moses journeyed toward Pharaoh's court, "it came to pass by the way in the inn, that the Lord met him, and sought to kill him" (Ex. iv. 24). Here indeed is one of the most wonderful things in scripture. The Lord *sought* to kill Moses, and could not! The human mind pauses in bewilderment. And then the

And it came to pass by the way in the inn, that the Lord met him, and sought to kill him. — Ex. iv, 24

field for conjecture as to the circumstances that is opened up. In just what manner did the Lord attempt the assassination? And how did the intended victim escape? Did the Lord chase his servant over the tavern, upsetting tables, wine-jugs, chairs, guests, the stove, and the baby? Did Moses scramble upon the roof and, crossing the adjoining tenements, dodge down a scuttlehole and steal into the next street? Did he perhaps clamber over the back-fence amid a shower of bootjacks, kettles, and bricks from the infuriated deity? Did he get word of the design and secrete himself in the dog-house, or get himself carried out in a basket of dirty clothes like Falstaff? Or did Jehovah lie in wait behind some door with a revolver and was his arm providentially knocked up by one of the hotel guests? But this is one of the things that a man may lie awake a whole night and think upon. Our artist's theory of the oc-currence is plainly to be seen from the picture with which he has seen fit to furnish us. We shall remark only that we consider it utterly below the dignity of the subject.

Finally Moses arrived at Pharaoh's court, and as to the happenings there, a neat little comedietta embodying the subject, written by Arthur B. Moss, may please our readers as well as anything that we can indite:

Pharaoh's Palace. A flourish of trumpets within. Enter MOSES (hat in hand, umbrella under arm), followed by BROTHER AARON.

HALL-PORTER. Your business, gentlemen?

MOSES. Is his majesty within?

HALL-PORTER. I believe 'e his, gentlemen.

MOSES. Thanks. Give him my card.

HALL-PORTER. Pleasure, gentlemen; pleasure. *(Bows himself off.)*

Another flourish of trumpets within.

HALL-PORTER *(returns: to MOSES and AARON).* This way, if you please, gentlemen.

SCENE II.—*Grand Reception Hall. PHARAOH dis-covered reading " The Maiden Tribute of Ancient Egypt." Enter MOSES and AARON.*

PHARAOH. Be seated, I pray you.

AARON. Your majesty, my brother, Moses here, has come, on behalf of Messrs. Jehovah & Co., to make a friendly demand of you.

MOSES. Oh, yes, perfectly friendly, I assure you.

AARON. In short, he has come to ask the re-

And the Lord did so: and there came a grievous swarm of flies into the houses of Pharaoh, and into his servants' houses, and into all the land of Egypt; the land was corrupted by reason of the swarm of flies.—Ex. viii. 24.

lease of the Israelites employed in your establishment. They have a little grievance, and the said firm has taken it up.

PHARAOH (smiling). Indeed!

MOSES. Yes, indeed, your majesty; and, if you don't release them quietly and at once, we shall have to take steps——

PHARAOH. What's that—a threat?

AARON. My brother may be a little impetuous, your majesty; but the fact is, we think the demand a reasonable one, and we have great hopes that you will concede our request.

PHARAOH. Concede, be hanged! How do I know who you are?

MOSES. Show him, Aaron; down with the rod.

AARON. Your majesty will observe that I hold in my hand a rod, which, if I do but cast it upon the ground, will instantly turn into a serpent.

PHARAOH (giggling). Indeed.

MOSES. Yes, indeed, your majesty.

AARON (throwing rod upon the ground). There, incredulous king; behold!

(PHARAOH bursts into a roar of laughter, and sends for his Magicians. Enter Magicians, each carrying in his hand a rod.)

PHARAOH. Magicians, you see what these tricksters have done. Now, give them a display of your power.

(Magicians simultaneously throw down their rods, which at once turn into serpents, and wriggle furiously on the floor of the palace.)

PHARAOH. (smiling to MOSES and AARON). You see my magicians can equal that.

MOSES. But look, your majesty, how my brother's serpent gobbles up all the rest.

PHARAOH. So it does; hungry, perhaps.

AARON. No, that's my power; I mean Jehovah's power.

(PHARAOH's heart being still hardened, AARON tries again.

AARON. But, your majesty, I respectfully declare that I will turn all the water in all the rivers, lakes, pools, vessels, and throughout the land into blood if you do not release these people.

PHARAOH (puts his hand to his heart, and murmurs that it is getting harder). Try it.

AARON (stretches forth his rod, and strikes all vessels containing water, from the wash-hand basin down to the spittoon). There! all blood.

MOSES. Yes; b—b—blood!

And the Lord said unto Moses, Stretch out thy hand toward heaven, that there may be darkness over the land of Egypt, even darkness which may be felt.—Ex. xi, 21.

PHARAOH (*chuckling*). Now, Magicians, try your hand.

(*Magicians throw down rods, and all the rest is turned into blood.*)

PHARAOH. That, gentlemen, surpasses your trick. Come, try another; I begin to enjoy them: saves patronizing Professor Anderson.

AARON (*strikes his rod*). Frogs, your majesty.

MAGICIANS (*striking rods*). Frogs, gentlemen.

PHARAOH. Good again.

MOSES. Now, Aaron, give it to them this time.

AARON (*vigorously throwing down rod*). Lice, your majesty.

MAGICIANS (*following; cannot produce anything*). We candidly confess, your majesty, that we cannot do this; we perceive that Jehovah has had a hand in it; but it is a very dirty trick.

AARON *and* MOSES *rush at Magicians, and strike them with rods; a fight ensues, during which* MESSRS. MOSES *and* AARON *get thrown out of the palace.*

———

Finally Jehovah's select corps of trained magicians surpassed Pharaoh's in their contest, and inflicted upon the Egyptians such dreadful plagues that Pharaoh consented to the departure of the Hebrews. There are two different narratives running through here. Sometimes they contradict each other and sometimes each one contradicts itself. The signification of the miracles is very different in the two narratives. In the first, they are especially intended as punishments. The disasters by which Egypt is afflicted are even colored so highly as to betray the writer into occasional contradictions. For example, he makes all the cattle of the Egyptians die of the murrain; but they reappear, to be killed by the hail; yet again, when the last plague comes Jehovah slays the first born of the beasts as well as of man. These disasters are intended, according to the first narrative, to move Pharaoh's heart and bring him to repentance. Their object is the same, according to the second, but they are to accomplish it in quite a different way; namely, by convincing the king that Jehovah is so mighty that all attempts at resistance are idle. In one account the plagues are ten; in the other eight. But both of them tell us, without a word of condemnation, how the Israelites at Jehovah's com-

AN OLD CONUNDRUM ANSWERED—WHERE MOSES WAS WHEN THE LIGHT WENT OUT.—See Ex. xii. 30.

mand took advantage of the bewildered state of the Egyptians, and the haste with which they were leaving the land, to borrow the goods of the native population, without the smallest intention of ever returning them. Here we have another proof that the ancient Israelites were not very particular about the truth, or keeping faith. Jehovah commands Moses to ask Pharaoh's leave for the Hebrews to go three days' journey into the desert to do honor to their god, while his real intention is to take them away from Egypt for good. At the same time he shows Moses how to plunder the land of bondage: every Hebrew woman is to ask her neighbors to lend her gold, silver, and apparel, and Jehovah is to incline the Egyptians to treat the request favorably. Actions for which we have no names except lying and stealing are here attributed to Jehovah. We cannot be surprised, then, that the writer tells us, without a word of disapproval, how Moses had deceived his father-in-law by telling him that his object in wishing to go to Egypt was to see whether his relatives were still alive (Ex. iv, 18).

So it came to pass that "all the hosts of the

Lord went out from the land of Egypt" (Ex. xii, 41). According to Christian statisticians, working on the data given in Exodus, observes the witty "Saladin" "the lowest estimate of the numbers of the Israelites who left Egypt is 3,000,-000. The Bible states that there were 600,000 fighting men, besides women and children, and men who were too old to fight. Besides, there were the flocks and herds which they took with them, which probably numbered 3,000,000 more, as they were a pastoral people. The Bible says they went up 'harnessed,' which the marginal reading explains as meaning 'five in rank.' Allowing only one square yard for each man and beast and picaninny, there would have been a procession over 691 miles long, all of which, we are solemnly assured, went out from Egypt in a single night without the departure being known to the Egyptians till the next morning. If the night in Egypt lasted ten hours, the Israelites must have traveled at the rate of over sixty-eight miles an hour, which is a good rate of speed even for a man with pretty long legs and arrayed in nothing save boots and a night shirt, and which is just a trifle too fast for a

And it came to pass at the end of the four hundred and thirty years, even the self-same day it came to pass, that all the hosts of the Lord went out from the land of Egypt.—Ex. xii, 41.

woman with sixty-eight children*—one on her back, one in each hand, and one behind holding on by her skirts, the next holding on by that one's skirts, and so on, in a long, long line of some sixty or seventy, almost as far as the maternal eye could reach, and all tearing along out of Egypt at the rate of seventy miles an hour. . . . This God that makes a woman pregnant with ten or twelve children, and, having one on her back, one in her arms, and thirty or forty in a row behind, ran out of Egypt at the rate of about seventy miles an hour, may be a suitable enough sort of God for those who find life a pantomime or burlesque; but he is not suitable for me, who find life a tragedy, solemn and earnest."

Here, again, the account is made up from two old legends that give us different representations of the event in many particulars. According to the one, God led his people southward into the desert, instead of straight to Canaan, because otherwise they would have come into immediate collision with the Philistines, and fear of this warlike tribe might have made them desire to turn back to Egypt (Ex. xiii, 17); whereas the other narrator says that Jehovah deliberately led the Israelites from Rameses to Succoth (Ex. xii, 37), thence to Etham, thence to Pi-Hachiroth, on the western shore of the sea, with the very dishonorable purpose of tempting Pharaoh to pursue the Israelites, since they appeared to have lost themselves. This would give Jehovah one more opportunity of showing by Pharaoh's destruction how mighty he, the God of Israel, was (Ex. xiv, 1-4). This writer also tells us of a special sign of the divine presence; namely, a column of fire by night and a column of smoke by day, which went in front of the army and showed it the way to go (Ex. xiii, 20-22).

* "Although the fathers were so plentiful that a journeyman carpenter like Joseph had two of them, the Lord, in his own blessed but mysterious way, made mothers alarmingly scarce. We find from a census taken at a particular period (See Ex. xxxvi, 20) that, making the usual allowance of five persons to each male over twenty, we have roughly, 3,000,000 people in all. There were, we are assured, 22,273 first-born males; allow for the same number of first-born females, and we get a total of 44,646. If you divide the 3,000,000 by the number of mothers, you get a total of about sixty-eight children for each mother. To please the Lord and give him something to write about, the women of the house of Israel must, then, like rabbits, have brought forth litters of eight or ten at a time" (Saladin).

And the children of Israel went into the midst of the sea upon the dry ground: and the waters were a wall unto them on their right hand and on their left.—Ex. xiv, 22.

Space fails us for recounting all the contradictions of this infallible record. According to one legend Israel went out " with uplifted hand," that is, in our military language, with " flying colors " (Ex. xiv, 8); according to the other they fled, and when they saw Pharaoh's troops drawing near were greatly terrified, until Moses quieted their fears (Ex. xiv, 10–14). One story makes a strong east wind dry the sea (Ex. xiv, 21); the other says that Moses dried it with a wave of his magic staff (Ex. xiv, 15–18). According to the one the hymn of triumph was sung by Moses's sister, Miriam the prophetess, who led the girls in the festal dance, timbrel in hand, and was the first to raise the alternating or responsive song (Ex. xv, 20, 21); the other puts into the mouth of Moses and all Israel an elaborate song of praise (Ex. xv), which could not possibly have been composed until some time after the passage of the Red sea, since it speaks of the conquest of Canaan as of something already accomplished (Ex. xv, 13).

Ex. xiv says that the waters of the Red sea were miraculously parted to give the Hebrews passage. This Red sea is subject to a violent ebb and flow of the tide, and a little north of Suez it is possible to wade across the gulf at low water, not indeed dry-footed, but yet without danger. It is remarkable that the tide rises and falls very suddenly there. These peculiarities of the place have probably given rise to the formation of our legend. The waters, the text says, reflowed and engulfed the pursuing Egyptians and their horses. However, observes Mr. Moss, "there could not have been many Egyptians, for had not almost all of them been slain several times by plagues, not to mention those of the first-born who went to bed and forgot to wake up on the following morning? Nor could there have been many horses, unless they were borrowed from the Israelites, or resurrected from the remains of those that were killed by the plague of murrain, or survived the tremendous pelting of hailstones."

We will add to the foregoing observations on the exodus that the truth of the matter appears to be that the Jews were driven from Egypt because they had leprosy. Some leader arose among them who figures in legend as Moses. Around him and around the whole event Jewish writers wove the miraculous accounts. Lysim-

And when the voice of the trumpet sounded long, and waxed louder and louder, Moses spake, and God answered him by a voice. And the Lord came down upon Mount Sinai, on the top of the mount: and the Lord called Moses up to the top of the mount; and Moses went up.—Exodus, 19, 20.

achus relates that "a filthy disease broke out in Egypt, and the Oracle of Ammon, being consulted on the occasion, commanded the king to purify the land by driving out the Jews (who were infected with leprosy, etc.), a race of men who were hateful to the gods." The whole multitude of the people were accordingly collected and driven out into the wilderness. Diodorus Siculus says: "In ancient times Egypt was afflicted with a great plague, which was attributed to the anger of God, on account of the multitude of foreigners in Egypt; by whom the rites of the native religion were neglected. The Egyptians accordingly drove them out." As to the passage of the Red sea, there are counterparts of it in many mythologies. Alexander and his army, Bacchus and his army, and Isis and a child each passed waters similarly. Besides, there is a Hindoo fable that when the infant Crishna was being sought by the reigning tyrant of Mathura his fosterfather took him and departed out of the country. Coming to the river Yumna, it was divided for them by the Lord. "Yasodha took the child Crishna, but, coming to the river Yumna, directly opposite to Gokul, Crishna's father perceiving the current to be very strong, it being in the midst of the rainy season, and not knowing which way to pass it, Crishna commanded the water to give way on both sides to his father, who accordingly passed dry-footed across the river."

When the procession of (God)assisted emigrants had got along to Sinai, a fish-horn was heard from the top of that lugubrious mount. "What! what! what!" ejaculated Moses, "it can't be Friday! Pshaw, no, what was I thinking of? the Roman Catholics and their customs are not in existence yet." "That doesn't matter," interposed the ecclesiastical scribe at his elbow; "you know ordinary difficulties of time never stop the Lord—or me." But Jehovah now called for Moses from the mount in his own voice, and that individual posted off.

Jehovah had drawn himself in from infinite space, that usual residence of his, and, bringing himself up close together, flopped down upon Mount Sinai; and here he, like other distinguished visitors, awaited in the expectation that the community would send up a reporter. Moses coming to serve as that functionary, the Lord opened a long interview, in which he conversed on many topics, and delivered the Ten

And Moses said unto the Lord, the people cannot come up to Mount Sinai; for thou chargedst us, saying, Set bounds about the mount, and sanctify it.—Ex. xix, 23.

Commandments. No one who has any knowledge of antiquity will be surprised at this, for similar beliefs were very common. All peoples who had issued from a condition of barbarism and acquired regular political institutions, more or less elaborate laws, an established worship, and maxims of morality, attributed all this—their birth as a nation—to one or more great men, all of whom, without exception, were supposed to have received their knowledge from some deity. Whence did Zarathustra (Zoroaster), the prophet of the Persians, derive his religion? According to the belief of his followers, and the doctrines of their sacred writings, it was from Ahuramazda (Ormuzd) the god of light. Why did the Egyptians represent the god Thoth with a writing-tablet and a pencil in his hand, and honor him especially as the god of the priests?—Because he was "the lord of the divine word," the fountain of all wisdom, from whose inspiration the priests, who were the scholars, the lawgivers, and the religious teachers of the people, derived all their wisdom. Was not Minos, the lawgiver of the Cretans, the friend of Zeus, the highest of the gods? Nay, was he not even his son, and did he not ascend to the sacred cave on Mount Dicte to bring down the laws which his god had placed there for him? From whom did the Spartan lawgiver, Lycurgus, himself say that he had obtained his laws?—From no other than the god Apollo. The Roman legend, too, in honoring Numa Pompilius as the people's instructor, at the same time ascribed all his wisdom to his intercourse with the nymph Egeria. It was the same elsewhere; and to take one more example—this from later times—Mohammed not only believed himself to have been called immediately by God to be the prophet of the Arabs, but declared that he had received every page of the Koran from the hand of the angel Gabriel.

According to Ex. xxxiv, 28, and Deut. ix, 18; x, 10, Moses during the forty days and nights of his interview "did neither eat bread nor drink water." This is quite different from the facts of modern fasters; if one of these should abstain from liquids as well as from solids he would speedily perish. But where the interview is without sense and the tale without consistency it is perhaps fit that the man who is its subject should be without water and everything be as we should not expect.

And when Aaron and all the children of Israel saw Moses, behold, the skin of his face shone; and they were afraid to come nigh him.—Ex. xxxiv, 30.

As a matter of fact no really thinking man in this age believes that any interview with a god was ever held. We can easily reason out how such claims came to be made. Throughout all history one will find in every department of affairs shrewd rogues trying to deceive their fellows into supporting them in luxury, in return for services really worthless but which they pretend are necessary to the welfare of the people. Kings have ever consumed the lion's share of the workers' produce, under the pretense that in some mysterious way they were owners of it all and their subjects too, and necessary to their existence; and many other like cheats will be easily brought to mind. But there is in particular one variety of these frauds that bears the closest resemblance to the one which is the subject of this paragraph. Here and there all through history we come across the class of favorites and courtiers of monarchs, extorting streams of money from outsiders in purchase of the good will of the monarch. Some of these represent their court influence as no higher than it is, and give satisfactory returns for their fees. Some hold out inducements that their influence is far greater than it is, and grossly deceive their petitioners. And vast numbers of others have made good livings upon representations of influence that they did not possess at all—often being not even so much as acquainted at court. Here, then, we have the main elements of the problem presented by the self-styled interviewers of gods with their monstrous claims. We can easily imagine certain cunning rogues spying about for another opening in the line of the courtier business, and finally hitting upon the device of claiming to be courtiers to an invisible monarch dwelling outside the world. On the strength of this pretense many an impostor has acquired ease and ' a good fair belly," and as shining a face as that of Moses in our engraving (Ex. xxxiv, 30). But how surpassing other fraudulent claims in sublime impudence is this one! The other courtiers could at least produce testimony of some good that had been effected for suppliants, or they could show that there actually were kings and nobles to appeal to. But the new pretenders could show none of these. The empire of the actual, the visible, had been all preëmpted by their brothers; all that remained for them was the domain of the invisible. It

And it shall come to pass while my glory passeth by, that I will put thee in a cleft of the rock, and will cover thee with my hand while I pass by: And I will take away my hand, and thou shalt see my back parts; but my face shall not be seen. — Ex. xxxiii. 22, 23

would seem that a scheme so hollow and unsupported by credentials must have required great efforts to maintain it. And so it has. It has had to shed oceans of blood. It has had to call in every aid, every device of intrigue and cruelty, that the most subtle ingenuity of its "inspired" founders and succeeding clergy could suggest. To silence the tongues of the sensible, observing men that have continually seen through and denounced its imposture, it has had to elaborate, from the few tortures occasionally employed by ancient peoples, a system of fiendish torments that as much surpass those ever used by the cruelest men for any other purpose, as a human being is surpassed by a devil in hell.

Ex. xxxiii. 11. says that "the Lord spake unto Moses face to face." In verse 20 of the same chapter the Lord says. "There shall no man see me, and live." Here is a sad contradiction. Suddenly a queer misgiving strikes us. Moses and the Lord were wrapped in a cloud forty days and nights without *water*. It does not say, without *liquids*. Can it be that they were supplied with *spirits*, and that the tangles in the narrative are the outcome of this? Dreadful conception! Without *water*, but surrounded

by the prodigious piles of hogsheads, puncheons, barrels, casks, kegs, flagons, demijohns, decanters, bottles, and flasks which the Great One's appetite, to say nothing of Moses's, would have required. A detachment of angels rushing about with white aprons, mopping tables, shouting "Waiter? waiter? who wants the waiter?" Shocking picture! And then what followed—the Lord showing Moses his back parts (Ex. xxxiii, 22, 23)—men after just such scenes of drunkenness often commit indecent exposure of their persons—let us draw the veil.

To the state of confusion in which we are already as to whether anyone ever saw God, there is an addition made when we consider Ex. xxiv. 9-11: "Then went up Moses, and Aaron, Nadab, and Abihu, and seventy of the elders of Israel: And they saw the God of Israel: and there was under his feet as it were a paved work of a sapphire stone, and as it were the body of heaven in his clearness. And upon the nobles of the children of Israel he laid not his hand: also they saw God, and did eat and drink." This account possesses, in many respects, the too common biblical vagueness and uncertainty; however, it surely does

And they saw the God of Israel. And **upon** the nobles of the children of Israel he laid not his hand: also they **saw** God, and did eat and drink.—Ex. xxiv. **10, 11.**

mean that human beings saw and hobnobbed with the creator of the universe.

To our citations already made of men conversing with gods, we may add further details upon the circumstance of a *mountain* being the place usually chosen. The idea of Moses receiving the commandments from the Lord on a *mountain* was perhaps taken from the Persian legend related of Zoroaster. Prof. Max Müller says: "What applies to the religion of Moses applies to that of Zoroaster. It is placed before us as a complete system from the first, revealed by Ahuramazda (Ormuzd), proclaimed by Zoroaster." The disciples of Zoroaster, in their profusion of legends of the master, relate that one day, as he prayed on a *high mountain*, in the midst of thunders and lightnings ("fire from heaven"), the Lord himself appeared before him, and delivered unto him the "Book of the Law." According to the religion of the Cretans, Minos, their law-giver, ascended a *mountain* (Mount Dicta) and there received from the supreme Lord (Zeus) the sacred laws. Almost all nations of antiquity have legends of their holy men ascending a *mountain* to ask counsel of the gods, such places being deemed

nearer to the deities than other portions of the earth. According to Egyptian belief, it is Thoth, the Deity itself, that speaks and reveals to his elect the will of God and the arcana of divine things. Portions of them are expressly stated to have been written by the very finger of Thoth himself. Diodorus, the Grecian historian, says: "The idea promulgated by the ancient Egyptians that their laws were received direct from the Most High God, has been adopted with success by many other lawgivers." The supreme God of the ancient Mexicans was Tezcatlipoca. His name is compounded of Tezcatepec, the name of a mountain (upon which he is said to have manifested himself to man), *tlil*, dark, and *poca*, smoke. They say that he once appeared on the top of a *mountain*. They paid him great reverence and adoration, and addressed him in their prayers as "Lord, whose servant we are." No man ever saw his face, for he appeared only "as a shade." Indeed, the Mexican idea of the godhead was similar to that of the Jews. Like Jehovah, Tezcatlipoca dwelt in the "midst of thick darkness."

There are two accounts of the giving of the

And it came to pass as soon as he came nigh unto the camp, that he saw the calf, and the dancing: and Moses's anger waxed hot, and he cast the tables out of his hands, and brake them beneath the mount.—Ex. xxxii, 19.

Commandments to Moses. The accounts lie in so tangled a state that we will not attempt to disinvolve them. Let anyone read Ex. xix and xx, and then xxxi, 18, and the three following chapters, and he will see that both narratives cannot be true. The Commandments are not the same in both cases. In the account in chapters xix and xx there is not a word about the making of a golden calf by the people or the breaking by Moses of the tables of stone.

In chapters xxxii to xxxiv, however, we learn about these events. The absence of Moses (we here adopt the language of Mr. Foote) was protracted enough to try the loyalty and patience of the most devoted adherents. Day after day the Jews looked up to "the mount of God," but all they saw was clouds, clouds, clouds; and by and by they concluded that Moses and Jehovah had both ended in the smoke. In this predicament they naturally wanted a fresh leader and a fresh god. Savages are like sheep in following their chief, and without a deity to worship they are like fish out of water. The Jews, therefore, requested Aaron to make them a few gods to ease their religious desolation.

Aaron accepted the offer with great alacrity.

Possibly he thought he might be able to establish his own authority before his brother's return, when he might successfully bid him defiance. Aaron was the elder brother, yet he had to play second fiddle; and as he was not yet consecrated high priest, he perhaps thought his own merits were not sufficiently recognized and rewarded. Here then was a glorious opportunity of promoting his own interest, and Aaron not unnaturally seized it. "I've played second fiddle to Moses long enough," he may have exclaimed, "and if ever he returns he shall play second fiddle to me."

Jehovah does not appear to have entered into our hero's calculations. That was not an age when religion presented only Hobson's choice. There were many gods, all independent of each other, and all warranted sound. What wonder, then, if Aaron thought he might, like Cain, go out from the presence of the Lord, and worship another deity?

Having agreed to make the Jews some new gods, Aaron desired them to furnish him with the material. "Bring your gold," said Aaron. Gold! It is the first demand of priests in every age and clime. They love gold. Judging by

A MODERN RENDITION OF AN ANCIENT DOCUMENT.

their practice, gold is their god. The felicities of heaven are for their dupes; they themselves wish "in health and wealth long to live." They read their title clear to mansions in the skies, but they prefer the actual possession of a snug rectory or vicarage in this miserable vale of tears.

The Jews brought Aaron their golden ear-rings, which were worn by men and women alike (Ex. xxxii, 2). With this precious metal he made a golden calf; or rather, we suspect, with so much of it as was left after he deducted his own liberal commission. The Jews took readily to the worship of the golden calf. Some people, indeed, say they worship it still.

Perhaps the calf was an imitation of the Egyptian god Apis, and thus the Jews simply returned to the religion of their old masters. Long after this they affected calf-worship. Jeroboam set up two golden calves at Dan and Bethel (1 Kings xii, 28, 29), and these were worshiped by Jehu even after he had "destroyed Baal out of Israel" (2 Kings x, 28, 29).

When Moses came down from the clouds and witnessed the saltatory worship of this calf, he not only broke all the Ten Commandments, but burnt the calf, ground it to powder, mixed it with water, and made the Jews drink the potion. Metallurgists would like to know how this was done, but scripture, which tells us many things we could dispense with, neglects to inform us of many things we are anxious to learn.

Moses instructed the Levites to slay the idolators. They did so, and "there fell of the people that day about three thousand men." Aaron, however, was only expostulated with. The chief sinner was spared because he belonged to the leader's family. During the colloquy between the two brothers, Aaron prevaricated in a manner worthy of his profession. "Look here, Moses," he said, "I didn't make that calf. 'Pon honor! I just put the gold into the fire, and the calf came out of itself" (Ex. xxxii, 24).

One of the many directions which the Lord gave Moses as supplementary to the Ten Commandments reads thus: "If thou buy an Hebrew servant, six years shall he serve: and in the seventh he shall go out free for nothing. If he came in by himself, he shall go out by himself: if he were married, then his wife shall

Then his master shall bring him unto the judges; he shall also bring him to the door, or unto the door post; and his master shall bore his ear through with an awl; and he shall serve him forever.—Ex. xxi, 6.

go out with him. If his master have given him a wife, and she have borne him sons or daughters; the wife and her children shall be her master's, and he shall go out by himself. And if the servant shall plainly say, I love my master, my wife, and my children; I will not go out free: Then his master shall bring him unto the judges; he shall also bring him to the door, or unto the door post; and his master shall bore his ear through with an awl; and he shall serve him for ever." Further instructions upon slavery are found in Lev. xxv, 45-6: "Of the children of the strangers that do sojourn among you, of them shall ye buy, and of their families that are with you, which they begat in your land; and they shall be your possession. And ye shall take them as an inheritance for your children after you, to inherit them for a possession." No wonder is it, in view of these and other Old Testament passages directing or countenancing slavery, that we find that institution defended in our own generation against the Abolitionists of America by citation of holy writ. In our antislavery agitation Rev. E. D. Simons, professor in Macon College, wrote: "These extracts from

holy writ unequivocally assert the right of property in slaves, together with the usual incidents of that right; such as the power of acquisition and disposition in various ways, according to municipal regulations. The right to buy and sell, and to transmit to children by the way of inheritance, is clearly stated. The only restriction on the subject is in reference to the market, in which slaves or bond men were to be purchased. Upon the whole, then, whether we consult the Jewish polity instituted by God himself, or the uniform opinion and practice of mankind in all ages of the world, or the injunctions of the New Testament and moral law, we are brought to the conclusion that slavery is not immoral." Rev. Wilber Fisk, D.D., late president of the Wesleyan University. Connecticut, wrote: "The general rule of Christianity not only permits, but, in supposable circumstances, enjoins a continuance of the master's authority." Rev. J. C. Postell, Orangeburg, S. C., in an address at a public meeting called for the purpose of opposing abolition, said: "From what has been premised the following conclusions result: 1. That slavery is a judicial visitation. 2. That it is not a

Thou shalt not suffer a witch to live.—Ex. xxii. 18.

moral evil. 3. That it is supported by the Bible. 4. It has existed in all ages. It is not a moral evil. The fact, that slavery is of divine appointment, would be proof enough with the Christian that it cannot be a moral evil. It is the Lord's doings, and it is marvelous in our eyes; and had it not been for the best, God alone, who is able, long since would have overruled it. It is by divine appointment." Rev. Mr. Crawler, of Virginia, in a General Conference, 1840, said: "Slavery is not only countenanced, permitted, and regulated, by the Bible, but it was positively instituted by God himself—he has in so many words enjoined it." The Charleston Union Presbytery: *Resolved,*—"That in the opinion of this Presbytery, the holding of slaves, so far from being a sin in the sight of God, is nowhere condemned in his holy word—that it is in accordance with the example, or consistent with the precepts, of patriarchs, apostles, and prophets, and that it is compatible with the most fraternal regard to the best good of those servants whom God may have committed to our charge." The Harmony Presbytery, South Carolina: *"Resolved,* unanimously—1. That, as the kingdom of our Lord

is not of this world, his church, as such, has no right to abolish, alter, or affect any institution or ordinance of men, political and civil merely, etc. 2. That slavery has existed from the days of those good old slaveholders and patriarchs, Abraham, Isaac, and Jacob (who are now in the kingdom of heaven), to the time when the apostle Paul sent a runaway slave home to his master Philemon, and wrote a Christian and fraternal epistle to this slaveholder, which we find still stands in the canons of the scriptures; and that slavery has existed ever since the days of the apostle, and does now exist. 3. That, as the relative duties of master and slave are taught in the scripture, in the same manner of those of parent and child, and husband and wife, the existence of slavery itself is not opposed to the will of God; and whosoever has a conscience too tender to recognize this relation as lawful, is 'righteous overmuch,' is 'wise above what is written,' and has submitted his neck to the yoke of man, sacrificed his Christian liberty of conscience, and leaves the infallible word of God for the fancies and doctrines of men." Rev. Thomas S. Witherspoon, of Alabama, wrote to the editor of the

Thou shalt not delay to offer the first of thy ripe fruits, and of thy liquors; the first-born of thy sons shalt thou give unto me.— Ex. xxii, 29.

Emancipator: "I draw my warrant from the scriptures of the Old and New Testament, to hold the slave in bondage. The principle of holding the heathen in bondage is recognized by God." Rev. Wilber Fisk, D.D., wrote to a friend: "This, sir [referring to the preceding letter], is doctrine that will stand, because it is Bible doctrine." Rev. R. Furman, D.D., South Carolina, to the governor of the state, 1833, wrote: "The right of holding slaves is clearly established in the holy scriptures, both by precept and example." On the death of Dr. Furman, which occurred soon after, among the property advertised by his executor to be sold at public auction, was a "library of miscellaneous character, chiefly theological, and twenty-seven negroes, some of them very prime."

School-children now would laugh at the person who asserted to them the reality of witches and their powers, yet the God of the Christians a few centuries ago believed it. He issued the order, "Thou shalt not suffer a witch to live." This text has caused the sacrifice of more lives and more unmerited suffering than any other line in any book in the world, except that other line in the same book, "They that do not believe shall be damned. The persecution of supposed witches arose from this text, it was continued by its support, and when growing intelligence bade fair to weaken the belief it was this text that was appealed to as conclusive proof and it was the clergy who appealed to it. Every attempt to substitute a lighter punishment for death was fiercely denounced as a direct violation of the divine law. Indeed, some persons went so far as to question the lawfulness of strangling the witch before she was burnt. Her crime, they said, was treason against the almighty, and therefore to punish it by any but the most agonizing death was an act of disrespect to him. Besides, the penalty in the Levitical code was stoning, and stoning had been pronounced by the Jewish theologians to be a still more painful death than the stake. We will relate here the chief instance of witchcraft persecution in our own country. As the skepticism increased a new and strenuous attempt was made to arrest it by accounts of fresh cases of witchcraft in America. The pilgrim fathers had brought to this country the seeds of superstition; and, at the same time when it was rapidly

And I will send hornets before thee, which shall drive out the Hivite, the Canaanite, and the Hittite, from before thee.—Ex. xxiii. 28.

fading in England, it flourished with fearful vigor in Massachusetts. Two Puritan ministers, named Cotton Mather and Parris, proclaimed the frequency of the crime; and, being warmly supported by their brother divines, they succeeded in creating a panic through the whole country. A commission was issued. A judge named Stoughton, who appears to have been a perfect creature of the clergy, conducted the trials. Scourgings and tortures were added to the terrorism of the pulpit, and many confessions were obtained. The few who ventured to oppose the prosecutions were denounced as Sadducees and Infidels. Multitudes were thrown into prison, others fled from the country abandoning their property, and twenty-seven persons were executed. An old man of eighty was pressed to death—a horrible sentence, which was never afterward executed in America. The ministers of Boston and Charlestown drew up an address, warmly thanking the commissioners for their zeal, and expressing their hope that it would never be relaxed.

The Lord is said to command in Ex. xxii. 29: "Thou shalt not delay to offer the first of thy ripe fruits, and of thy liquors: the first-born of thy sons shalt thou give unto me." The offering of sons was elsewhere commuted to one of beasts, but except in this particular the statute remained in full operation, and was always a favorite one with the priests, for the very simple reason that it was *they* who enjoyed the offerings which they pretended were for the Lord. For in Num. xviii we find: "Every oblation of theirs, every meat offering of theirs, and every sin offering of theirs, and every trespass offering of theirs, which they shall render unto me, shall be most holy for thee and thy sons. In the most holy place shalt thou *eat it*; every male shall *eat it*; it shall be holy unto thee. And this is thine; the heave offering of their gift, with all the wave offerings of the children of Israel: I have given them unto thee, and to thy sons and to thy daughters with thee, by a statute forever: every one who is clean in thy house shall *eat* of it. All the best of the oil, and all the best of the wine, and of the wheat, the first-fruits of them which they shall offer unto the Lord, them have I given thee. And whatsoever is first ripe in the land, which they shall bring unto the Lord, shall be thine: every one

And the cherubims shall stretch forth their wings on high, covering the mercy-seat with their wings, and their faces shall look one to another; toward the mercy-seat shall the faces of the cherubims be.—Ex. xxv, 20.

that is clean in thine house shall *eat of it.*
Every thing devoted in Israel shall be thine."
"Thou shalt sprinkle their blood upon the
altar, and shall burn their fat for our offering
made by fire, for a sweet savor unto the Lord.
And the flesh of them shall be thine, as the
wave breast and right shoulder are thine. All
the heave offerings of the holy things, which
the children of Israel offer unto the Lord, have
I given thee, and thy sons and thy daughters
with thee, by a statute forever, it is a covenant
of salt forever before the Lord unto thee and thy
seed with thee." It appears then that the sacrifice originated in priestcraft, and that the
priests and their children lived on the firstlings
of cows, sheep, goats, early vegetables, the best
wine, etc., and it was quite as natural for them
to say to their followers, "Bring your best
sheep, and your heifers, and goats, without
blemish, unto the Lord," as it is for the same
sort of gentlemen now to urge their congregations to "put money into the Lord's treasury,"
meaning their own purses.

In Ex. xxiii. 28, the Lord promises his people:
" I will send hornets before thee, which shall
drive out the Hivite, the Canaanite, and the

Hittite, from before thee." On this text
Colonel Ingersoll says: "Must we believe that
God made arrangements with hornets for the
purpose of securing their services in driving the
Canaanites from the land of promise? Is this
belief necessary unto salvation? Must we believe that God said to the Jews that he would
send hornets before them to drive out the
Canaanites, as related in the twenty-third chapter of Exodus and the seventh chapter of Deuteronomy? How would the hornets know a
Canaanite? In what way would God put it in
the mind of a hornet to attack a Canaanite?
Did God create hornets for that especial purpose, implanting an instinct to attack a Canaanite, but not a Hebrew? Can we conceive of the
Almighty granting letters of marque and reprisal
to hornets? Of course it is admitted that nothing in the world would be better calculated to
make a man leave his native land than a few
hornets. Is it possible for us to believe that an
infinite being would resort to such expedients
in order to drive the Canaanites from their
country? He could just as easily have spoken
the Canaanites out of existence as to have spoken
the hornets in. In this way a vast amount of

And for Aaron's sons thou shalt make coats, and thou shalt make for them girdles, and bonnets shalt thou make for them, for glory and for beauty. And thou shalt make them linen breeches to cover their nakedness; from the loins even unto the thighs they shall reach.
—Ex. xxviii, 40, 42.

trouble, pain and suffering would have been saved. Is it possible that there is, in this country, an intelligent clergyman who will insist that these stories are true; that we must believe them in order to be good people in this world, and glorified souls in the next? We are also told that God instructed the Hebrews to kill the Canaanites slowly, giving as a reason that the beasts of the field might increase upon his chosen people. . . . What would we think of a general, invading such a state, if he should order his soldiers to kill the people slowly, lest the wild beasts might increase upon them? Is it possible that a God capable of doing the miracles recounted in the Old Testament could not in some way have disposed of the wild beasts? After the Canaanites were driven out, could he not have employed the hornets to drive out the wild beasts? Think of a God that could drive twenty-one millions of people out of the promised land, could raise up innumerable stinging flies, and could cover the earth with fiery serpents, and yet seems to have been perfectly powerless against the wild beasts of the land of Canaan! Speaking of these hornets, one of the

good old commentators, whose views have long been considered of great value by the believers in the inspiration of the bible, uses the following language:—'Hornets are a sort of strong flies, which the Lord used as instruments to plague the enemies of his people. They are of themselves very troublesome and mischievous, and those the Lord made use of were, it is thought, of an extraordinary bigness and perniciousness. It is said they live as the wasps, and that they have a king or captain, and pestilent stings as bees, and that, if twenty-seven of them sting man or beast, it is certain death to either. Nor is it strange that such creatures did drive out the Canaanites from their habitations; for many heathen writers give instances of some people driven from their seats by frogs, others by mice, others by bees and wasps. And it is said that a christian city, being besieged by Sapores, king of Persia, was delivered by hornets; for the elephants and beasts being stung by them, waxed unruly, and so the whole army fled.' Only a few years ago, all such stories were believed by the christian world; and it is a historical fact, that Voltaire was the third man of any note in Europe, who took the

Keeping mercy for thousands, forgiving iniquity and transgression and sin, and that will by no means clear the guilty; visiting the iniquity of the fathers upon the children, and upon the children's children, unto the third and to the fourth generation. — Ex. xxxiv, 7.

ground that the mythologies of Greece and Rome were without foundation. Until his time, most christians believed as thoroughly in the miracles ascribed to the Greek and Roman gods as in those of Christ and Jehovah."

On page 177 is an illustration, with a comical addition (though not more comical than the original, of a queer old box, cage, or cupboard which the Israelites used to carry about with them. It was known by the name of "ark," which word means simply chest. The fairy creatures that we see upon it are thus described in Ex. xxv, 20: "And the cherubim shall stretch forth their wings on high, covering the mercy-seat with their wings, and their faces shall look one to another; toward the mercy-seat shall the faces of the cherubim be." Just what the purpose of the ark was is not settled by commentators. It is in one place spoken of as a chest containing the stone tables on which the Ten Commandments were cut (Deut. x, 1-5). Elsewhere it seems to have been a residence of the deity, in which he dwelt most of the time and was conveyed about by his subjects. Late scholars conjecture that the god in it was a stone. The fact is, the Israelites, whom our

preachers would represent to us to have been of so elevated a mind, were practicers of the very lowest form of religion, fetichism, the worship of inanimate objects in nature, usually stones. Surrounding tribes were given to this custom, and the old stone-worship has left traces behind it in Israelitish proper names; as Elitsur, i. e., "the rock is my god;" Tsurishaddai, "Shaddai, or 'the mighty one,' is my rock;" Tsuriel, "God is my rock;" Pedatsur, "the rock delivers." Jehovah too is frequently called the rock of his worshipers, or the rock of Israel. Now, it is quite true that this is metaphorical; just as Jehovah is often called the mountain, the shield, or the fortress of those that trust in him; but the marked preference shown for the expression "Israel's rock," and the emphasis with which it is used, show that there must have been a special reason for selecting just this metaphor so often; and we can find no other than that derived from the ancient worship of blocks of stone. Here is one out of many examples:

The Rock, his work is pure,
   For all his ways are right. . . .
The Rock that produced thee thou hast rejected,
   And thou hast forgotten the god that bare thee. . . . .

And ye shall eat the flesh of your sons, and the flesh of your daughters shall ye eat. — Lev. xxvi. 29

How should one (Israelite) pursue a thousand,
And two put ten thousand to flight,
Except their (the enemies') Rock had sold them,
And Jehovah delivered them up!
For their rock is not as our Rock.—(Deut. xxxii, 4–31).

In these lines "the Rock" is used in exactly the same sense as the word, god. Sacred stones are found in great numbers by most altars and also standing alone, being called *massebah*, a word the literal meaning of which is simply "something which is set up." In the Authorized Version it is translated "an image." The Romans called them "anointed stones" on account of the manner in which they were usually worshiped.

"And for Aaron's sons thou shalt make coats, and thou shalt make for them girdles, and bonnets shalt thou make for them, for glory and for beauty. And thou shalt make them linen breeches to cover their nakedness; from the loins even unto the thighs they shall reach" (Ex. xxviii, 40–42). I cannot believe, says Ingersoll, that God told Moses how to cut and trim a coat for a priest. Why should a God care about such things? Why should he insist on having buttons sewed in certain rows, and

fringes of a certain color? On other directions of God upon equally frivolous matters, Ingersoll says: "There must be some mistake. I can not believe that an infinite intelligence appeared to Moses upon Mount Sinai having with him a variety of patterns for making a tabernacle, tongs, snuffers, and dishes."

Ex. xxxiv, 7, speaks of the **Lord** as "visiting the iniquity of the fathers upon the children, and upon the children's children, unto the third and to the fourth generation." To a civilized man, no proposition can appear more self-evident than that a man can be guilty only of acts in the performance of which he has himself had some share. Yet, the conceptions both of hereditary guilt and of hereditary merit pervade the belief and the institutions of all nations, and have clung to the mind with a tenacity which is even now but beginning to relax. We find them in every system of early punishment which involved children in the destruction of a guilty parent, in every account of curses transmitted through particular families or particular nations, in every hereditary aristocracy, and in every legend of an early fall. All these rest upon the idea that there is something in the

And I will make your cities waste, and bring your sanctuaries unto desolation, and I will not smell the savour of your sweet odours.— Lev. xxvi, 31.

merit or demerit of one man that may be reflected upon his successors altogether irrespectively of their own acts. This idea seems to be strongest in ages when civilization is very low, and to decline with the intellectual advance. There seems to be a period in the history of every nation when punishments involving the innocent child with the guilty parent are acquiesced in as perfectly natural, and another period when they are repudiated as manifestly unjust. A vast aristocratical system has probably contributed more than any other single cause to consolidate the doctrine of hereditary merit. For the essence of an aristocracy is to transfer the source of honor from the living to the dead, to make the merits of living men depend not so much upon their own character and actions as upon the actions and position of their ancestors; and as a great aristocracy is never insulated, as its ramifications penetrate into many spheres, and its social influence modifies all the relations of society, the minds of men become insensibly habituated to a standard of judgment from which they would otherwise have recoiled. When in the sphere of religion the rationalistic doctrine of personal merit and

demerit at last completely supersedes the theological doctrine of hereditary merit or demerit, the change will be largely effected by the triumph of democratic principles in the sphere of politics. The origin of this widely diffused habit of judging men by the deeds of their ancestors is one of the most obscure and contested points in philosophy. Some have seen in it a dim and distorted tradition of the Fall; others have attributed it to that confusion of misfortune with guilt which is so prominent in ancient beliefs. Partly in consequence of the universal conviction that guilt deserves punishment, and partly from the notion that the events which befall mankind are the results not of general laws but of isolated acts directed to special purposes, man imagined that whenever they saw suffering they might infer guilt. They saw that the effects of an unrighteous war will continue long after those who provoked it have passed away; that the virtue or vice, the wisdom or folly, of the parent will often determine the fortunes of the children; and that each generation has probably more power over the destiny of that which succeeds it than over its own. They saw that there was such a thing as trans-

And the Lord came down in a cloud, and spake unto him, and took of the spirit that was upon him, and gave it unto the seventy elders: and it came to pass, that, when the spirit rested upon them, they prophesied.—Num. xi, 25.

mitted suffering, and they therefore concluded that there must be such a thing as transmitted guilt. Besides this, patriotism and church feeling, and every influence that combines men in a corporate existence, makes them live to a certain degree in the past, and identify themselves with the actions of the dead. The patriot feels a pride or shame in the deeds of his forefathers very similar to that which springs from his own. Connected with this, it has been observed that men have a constant tendency, in speaking of the human race, to forget that they are employing the language of metaphor, and to attribute to it a real objective existence distinct from the existence of living men. It may be added too that that retrospective imagination which is so strong in some nations, and which is more or less exhibited in all, leads men to invest the past with all the fascination of poetry, to represent it as a golden age incomparably superior to their own, and to imagine that some great catastrophe must have occurred to obscure it. These considerations, and such as these, have often been urged by those who have written on the genesis of the notion of hereditary guilt. We will not pursue farther these attempts to

188

account for the notion, but will conclude by remarking that an application of it made in religion, still more important than that shown in the Old Testament, is that made by the church in the early and middle ages. According to the unanimous belief of the church, all who were external to Christianity were doomed to eternal damnation, not only on account of their own transgression, but also on account of the transmitted guilt of Adam; and therefore even the new-born infant was subject to the condemnation until baptism had united it to the church. To conclude, this notion of visiting parents' sins on their descendants is the production of erratic and confused reasoning, dim and muddled notions; it is highly unjust; and its practice by Jehovah and by the church is a gross blot of blame upon them.

"Even of these," says God to his people in Lev. xi, 22, "ye may eat; the locust after his kind, and the bald locust after his kind, and the beetle after his kind, and the grasshopper after his kind." Notwithstanding the Lord's approval of his followers' eating these species of diet, they do not seem to patronize them much at the present day. They evidently believe themselves

And Miriam and Aaron spake against Moses because of the Ethiopian woman whom he had married: for he had married an Ethiopian woman. —Num. xii, 1.

to know more about propriety in the *cuisine* than Jehovah, which is confirmation of the dreadful nature of that pride of man which is so often censured in the holy books. Jehovah also gave divers other directions as to food. Many of them are ridiculous. Many of his prohibitions of certain foods are unwarranted. We may profitably here explain the origin of the fables that he fed his people on quails and manna. The stories of the extraordinary abundance of these birds and of the manna-dew are alike borrowed from real phenomena of nature. Innumerable flocks of quails are often seen in Arabia, Palestine, Asia Minor, and Italy, and not unfrequently they fall to the ground by thousands from sheer exhaustion, or at least can be caught without difficulty. Manna is a substance well known in southern Europe and central Asia, and is used by apothecaries. It is a sticky, sweet-tasting sap, that flows in June and July from the bark of several trees, especially that of a species of tamarisk. At night it is liquid, but it thickens toward morning. After sunrise it melts, and is then more difficult to collect. The ancients believed it to fall from the air, as honey also was sometimes supposed to do; and there are cer-

tain facts which seem to prove that the manna juice is really suspended and carried away in a finely-divided condition by the air, and then deposited, in damp weather, as a sweet dew. It may sometimes be useful as a medicine, but if used as the chief article of food it would be most injurious. Around this natural phenomenon grew the legend that the manna was miraculously abundant, and was safely eaten in large quantities, and the quails tradition had a similar origin.

"And ye shall eat the flesh of your sons, and the flesh of your daughters shall ye eat." Thus speaks the Lord to his people in Lev. xxvi, 29. One would think that the deity might have found means of bringing things about so that his people would behave, less extreme than punishing them with the necessity of cannibalism. Governments nowadays find it possible to rule their subjects without such measures. But then, the world has advanced and governments have grown more experienced. The Lord was new to his business in those days, and perhaps is to be expected, like all young rulers, to have been rash and heady. Still, we think that he might have taken such records out of his book

And there we saw the giants, the sons of Anak, which come of the giants: and we were in our own sight as grasshoppers, and so we were in their sight.—Num. xiii. 33.

before letting us have it for present-day use, for these accounts are not the most humanizing things in the world for our youth.

To be sure, cannibalism may not have been any particular hardship to the ancient Jews, as there are many passages in their records which have given rise among learned men to the belief that they were to some extent cannibals. At any rate, they practiced human sacrifice, which is no better. Another way of looking at it is that the whole Christian religion is a cannibalistic one. Thos. Rush writes: "The Egyptians worship crocodiles and calves; the Greeks made their gods of marble or gold: the Persian made the sun his god; the Hottentots make their gods with whalebone, and go far through the storm to adore them; the church of Rome makes her god of a wafer and eats him. This is the worst kind of cannibalism, and is also base ingratitude. Think of a man eating his dearest friend, and then you have transubstantiation in a nutshell."

In Lev. xxvii, 31, we are presented with the unseemly spectacle of Jehovah in a pet and declaring that he "will not smell the savor of [the Jews'] sweet odors." This deity it seems was constantly falling into like fits of sulkiness. No wonder that Ingersoll in enumerating the causes why he pities the Hebrews, mentions as one that "their God was quick-tempered, unreasonable, revengeful, and dishonest." By this God, says Ingersoll, they were "cheated, deceived, and abused. He was always promising but never performed. He wasted time in ceremony and childish detail, and in the exaggeration of what he had done. It is impossible for me to conceive of a character more utterly detestable than that of the Hebrew god. He had solemnly promised the Jews that he would take them from Egypt to a land flowing with milk and honey. He had led them to believe that in a little while their troubles would be over, and they would soon in the land of Canaan, surrounded by their wives and little ones, forget the stripes and tears of Egypt. After promising the poor wanderers again and again that he would lead them in safety to the promised land, of joy and plenty, this God, forgetting every promise, said to the wretches in his power: 'Your carcasses shall fall in this wilderness and your children shall wander until your carcasses be wasted.' This curse was the conclu-

MOSES APPEALS TO THE LORD'S VANITY AND URGES HIM NOT TO MAKE HIMSELF RIDICULOUS. Num. xiv, 13-16

sion of the whole matter. Into this dust of death and night faded all the promises of God. Into this rottenness of wandering despair fell all the dreams of liberty and home. Millions of corpses were left to rot in the desert, and each one certified to the dishonesty of Jehovah. . . . No wonder that they longed for the slavery of Egypt, and remembered with sorrow the unhappy day when they exchanged masters. Compared with Jehovah, Pharaoh was a benefactor, and the tyranny of Egypt was freedom to those who suffered the liberty of God. While reading the Pentateuch, I am filled with indignation, pity and horror. Nothing can be sadder than the history of the starved and frightened wretches who wandered over the desolate crags and sands of wilderness and desert the prey of famine, sword, and plague. Ignorant and superstitious to the last degree, governed by falsehood, plundered by hypocrisy, they were the sport of priests, and the food of fear. God was their greatest enemy, and death their only friend."

The jug in the picture on page 187 gives an idea of what Mr. Heston supposes the "spirit" so often spoken of in scripture to have been.

The text runs: "And the Lord came down in a cloud . . . and took of the spirit that was upon him, and gave it unto the seventy elders: and it came to pass, that, when the spirit rested upon them, they prophesied" (Num. xi, 25). Certainly scripture reads as though dictated at the inspiration of just the kind of spirit that we see in the picture.

We are told in Num. xii, 1, that 'Miriam and Aaron spake against Moses because of the Ethiopian woman whom he had married: for he had married an Ethiopian woman" (Num. xii, 1). In bringing the readers into full acquaintance with this event, we shall temporarily step down from our platform as Silver-Tongued Lecturer to the Panorama of Bible Wonders, in favor of G. W. Foote, who mounting the pedestal and trying to hide the monkey with his long pointing-staff as he extends it across the picture, discourseth thus: "Moses was so great a favorite of God that all who insulted or opposed him were badly punished. When he married an Ethiopian woman, Miriam and Aaron set their backs up, and sneeringly inquired whether the Lord had not spoken by them as well as by Moses. Scripture does not

And they that found him gathering sticks brought him unto Moses and Aaron, and unto all the congregation. And the Lord said unto Moses, The man shall be surely put to death; all the congregation shall stone him with stones without the camp.—Num. xv. 33–35.

go to the bottom of the quarrel, nor tell us whether Zipporah was still alive. She may have been dead, or Moses may have taken another wife during her lifetime, for he was a lusty old fellow and Zipporah's withered charms must have lost their attraction. Be that as it may, Miriam and Aaron took to nagging. This is a common incident in domestic circles, and it was scarcely worth the fuss God made about it. He was especially angry with the female sinner, and punished her with the loathsome and ghastly disease of leprosy, which was only removed at her brother's intercession (Num. xii). Here, again, the Lord flies into a fury, and Moses has to cool him down."

An expedition which had been sent out from the camp of the main body of the Israelites returned telling this truly biblical yarn: "We saw the giants, the sons of Anak, which come of the giants, and we were in our own sight as grasshoppers, and so we were in their sight." In 1846 Rev. Dr. Cruden wrote: "It is very probable, that the first men were all of a strength and stature much superior to those of mankind at present, since they lived a much longer time; long life being commonly the effect of a strong and vigorous constitution. And that formerly there were men of a stature much above that of common men, cannot be denied, at least not without contradicting the holy scriptures. Moses speaks of Og the king of Bashan's bed, which was nine cubits long, and four wide; that is, fifteen feet four inches and a half long (Deut. iii. 11). These sorts of giants were still common in Joshua's and David's times, when the life of men was already so much shortened, and, as may be presumed, the size and strength of human bodies were very much diminished." Thus were men who under proper instruction might have added something to the good of mankind perverted by scriptural fables into writing the utterest trash and falsehood.

The spies who had been sent out and had seen the giants, "the children of the Anak," gave marvelous accounts of the fertility and pleasantness of the land wherein those dime museum wonders dwelt. It was, they said, a land flowing with milk and honey. All the camp longed to go there, intending, no doubt, to swim through the ocean of milk with their

And the Lord sent fiery serpents among the people, and they bit the people; and much people of Israel died. Num. xxi, 6.

mouths open catching the honey. Then, the spies had brought back a bunch of grapes so big that two men had to bear it between them on a staff (Num. xiii, 23). No wonder Israel wished to enter a land which could produce such grapes. Grapes of that sort would tempt any modern vineyardman. But they are not common now. They were Bible grapes. Bible grapes, giants, cattle, human fecundity, chronology—how different were all things from what they are now. But we were telling that the Israelites said, "If the Lord delight in us, then he will bring us into this land, and give it to us." Their notions as to the justice of taking the land from its original possessors are seen from their saying to one another, "Neither fear ye the people of the land; for they are bread for us: their defense is departed from them, and the Lord is with us: fear them not." But they were counting their chickens before they were hatched. The Lord stole up to the outskirts of the camp behind the tabernacle, set a chafing-dish on the ground, and sprinkling on the live coals in it some sulphur and other chemicals such as emit a thick smoke, produced one of those "glories" in which it was his fad to appear. Out of this glory he spoke, railing like a fishwife against the poor devils who wanted to leave the desert in which their self-styled protector kept them wandering, and settle in the fertile region discovered. As he was threatening to kill off the whole lot, Moses stepped to the side of the glory and reaching in patted the old fellow soothingly on the back, and between coughs produced by the fumes advised him thus: "Then the Egyptians shall hear it, (for thou broughtest up these people in thy might from among them); and they will tell it to the inhabitants of this land: for they have heard that thou Lord are among this people, that thou Lord art seen face to face, and that thy cloud standeth over them, and that thou goest before them, by day time in a pillar of a cloud, and in a pillar of fire by night. Now if thou shalt kill all this people as one man, then the nations which have heard the fame of thee will speak, saying, Because the Lord was not able to bring this people into the land which he sware unto them, therefore he hath slain them in the wilderness." The following text seems to convey that Jehovah relented. Similar cases, in which he did change his unchangeable intents

And Moses made a serpent of brass, and put it upon a pole: and it came to pass, that if a serpent had bitten any man, when he beheld the serpent of brass, he lived.—Num. xxi, 9.

on being argued with, are to be found in Ex.
xxxii and Num. xii, 10–16.

For even gathering a few sticks on the Sabbath, with which to kindle a fire for the comfort of his little ones in very cold weather, a poor man, who could not otherwise protect his children from cold, had to be beaten to death with stones: "Six days may work be done, but in the seventh is the Sabbath of rest, holy to the Lord: whosoever doeth any work in the Sabbath-day he shall surely be put to death" (Ex. xxxi, 15). "Ye shall kindle no fire throughout your habitations upon the Sabbath-day" (Ex. xxxv, 3). "And while the children of Israel were in the wilderness, they found a man that gathered sticks upon the Sabbath-day. . . . And the Lord said unto Moses, The man shall surely be put to death; all the congregation [including his nearest and dearest friends and relatives] shall stone him with stones without the camp. And all the congregation brought him without the camp, and stoned him with stones and he died; as the Lord commanded Moses" (Num. xv, 32–36). The burdens of these Sabbath laws fell almost entirely upon the poor alone. As we elsewhere

learn, the priests, who filled all the offices, were permitted, or rather permitted themselves, to go right on performing their ordinary work, the offering of sacrifices, the cooking and eating of rich viands, etc., on the Sabbath, the same as on any other day. Indeed, like our clergy with their Sunday, those priests derived far greater profits from their trade on the Sabbath than on any other day. In this fact, therefore, we have strong presumptive evidence that the institution called the Sabbath was invented by the priests themselves for their own special benefit.

With all the offerings and similar little amenities, the life of the Jewish priesthood was not altogether a happy and untroubled one. No age has been without its bad people, and those ages had their Infidels as well as the present. Men have been found in every period so wrong-headed as to set themselves against the lawful and beneficent rule of God's friends. Moses and Aaron found their case no exception. There were in each of the thirteen tribes restless spirits continually seeking escape from the new government. Some retained an affection for Egypt, their native land, and these exclaimed against

And the Lord said unto Moses, Take all the heads of the people, and hang them up before the Lord against the sun, that the fierce anger of the Lord may be turned away from Israel.—Num. xxv, 4.

what they called inconveniences and hardships, and against their leaders as the authors of their troubles, and even wished to stone their benefactors (Num. xiv). Notwithstanding that we are now told in legends that their new God showed his power and care in frequent miracles that should have convinced the most skeptical, it seems that those who were there, and should have known if anyone should, by no means exhibited such a faith as we should expect. Some wanted to worship other gods. Others had more confidence in golden serpents. But there is no accounting for the waywardness of man. Then many of the chiefs said that a trust and an unrightful and unlawful combination was being set up in the God's friendship business. This branch of industry being such a profitable one in those days, no wonder they invoked opposition to the bloated monopolists. Many and bitter were the complaints they made that the new constitution would be injurious to their particular interests, and that the profitable places would be engrossed by the families and friends of Moses and Aaron, and others equally well born excluded (Num. xvi, 3). Finally the Lord, exasperated beyond endurance at these

indignities shown to himself and his lieutenants, "sent fiery serpents among the people, and they bit the people : and much people of Israel died" (Num. xxi, 6).

On page 199 we behold other "much people" who were bitten getting cured. Moses made a serpent of brass—that particular substance always being on hand in the priesthood in inexhaustible quantities—and put it on a pole, "and it came to pass, that if a serpent had bitten any man, when he beheld the serpent of brass he lived" (Num. xxi, 9).

In Josephus and the Talmud we learn some particulars as to these rebellions of the people that are not so fully narrated in scripture. We are there told that one Korah made public objections to Moses's conferring the priesthood upon Aaron, and this, he said, without the consent of the people. He accused Moses of having obtained the government by fraudulent artifice, and having deprived the people of their liberties; and of conspiring with Aaron to perpetuate the tyranny in their family. The people then began to cry out: "Let us maintain the liberty of our tribes; we have freed ourselves from one slavery, and shall we allow our-

And Moses spake unto the people, saying, Arm some of yourselves unto the war, and let them go against the Midianites, and avenge the Lord of Midian.—Num. xxxi, 3.

selves to be deceived and subdued by Moses?" And so these Infidel doubters clamored on, at great length. The more hardened called in question the reality of Moses's conferences with God; objecting to the privacy of the meeting, and the preventing of any of the people from being present at the colloquies, or even approaching the place, as grounds of great suspicion. This seems strange when other passages of scripture represent God every now and then appearing to the whole people. It would seem that if he had really done so these men would not have doubted. Modern Infidels may go so far as to insinuate that the supernatural events did not occur; that the only possibly truthful parts of the account are those treating of the doubts, and natural events such as we see around us every day, and that the supernatural element was inserted in the legends later to subdue future generations. But these scoffers should take warning from the horrid fate that befell their brother Infidels of those days, Korah and his associates. Priesthoods have always had their little ways of getting rid of the contumacious and unsubduable, and let it be remembered that our own days present

plentiful examples. But this is getting too far ahead. The intractable Korah and friends made many other charges that are to be named. They accused Moses of peculation; as, embezzling part of the golden spoons and the silver chargers that the princes had offered at the dedication of the altar (Num. vii); and the offerings of gold by the common people (Ex. xxxv. 22), as well as most of the poll-tax (Num. iii; Ex. xxx). Aaron they accused of pocketing much of the gold of which he pretended to have made a molten calf. Besides peculation, they charged Moses with ambition; to gratify which passion he had, they said, deceived the people, by promising to bring them to a land flowing with milk and honey, instead of which he had brought them from such a land. All this, they said, he thought light of, provided he could make himself an absolute prince (Num. xvi, 13). Malcontents urged as a grievance that, to support with splendor the new dignity in the family, the partial poll-tax already levied and given to Aaron (Num. iii) was to be followed by a general one (Ex. xxx), which would probably be augmented from time to time, if Moses were suffered to go on promulgating new laws on

And Moses said unto them, Have ye saved all the women alive?—Num. xxxi. 15.

pretense of new revelations of the divine will, till the people's whole fortunes were devoured by the hierarchy. In fine, no less than two hundred and fifty men, "famous in the congregation, men of renown," forming themselves into a Hebrew Secular Society, led the people against God's just 'and regularly ordained government, for all the world as similar intractable persons are doing to-day, and worked the mob up to such a pitch of frenzy that they called out, "Stone 'em, stone 'em, and thereby secure our liberties; and let us choose other captains to lead us back into Egypt, in case we do not succeed in reducing the Canaanites." In Num. xvi, 23-35, we learn that the ground opened and swallowed up the malcontents and "all that appertained unto them." Shocking fate! Dread warning! Let us take it, to the extent of behaving and poking no fun at divinity for at least half a page, but confine ourselves to a decent narration of the incidents represented in our picture. When Israel came to dwell in Shittem, they bowed down unto strange gods. "And the anger of the Lord was kindled against Israel. And the Lord said unto Moses, take all the heads of the people, and hang them up be-

fore the Lord against the sun, that the fierce anger of the Lord may be turned away from Israel" (Num. xxv, 3, 4).

A visitor to a penitentiary once asked a convict, "I s'pose they treat you well here, my friend?" "Yes, sir;" said the convict, "I have no complaints to make, but there is one thing I don't like. Every Sunday mornin' in the chapel, they set me next to one of these ere shoutin' Methodists, an' t'ain't pleasant for a man wot was born an' brought up a 'Piscopalian." Likewise that band of plundering cut-throats the old Israelites, though steeped in every crime, had religious feeling in such strength as to be highly shocked at the neighboring Midianites' having a different religion. Actuated by their horror at anyone's choosing to believe differently from themselves in religion, and also impelled by lust for the heretics' rich possessions, they declared war against them, in the name of that deity whose name has furnished a sanction for all of the European and half of the Asiatic wars for a score of centuries.

The Israelites conquered, but as they had saved all the women alive, Moses became wroth with them, and (Num. xxxi, 17, 18) directed:

AN INSPIRED WAY OF GETTING RID OF TEMPTATION

"Now, therefore, kill all the males among the little ones, and kill every woman who hath known man by lying with him. But all the women-children that have not known a man by lying with him, keep alive for yourselves." On this part of holy writ John Peck says: "There are thousands of Christians who never read these verses. Their minds have been studiously turned away from them and many othersimilarly savage passages of scripture by their ecclesiastical trainers.

"Now, I want to make a missionary of every Liberal, and this is the way I propose to do it—mark the passages as I have directed, and as you find fitting occasions call the attention of Christians to them. Ask them to consider the unreasonableness of God giving utterance to such indecent language and giving such brutal commands. A few passages will make every Christian feel, if he have a thimbleful of brains, as though he ought to take a purgative. Verse 35: 'And thirty and two thousand in all, of women that had not known man by lying with him.'

"Think of it! Thirty-two thousand young women to be kept alive for 'yourselves'—that is, handed over to the lustful embrace of the soldiery! Write this hideous command upon every gatepost along the wayside, that every Christian may see it. In all the books I ever read I never found anything more brutal and demoralizing. If we are justifiable in giving homage to a God who gave such a savage command, then we should take off our hats and make the lowest bow when we meet the lowest and most brutal savage.

"After Probst had murdered a whole family he was asked why he killed the little children, and if it was possible that they had ever done anything to injure him. 'Why, no;' he replied, 'but when I got my hand in I rather liked it.'

"Probably Moses, who was on such familiar terms with the Lord, was about on a level with the man Probst. No doubt he enjoyed the killing of 'all the males among the little ones.' But the horror of believing that such a ghastly sight would turn away the 'fierce anger of the Lord' is enough to nauseate any but a Christian stomach. It is bad enough to be compelled to believe that human beings are savages. But to

And thou shalt bestow that money for whatsoever thy soul lusteth after, for **oxen**, or for sheep, or for wine, or for strong drink.—Deut. xiv. 26.

believe that God is a savage can have no other result than to produce Christian savages."

In Deut. xiii, 6–10, we find this command: "If thy brother, the son of thy mother, or thy son, or thy daughter, or the wife of thy bosom, or thy friend, which is as thine own soul, entice thee secretly, saying, Let us go and serve other gods, . . . thou shalt surely kill him; thine hand shall be first upon him to put him to death, and afterward the hand of all the people. And thou shalt stone him with stones, that he die." Can we believe, asks Ingersoll, "that any such command was ever given by a merciful and intelligent God? Suppose, however, that God did give this law to the Jews, and did tell them that whenever a man preached a heresy, or proposed to worship any other god, that they should kill him; and suppose that afterward this same god took upon himself flesh, and came to this very chosen people and taught a different religion, and that thereupon the Jews crucified him; I ask you, did he not reap exactly what he had sown? What right would this God have to complain of a crucifixion suffered in accordance with his own command? . . . In the Old Testament no one

is told to reason with a heretic, and not one word is said about relying upon argument, upon education, nor upon intellectual development— nothing except simple brute force. Is there to-day a christian who will say that four thousand years ago, it was the duty of a husband to kill his wife if she differed with him upon the subject of religion? Is there one who will now say that, under such circumstances, the wife ought to have been killed? Why should God be so jealous of the wooden idols of the heathen? Could he not compete with Baal? Was he envious of the success of the Egyptian magicians? Was it not possible for him to make such a convincing display of his power as to silence forever the voice of unbelief? Did this God have to resort to force to make converts? Was he so ignorant of the structure of the human mind as to believe all honest doubt a crime?"

The Lord instructs his subjects in Deut. xiv, 26: "Thou shalt bestow that money for whatsoever thy soul lusteth after, for oxen, or for sheep, or for wine, or for strong drink." The Bible is full of such sanctions of indulgence in spirituous liquor. In Deut. vii, 13, God, through Moses, said to his chosen people: "And he will

A QUESTION FOR CHRISTIANS TO CONSIDER.

love thee, and bless thee, and multiply thee; and he will also bless the fruit of thy womb, and the fruit of thy land, thy corn, and thy wine, and thine oil," etc., etc. Deut. xi, 14: "That I will give you the rain of your land in his due season, the first rain and the latter rain, that thou mayest gather in thy corn, and thy wine, and thy oil." Deut. xv, 14: "Thou shalt furnish him liberally out of thy flock, and out of thy floor, and out of thy wine-press; of that wherewith the Lord thy God hath blessed thee thou shalt give unto him." This is said regarding the manumitted Hebrew slave. And so it is a *blessing* for God to give the fruit of the wine-press to his children? And we are to emulate him. Deut. xxviii, 39: "Thou shalt plant vineyards, and dress them, but thou shalt neither drink of the wine, nor gather the grapes, for the worms shall eat them." Verse 51 of the same chapter tells the people that their cattle and wine and oil shall be taken from them if they disobey God's commands. E. C. Walker thus sums up scriptural teachings on liquor-drinking: "There are but a very few passages, none of which are found in the New Testament, which condemn the use of intoxicants; more

than five times as many encourage or enjoin their use; a few condemn the use of wine on stated occasions by certain persons, or in excess, while a large number of other passages make mention of its use as a matter of course, and with no hint of censure or of its evil effects."

"But the women and the little ones, and the cattle and all that is in the city, even all the spoil thereof, shalt thou take unto thyself; and thou shalt eat the spoil of thine enemies which the Lord thy God giveth thee" (Deut. xx, 14). Could a savage or even a devil do worse?

The Lord in Deut. xxiv, 1, issued this ordinance on divorce: "When a man hath taken a wife, and married her, and it come to pass that she find no favor in his eyes, because he hath found some uncleanness in her; then let him write her a bill of divorcement, and give it in her hand, and send her out of his house." Such are the notions of the God of the Bible on this question which is so much vexed of late. When a husband for any reason desires to be rid of his wife, when she has spent on him her youth and beauty and he fancies a younger damsel, he has only to write a bill of divorce and dismiss her, to perish if fate so will it. But not a word is

When a man hath taken a wife, and married her, and it come to pass that she find no favor in his eyes, because he hath found some uncleanness in her; then let him write her a bill of divorcement, and give it in her hand, and send her out of his house.—Deut. xxiv, 1.

devoted to assigning to the wife equal rights or any rights at all. Talbot W. Chambers, a member of the American Old Testament Co., has written a "Companion to the Revised Old Testament," in which he makes this peculiar defense of our text: "It is further objected that the Old Testament tolerated polygamy and extra-judicial divorce. In regard to the latter of these we have a full and satisfactory explanation from our Lord. He points back to the monogamy established in paradise as the true family constitution. But in the case of the Jews the statute was relaxed, not because it was wrong, but because of the 'hardness of the people's hearts.' The same thing may be said of polygamy. Yet, upon the whole, in a country like Palestine and in an age when women were cut off from all the social life of both sexes, it was doubtless expedient to allow a departure from the law laid down at the creation, and permit a man to have more wives than one, on the ground that this imperfect arrangement was better than general and promiscuous concubinage, and that the habit being so deeply rooted, it was wiser to regulate and control it than to meet it by an absolute prohibition in that rudi-

mentary stage of human progress." What uproarious laughter can do justice to the ludicrousness of a subterfuge like this? The all-powerful God would abolish unjust divorce, and polygamy, but is thwarted by "the hardness of the people's hearts," and compelled to await the bringing around of mankind to sentiments of justice by the gradual and natural growth of morals, civilization—and Rationalism!

Soon we cross again one of the Lord's favorite institutions, slavery. Sometimes it appears in the form of the reduction of foreigners to bondage; sometimes in that of enslavement of individuals among the Hebrews themselves, for no fault of their own: while here we come upon a contemplated deliverance of the whole Hebrew nation into slavery. That nation is thus threatened in case of disobedience: "And the Lord shall bring thee into Egypt again with ships, by the way whereof I spake unto thee. . . . There you shalt be sold into your enemies for bondmen and bondwomen, and no man shall buy you" (Deut. xxviii, 68). The ludicrous contradiction, that they were to be sold yet no one was to buy them, was perhaps introduced to help in giving the inspired book that humorous

And the Lord shall bring thee into Egypt again with ships, by the way whereof I spake unto thee, Thou shalt see it no more again: and there ye shall be sold unto your enemies for bondmen and bondwomen, and no man shall buy you.—Deut. xxviii, 68.

element without which no novel, whatever its other merits of adventure or romance, can hope to find an extended sale. We are willing, for our part, to express a belief that the romance which we are now reviewing will never be impeded in sale by lack of the comic element.

Jehovah in the text inscribed on page 217 complains in sad lass-lorn—or Jew-lorn—strains of being so unfortunate as to be subjected to the pangs of jealousy. We have been jealous ourselves, in our callow days, and as these were the Lord's unfledged years also, we perhaps should not count it against him in our column of black marks. We have always felt sympathy with anyone to whom fate had decreed this vexatious experience, and though we never expected to have to bestow that feeling upon a god, yet we do not refuse to do so. So forgetting any little past differences, Jehovah, we heartily extend you our compassion and fellow-feeling. Come, old boy, cheer up! Never say die! What, ne'er pull thy hat upon thy brows! There are as good fish in the sea as have ever been caught! Come, the company of friends is good for anyone in trouble. Come and take a walk—come (bend your ear closer)—come on to the café

round the corner and you'll soon feel better.

Truly poor Jehovah had a hard time struggling against all his rivals. No wonder that in his harassment he so often fell into the bluster of a low-ward city tough, and cocking the cigar in his mouth and clapping his arms akimbo, called out, "Am I a God at hand, and not a God afar off? Can any hide himself in secret places that I shall not see him? Do I not fill heaven and earth? Is not my word like as a fire? and like a hammer that breaketh the rock in pieces" (Jer. xxiii, 23, 24, 29)? We are willing to pardon some exaggerations used in passion, but of course Jehovah knew that he did not "fill heaven and earth." For there was a multitude of other gods around him on every hand. His followers never thought of doubting that there was, only believing—or hoping—that they had chosen the doughtiest one of the candidates for their favor in that line. Jehovah admits this himself in many places, for instance in Ex. xii, 12, where he declares, "Against all the gods of Egypt I will execute judgment!" Of course, the Israelites followed their best knowledge in regard to the merits of the competing deities, and if they erred it was the fault of him who had created

PARALLEL CASES

their faculties so that they would, and they
should no more have been punished therefor
than the honest mistaking youngster in our
illustration on page 217.

Moses died at the age of one hundred and
twenty. "His eye was not dim, nor his natural
force abated" (Deut. xxxiv, 7). Truly a marvelous old man! Indeed, he had intended to keep
right on living, but the Lord intervened and cut
him off for a special reason. Jehovah's motive
in this was revenge, but we are given two different transgressions each of which was the sole
cause of this revenge, and as we must be sure to
choose the correct one of these for our belief
or be damned, prudence dictates that we give
them some attention. The writer of Deuteronomy tells us in i, 37, 38; iii, 26, that the refrac-
toriness of all the Israelites is the sin for which
Jehovah exacts the premature death of Moses.
While the writer of Numbers in xxvii, 12-14,
imputes the guilt to Moses's conduct when
bringing water from the rock (Num. xx, 7-11)—
using incredulous language and striking the
rock instead of simply speaking to it as he had
been commanded.

The Pentateuch, or the books of Genesis,

Exodus, Leviticus, Numbers, and Deuteronomy,
was ascribed to Moses by divinity writers till
recent criticism forced the more intelligent of
them to drop the claim and make the unpleasant
admission that that part of scripture is utterly
anonymous. In Gen. xxxvi, 31, we read, "And
these are the kings that reigned in Edom, before there reigned any king over the children of
Israel." But no kings ruled over Israel till
centuries after Moses's death. In Ex. xvi, 35,
we read. "And the children of Israel did eat
manna forty years, until they came to a land inhabited: they did eat manna until they came
into the borders of the land of Canaan." But
these events did not occur till some time after
the death of Moses (Josh. v, 12). Our space
excludes other disproofs of the Mosaic authorship of the Pentateuch, except mention of the
fact that to have written the last chapter of
Deuteronomy Moses would have had to describe
his own death and burial.

Jude i, 9, mysteriously speaks about "Michael
the archangel, when contending with the devil
he disputed about the body of Moses." Had
we been arbitrator of that dispute the devil
would not have gone off empty-handed.

MICHAEL THE ARCHANGEL DISPUTETH WITH SATAN OVER THE BODY OF MOSES.—Jude 9.

CHAPTER XIV.

BALAAM THE DIVINER.

Our present story opens with the sojourning of several men at the house of one Balaam, whereat the Lord, being omniscient and therefore not knowing who they were, called Balaam up in the night and asked, "What men are these with thee" (Num. xxii, 9)?

Balaam civilly enlightened the Lord on the subject of his inquiries. The strangers were embassadors from Balak, king of the Moabites, who had sent them to solicit Balaam, who was a soothsayer and wizard on his own account as well as an oracle of Jehovah, to come and put a curse on a strange and fierce nation which had entered the neighborhood and threatened to exterminate that king's subjects. Now, it so happened that this invading nation was the Israelites, and consequently Jehovah refused to allow his sorcerous acquaintance to curse them, "for," expostulated that deity, "they are blessed." So Balaam in the morning said to the embassadors of King Balak, "Git out! scat! git out now!"—or, as we believe the text more nearly runs, "Get you into your land" (Num. xxii, 13)! The embassadors returned to Balak and reported. That king "sent yet again princes, more, and more honorable than they." This second embassy made Balaam promise of munificent rewards in case of his compliance. These rich prospects seem to have shaken his resolution and induced him to hope that he could change the Lord's mind and make him consent to his friend's going over and cursing his people. Perhaps Balaam contemplated offering Jehovah half of the reward. For a plenty of gold and silver, and burnt offerings, and wine, and oil, no doubt that disrespectable old deity would have allowed his people to have a curse or pretty much anything else inflicted on them. Balaam's reply was: "If Balak would give me his house full of silver and gold, I cannot go beyond the word of the Lord my God, to do less or more." Here he paused, and—we suppose with a wink at Balak's diplomats, while they, catching the hint, poked him roguishly in the ribs—added, "I pray you, tarry ye also here this night, that I may know what the Lord will say unto me more." Balaam then rung up the telephone communication: "Hello, Central!"

And he said unto them, Lodge here this night, and I will bring you word again, as the Lord shall speak unto me: And the princes of Moab abode with Balaam. And God came unto Balaam, and said, What men are these with thee?—Num. xxii, 8, 9.

"Hello!" "Give me Jehovah!" (After a pause) "Can't ring him up—must be out—no other god do?—can give Dagon, Baal, Bel, Chemosh, Molech—oh, here he is himself!" Jehovah: "Hello!" "Important business! Must see you again to-night. Come by 11:30 express." "Oh, pshaw, really can't. Beastly headache! Do you fellows think I *never* want to sleep?" "Well, it's those chaps from Balak again. If you don't take the job, the god of the Mo——" Jehovah, his strongest motive, that of jealousy, being now touched, interrupted to say that he would be along by 12 sharp. When he arrived, he listened to Balaam's representations, and finally said, "If the men come to call thee, rise up, and go with them; but yet the word which I shall say unto thee, that shalt thou do." By this he would seem to have wavered in his resolution, tempted by the gold and silver. But to give him his due, he finally withstood all offers and refused to allow his people to be cursed, as we shall see. "And Balaam rose in the morning, and saddled his ass, and went with the princes of Moab" (Num. xxii, 21).

Notwithstanding that Balaam had received the clearest of authorization to go to Balak, we read in Num. xxii, 22, that God's "anger was kindled because he went." Perhaps the deity was still fluctuating between temptation to allow his people to be cursed and reflections on the disadvantages that must attend such an action. For it would cause the loss of the little honor and reputation that he had left. It would make him a by-word among other gods. Then, too, Balaam's powerful curse would destroy him people—a thing which we see happening around us every day—awfully common, you know—and he would be left without anyone to provide him with the sweet savors which so delighted him (Gen. viii, 21), or with the "wine which cheereth God and man" (Judges ix, 14). And think of him—Lim, Jehovah, who aspired to be "a God of gods" (Dan. ii, 47) as Bonaparte desired to be called emperor of the kings of Europe—him who had so often made great boasts and blusters to mortals—think of him left without a people, to be laughed at by all his rivals who retained theirs! Yet on the other hand, how alluring were King Balak's offers! Perhaps Jehovah was short of cash—verging toward the necessity, it may be, of hiring out as a journeyman barber (Isa. vii, 20) to earn a few cents to keep body

And Balaam rose up in the morning and saddled his ass, and went with the princes of Moab.—Num. xxii, 21.

and soul together. These conflicting desires, we have supposed, threw the Lord into one of those fits of vexation so common to that ill-tempered individual; and, like many a petulant and mean-minded man, he spent his anger upon the nearest unoffending person. Be this as it may, the fact that he was enraged with Balaam for obeying his order stands there in Num. xxii in the most unmistakable of language, and Christians may justify it if they can.

So Jehovah sent an angel to stand across the way with drawn sword, "and the ass saw the angel of the Lord standing in the way, and his sword drawn in his hand; and the ass turned aside out of the way, and went into the field; and Balaam smote the ass, to turn her into the way" (Gen. xxii, 23).

To Balaam the angel continued invisible, as also to the embassadorial princes and their servants who accompanied him. The seraphic intruder was visible only to the ass. Perhaps the story of Balaam is the work of an ancient Infidel, written to convey, in a cloaked and safe manner, his opinion that supernatural visions have no existence for sensible men and are sensible only by asses. Such a production

might easily have got included in the "sacred canon" by the bungling rabbis and afterward the equally blundering councils who huddled together the old legends and fragments, the same as they made the mistake of inserting other pieces of literature which as fatally contradict their doctrines—viz., Job and Ecclesiastes, wherein it is declared that "he that goeth down to the grave shall come up no more" and "a man hath no preëminence above a boast, for . . . all go unto one place."

Next the angel stood between two walls, whereupon the inspired ass thrust herself against one wall, in order to get by, so that Balaam's foot was crushed. "And he smote her again"—good treatment for every ass who thinks he sees supernatural things and in his wild freaks owing thereto puts us in danger. Then the angel half waddled and half flopped with his wings, as we see geese do in exigencies, up between the walls into a place as narrow as the heart of a petitioner for Sunday closing of museums to the working-people. At this the ass threw herself down, as we have seen many of her kind do at the pitch of excitement in a colored church service. The freakish jenny

And the ass saw the angel of the Lord standing in the way, and his sword drawn in his hand; and the ass turned aside out of the way, and went into the field; and Balaam smote the ass, to turn her into the way.—Num. xxii, 23.

now received such a thumping from the stick of the infuriated necromancer that "the Lord opened her mouth." This was not to tell her age, but to enable her to speak. Those who have seen an ass speak and observed the width to which it is necessary for one to open his or her mouth, realize why the Lord's assistance came in handy. While Jehovah was standing there—of course invisible to the travelers—holding jenny's mouth stretched with one hand while with the other he brushed from his black broadcloth the lather which she kept foaming forth, she administered to Balaam this rebuke: "What have I done unto thee, that thou hast smitten me these three times" (Num. xxii, 28)?

Balaam showed no surprise at this use of speech by a beast. We ourselves, to be sure, have frequently—only too frequently—heard asses discourse touching the actions of the Lord and his angels, but they were all two-legged ones, and we think this cool reception by Balaam of his ass's speech the very queerest part of a story where all is queer. However, the worthy magician unhesitatingly entered into an animated controversy with his ass. The

dialogue ran thus: Fortune-teller Balaam (in reply): "Because thou hast mocked me: I would there were a sword in mine hand, for now I would kill thee." Jenny Ass: "Am not I thine ass, upon which thou hast ridden ever since I was thine unto this day? was I ever wont to do so unto thee?" Fortune-teller Balaam: "Nay." At this moment the Lord revealed to Balaam the angel standing in the way with drawn sword, his wings flapping in anger.

But after all that fuss the angel merely repeated the Lord's command to Balaam to speak nothing but what he was inspired to, and departed—

<pre>
     A good-bye wink he wunk,
     A line of song he sung,
     A sudden thought he thunk—
     Off on his wing he wung.
</pre>

As the last rays of the setting orb of day glowed upon the gloomy cloud-pile which filled the western horizon, but were gradually muffled in by the envious vapors, while grim shadows stole up from the valleys like assassins until they had shrouded all, a solitary

And the Lord opened the mouth of the ass; and she said unto Balaam, What have I done unto thee, that thou hast smitten me these three times?—Num. xxii, 28, 29, 30.

horseman might have been seen (we mean, during the first part of .this transaction, not during the last) to emerge from the distance (of course, he couldn't have emerged from the center of the place) and ride over the dreary waste with anxious glances as if for some wayside inn to shelter his weary steed and himself during the somber night.

It was Balaam! However, he wasn't so very solitary after all, for the embassador princes and their servants were with him. But as they kept pretty well behind, to avoid any more inhumane angels with invisible swords across pathways (this is what B.'s anxious glances were for); and as we deemed it necessary to the romanticness of the thing to have the traveler alone, we took the liberty to term him so. We shall have to confess, also, that there were no valleys for shadows to steal from. B.'s journey lay across a desert. We had previously had tales of war, of court intrigue, of love and ladye fair, and of supernatural apparition, and we had intended to serve up this journey as one of that good old romantic class, to be read on wild winter nights, in which lonely travelers

manage to gain through the shades of eve secluded and moldering inns, with suspicious-faced landlords, where ensue at midnight adventures of the most delightfully blood-curdling character. But if we can't do it without making so many mistakes we shall drop it. We don't intend to make this a Bible.

Let us pause to castigate a certain gross error in the inspired narrative. The journey from Balak's land to Balaam's is known to modern investigators to have been beset with difficulties, across a desert, and requiring at least fourteen days each way. To make it four times must have taken the embassies fifty-six days, without counting the delays at each termination. Yet we are to imagine the Israelites waiting all this time with their hands folded to see what would be the outcome of Balak's machinations.

Balaam arrived safe and hearty, and "when Balak heard that Balaam was come, he went out to meet him unto a city of Moab, which is in the border of Arnon, which is in the utmost coast" (Num. xxii, 36).

"And it came to pass on the morrow, that

Then the Lord opened the eyes of Balaam, and he saw the angel of the Lord standing in the way, and his sword drawn in his hand. – Num. xxii, 31.

Balak took Balaam, and brought him up into the high places of Baal, that thence he might see the uttermost parts of the people" (Num. xxii, 41). Balaam wished to have a little confabulation with his heavenly papa before beginning to curse or otherwise violate the city ordinances. So, conjecturing that said paternal ancestor might be hungry, and therefore enticeable by means of a fine roast dinner, he had Balak build seven altars and cook thereon seven bullocks and seven rams. Here was a precious feed, and anyone knowing the irresistible attraction of fine banquets for public dignitaries would confidently have expected the arrival of this one.

"And Balaam said unto Balak, Stand by thy burnt-offering, and I will go; peradventure the Lord will meet me: and whatsoever he showest me I will tell thee. And he went to a high place" (Num. xxiii, 3). The event justified the expectations that Balaam had placed upon the Lord's alimentiveness, for soon that worthy rolled in, puffing and blowing, and, having gracefully resigned his shiny silk hat to a colored servant, seated himself to the good cheer. Balaam before long managed to get out of him, between mouthfuls, the following directions: "Return (taking a side of mutton) unto Balaam, (" hum, yum," licking his chaps) and thus ("another leg of beef, waitaw ") then ("well, that *is* good—say, Baaly, who's your cook?") shalt speak." The Lord being now deep in the wine, and showing signs of soon being under the table, his host forbore to inquire what the "thus" meant, and concluding that the Lord intended to inspire him at the right moment, returned to Balak. On puffing up his cheeks and straddling his legs apart ready to be delivered of the inspired vaticination, he found himself destined, instead of cursing Israel, to bless it. And he burst into this song of praise :

From Syria has Balak brought me,
  Moab's king from the eastern heights:
"Come, curse me Jacob,
  Come, defy me Israel !"
How shall I curse whom God curses not,
  And defy whom Jehovah defies not?
From the top of the rocks I see him,
  From the hills I look down upon him:
See! It is a people that dwells apart,

And the angel of the Lord said unto Balaam, Go with the men: but only the word that I shall speak unto thee, that thou shalt speak. So Balaam went with the princes of Balak.—Num. xxii, 35.

And is not reckoned among the nations
Who can measure the dust of Jacob
Or count the fourth part of Israel?
May I die the death of the Upright,
May my seed be like him!

Let us be serious for a moment. It will be noticed in the above song that the thought which is in one line is usually repeated in slightly altered words in the next. This is very common in Hebrew poems; for they seldom or never have any measure or rhyme, but are distinguished from prose, in outward form, by the repetition of the same thought in different words two or three times in succession. This may well seem strange to us, for we are accustomed to rhyme and rhythm, or at any rate the latter, in all our verses. Yet neither the one nor the other is by any means inseparable from poetical language. The peculiarity of poetry is that in it a man who is inspired by some passion, whether noble or the reverse, gives expression to his feelings; and the more artificial the form in which he does so the smaller the chance of the substance being really poetical. And when a man, in a highly wrought

frame of mind, is driven by pressure from within to utter what is going on in his heart and to pour out his soul in words, nothing is more natural than for him to repeat the same thing in different forms two or even three times over; for passion rarely stints its words. This repetition by which the second member of a sentence fills in the first, even a third being sometimes added, is called "parallelism." Now, although these lines are in our ordinary Bibles run together like prose, their poetical character is better seen when printed as above, and we shall accordingly take all of Balaam's prophecies or songs through this story from a translation which arranges them thus. The words themselves differ somewhat from those of the King James translation; they more nearly approach the Revised Version, and are rendered by the best Hebrew scholars.

Balak at this effusion very naturally exclaimed, "What hast thou done unto me? I took thee to curse mine enemies, and, behold, thou hast blessed them altogether." They changed their situation, Balaam hunted up the

And when Balak heard that Balaam was come, he went out to meet him unto a city of Moab, which is in the border of Arnon, which is in the utmost coast. Num. xxii, 36.

Lord and received more instructions, as we see in the illustration, and prophesied thus:

> Stand up, O Balak! and hear.
> Hearken to me, O son of Zippor!
> God is not a man that he should lie,
> Or a son of man that he should repent.
> Would he say a thing and then not do it?
> Would he promise and not perform?
> Behold! I was bidden to bless,
> And this blessing I may not recall.
> No misery is seen in Jacob,
> Nor sorrow perceived in Israel;
> Jehovah, his god, is with him,
> A right royal shout in his midst.
> God has led him out of Egypt;
> His might is like to a buffalo's
> No charm has force against Jacob,
> Nor magic power on Israel;
> When it is said of Jacob
> And of Israel: "God does wonders!"
> See! it is a people that stands like a lioness
> And rises up like a lion,
> Who lies not down till he has eaten the prey
> And drunk the blood of the slaughtered.

Balak now grew so indignant that he wouldn't play any more, but turned away to go over into his own yard. But Balaam persuaded him to let him try again and see whether he could not curse Israel. Most godly persons whom we

have seen have much less difficulty in cursing. Balaam's deliverance this time was:

> The oracle of Balaam, son of Beor;
> The word of the man of unclosed eyes,
> Who hears the word of God,
> And knows the knowledge of the Most High,
> Who sees the sight of the Almighty;
> Who bows down, and his eyes are unveiled:
> How goodly are thy tents, O Jacob!
> Thy dwellings, Israel!
> Like spreading streams;
> Like gardens by the river;
> Like aloes planted by Jehovah;
> Like cedars by the streams.
> Water flows out from his buckets,
> And his new-sown fields are richly watered.
> His king is taller than Agag;
> His kingdom is exalted.
> His god brought him forth from Egypt;
> And he has a buffalo's strength.
> He devours the peoples that oppose him;
> He grinds their bones;
> He breaks their loins.
> He crouches like a lion for the spring;
> Like a lioness;—who shall provoke him?
> A blessing shall rest upon him who blesses you;
> A curse upon him who curses!

"And Balak's anger was kindled against Balaam, and he smote his hands together: and Balak said unto Balaam, I called thee to curse

And Balaam said unto Balak, Stand by thy burnt-offering, and I will go; peradventure the Lord will come to meet me: and whatsoever he showeth me I will tell thee. And he went to a high place.—Num. xxiii. 3.

mine enemies, and, behold, thou hast altogether
blest them these three times. Therefore now
flee thou to thy place" (Num. xxiv, 10, 11). But
the seer before leaving felt himself moved to say
a last word, and accordingly, without waiting for
Balak's permission, launched into this lofty
strain :

The oracle of Balaam, son of Beor;
  The word of the man of unclosed eyes.
Who hears the word of God,
  And knows the knowledge of the Most High;
Who sees the sight of the Almighty:
  Who bows down, and his eyes are unveiled:

I see him, but not as he now is ;
  I behold him, but not from near;
There is a star rising out of Jacob,
  A scepter comes up out of Israel,
Smiting the temples of Moab,
  The skull of all sons of the war-cry !
Edom shall be a conquered province;
  Seir, his enemy, a possession ;
  And Israel shall wax mighty.
A ruler shall come out of Jacob
  And destroy them that flee from the city.

Though Amalek be the first of peoples,
  Yet shall his children fall in ruin !
236

Though thy dwelling be so firm
  And thy nest (lies) built on the rock ;
Yet shall ken be slowly destroyed
Till Ashur take him captive away.

Alas! but who shall live
  Longer than God allows !
Ships that come from Cyprus   .   .   .
  They shall oppress Ashur,
Shall oppress that people beyond Euphrates,
  And it too shall be destroyed !

These utterances of Balaam are really good
as poetry. They are, as Herder remarks, "distinguished for dignity, compression, vividness,
and fulness of imagery ; there is scarcely anything equal to them in the later prophets, and
nothing in the discourses of Moses." As about
the only good things in the Bible are bits of
poetry here and there, we have given them in
full, hoping that our readers may enjoy them.

After this last glorification of his God, Balaam
"rose up, and went and returned to his place;
and Balak also went his way" (Num. xxiv, 25).

With these events the narrative of Balaam in
the Old Testament ceases, and the only farther
event of his life that is recorded is his death in
battle, several chapters after. Now, the point

And God met Balaam: and he said unto him, I have prepared seven altars, and I have offered upon every altar a bullock and a ram. And the Lord put a word in Balaam's mouth, and said, Return unto Balak, and thus thou shalt speak.—Num. xxiii, 4, 5.

where his main story ceases is at the end of chapter xxiv, and the next chapter begins with an account of a perversion of the Israelites to idolatry of the god Baal-peor; and there are intimations in two parts of the Old Testament that Balaam was the cause of this sin. Christian writers in their anxiety to find model men of God to hold up as ideals to their congregations, are prone to ignore all flaws in the characters whom they would exalt, and so they slur over these ill reports of Balaam. But the records are there, and it remains an open question whether Balaam was not throughout a secret server of Balak and a worker against Israel and its God. Num. xxxi, 16, says: "These caused the children of Israel, through the counsel of Balaam, to commit trespass against the Lord in the matter of Peor." And Num. xxi, 8, relates that the Israelites "slew the kings of Midian, . . . Balaam also, the son of Beor, they slew with the sword." Balaam's being enlisted against the Israelites here, and enticing them to "false worship" in the former verse, show that he at least turned against "the true God"

and his people after the affair with Balak, if indeed he was not hostile to them throughout. Josephus says that before Balaam returned from Moab he advised Balak to undo the Israelites by tempting them to join the licentious worship of Baal-Peor. The conception of Balaam as a deceiver, a false prophet bribed by Balak, a typical enemy of the kingdom of God, is held by the Jews, and was current among the Christians of the first centuries (Rev. ii, 14: 2 Pet. ii, 15, 16).

Wishers of farther conjecture on Balaam may consult the following treatises wherein men who should have been at the plow or the chisel wasted time in guesses about him: Dr. Jortin's "Six Dissertations, Lond. 1755, pp. 171-194; Bishop Butler's "Sermons at the Rolls' Chapel," Serm. vii. Bishop Newton "On the Prophecies," vol. i, ch. 5. "Discours Historiques, etc.," par M. Saurin, Amst. 1720, tome ii. "Disc." 64. "Die Geschichte Bileams und seine Weissagungen erläutert." von E. W. Hengstenberg. 1842. "Origenis Opera," Berl. 1840, tom. x. pp. 168-258.

And they slew the kings of Midian, besides the rest of them that were slain: namely, Evi, and Rekem, and Zur, and Hur, and Reba, five kings of Midian: Balaam also, the son of Beor, they slew with the sword.—Num. xxxi, 8.

CHAPTER XV.

BLOODY JOSHUA

In treating the mixed-up books of the Bible as they come we have been led away from the true thread of the narrative. The episode of Balaam occurred while the wandering children of Israel were yet under the leadership of Moses, but as its place of narration in scripture is after that chief's death we have related it after. Now, however, we start from Moses's death. The Israelites must have a new leader in his place to direct their farther meanderings. Moses has recommended Joshua, probably as being, next to himself, the most audacious scoundrel and on the best understanding with the priests. The Lord, doubtless on the same grounds, accepts him, and begins to instruct him, telling him about "the land which I do give to them, even to the children of Israel. Every place that the sole of your foot shall tread upon, that have I given unto you" (Josh. i, 2, 3). This has always been a favorite trick of the Lord's, giving to his flunkies and flatterers the possessions of other people. At present he has given to his sycophants

vast amounts of land and other things of value in America and Europe, for which the independent and honest men have to pay taxes and other charges. We wish that he would get out of this habit. However, his favorites possess less than they used to. The Lord next commands Joshua to "observe to do according to all the law which Moses my servant commanded thee." That law, given by God to Moses, directed, as we know, all manner of inhumanity. Here, for instance, is a sample from it: "When thou comest nigh to a city to fight against it, then proclaim peace unto it. And it shall be, if it make thee answer of peace, and open unto thee, that all the people that is found therein shall be tributaries unto thee, and they shall serve thee. And if it will make no peace with thee, but will make war against thee, then thou shalt besiege it; and . . . thou shalt smite every male, . . . but the women, . . . thou shalt," etc.—we know how all these commands run. This butchery was to be the fate of an unoffending people whom God's pets had taken a fancy to make slaves, if they did not willingly embrace bondage.

Joshua's first step in carrying out these com-

And Joshua the son of Nun sent out of Shittim two men to spy secretly, saying, Go view the land, even Jericho. And they went, and came unto a harlot's house, named Rahab, and lodged there.—Joshua ii, 1.

mands was to send two spies into the city of Jericho, who "came unto a harlot's house, named Rahab, and lodged there" (Josh. ii, 1).

We strive to keep the moral character of this book as high as possible, but to do so is truly an arduous task, as must appear when the nature of our subject is considered. A progress through the Bible is simply a stumbling from one criminal to another, from one variety of ill deed to another, with the experience unrelieved by a single great and good character, a single benefactor of mankind, a single Jefferson, Franklin, Paine, Ingersoll, Darwin, or Edison. Our narrative, we will admit, can be made to wear a character little above that of a police court register. Like such a register, it must now alternate its records of crimes of violence with the ease of a prostitute. Rahab, who received the spies of the people of God, was a harlot. On account of her being on the Lord's side Christians have always sung her praise, and commentators have searched anxiously for some subterfuge by which she could be made out to be not a harlot. Some have flatly declared her not one, when they have not the slightest shadow of excuse for thus contradicting the plain language of scripture. The historian Josephus, for instance, calls her an innkeeper. Milman tries to give the same impression, saying that she kept "a public caravansary." Whiston attempts her exculpation. But these are about all who have had the impudence to make such a baseless assertion. It is now admitted by every Hebrew scholar that the word employed in the scripture to designate Rahab means "harlot," not "hostess." It signifies "harlot" in every other text where it occurs. The idea of hostess is not represented by this or any other word in Hebrew, as the function of such a person did not exist. There were no inns, and when quasi-inns came into use they were never in any Eastern country kept by women.

This precious lady, when natives came seeking the Lord's spies, "brought them up to the roof of the house, and hid them with the stalks of flax, which she had laid in order upon the roof" (Josh. ii, 6).

Rahab's motive in befriending the Lord's spies perhaps was piety. She displays that quality strongly in her conversation with them. It is a notorious fact that every member of her profession is a strong religious believer. Be-

But she had brought them up to the roof of the house, and hid them with the stalks of flax, which she had laid in order upon the roof.—Joshua ii, 6.

sides her devoutness, fear may have operated on her. She said to the spies: "I know that the Lord hath given you the land, and that your terror is fallen upon us. . . . For we have heard how the Lord dried up the water of the Red sea for you, when ye came out of Egypt; and what ye did unto the two kings of the Amorites, that were on the other side Jordan, Sihon, and Og." It is little wonder that she wished to ingratiate herself with a god and a people who did such things. This Og was a giant. If the United States were invaded by a coalition of supernatural and natural beings, who dried up the waters—strong and other—that they came across, and got the better of giants, we should be filled with concern also. Giants abound through this veritable story. In xii, 4, we read of a lot of those gruesome characters— "the remnant of the giants that dwelt at Ashtaroth and at Edrei." In xvii, 15, we learn of a country which we shall always avoid in our wanderings, "the land of the Perizzites and the giants." In xviii, 16, our nerves are set atremble by an account of "the valley of the giants on the north."

Rahab finally, after telling a lot of lies to the searchers (lies in the cause of the Lord are not lies), let the spies "down by a cord through the window," and they effected their escape.

Thus we see that this lady was not only a harlot but a traitress. We will insert the monstrous sentiment of one of the theological commentators: "With regard to her taking part against her own countrymen, it can only be justified, but is fully justified, by the circumstances that fidelity to her country would, in her case, have been infidelity to God, and that the higher duty to her maker eclipsed the lower duty to her native land." The "Ungodly Woman of the Nineteenth Century" writes of Rahab: "Benedict Arnold—execrated by the entire world, and whose name is consigned to eternal infamy—betrayed only his own command into the hands of the British, while this harlot, as she is always called as if fearful her character and vocation would not be known, betrayed her whole nation, and the city of her nativity, into the bloody jaws of the most villainous cutthroat filibusters on the face of the earth. Yet she is exalted to the skies, both in the Old Testament and the New, and by no means today held in execration by the world—for she is

Then she let them down by a cord through the window: for her house was upon the wall
and she dwelt upon the wall. - Josh. ii. 15.

one whom the Christians venerate as one of the grandmothers of 'Our Blessed Lord and Savior Jesus Christ.' Let it be remembered whenever man or woman lied for Jehovah or Israel, they were blessed; whenever against them, they were accursed. The infamous Jezebel, whose name is a synonym of treachery, deceit, and wickedness, did but exalt her own people and family by foul means, while Rahab sacrificed her own and saved her would-be assassins by turning state's evidence against them. Jezebel was thrown to the dogs as an ungodly woman (2 Kings ix, 30 37), while Rahab, the harlot, is held in everlasting remembrance for her good works. Yea, farther, this abominable treachery was rewarded by God and his earthly saints, not only by preserving Rahab and family and giving them a home among them 'unto this day' (be that day when it may), but, under the cognomen of Rachab (Matt. i, 5), this Rahab, this harlot, married Salmon, became the mother of Boaz, and the great-great-grandmother of David, thus being, as the Christians claim, an ancestress of the Messiah."

"So the two men returned, and descended from the mountain, and passed over, and came to Joshua the son of Nun, and told him all things that befell them" (Josh. ii, 23). Preparations for the campaign against the unoffending city of Jericho began straightway. Joshua commanded: "Sanctify yourselves; for to-morrow the Lord will do wonders among you." Said Lord we may conceive at about that time as working himself up to do those wonders outside the camp in a field where he could exercise without hurting anything, ramping up and down, snorting smoke and belching fire (Ps. xviii, 8), sharpening his horns (Hab. iii, 4), and scouring his sword (Rev. i, 16). The next morning the confusion grew. Soldiers polished, corporals swore, captains flew about, the brevet-general Joshua cogitated, and the general—i. e., the Lord—took his position at the head of his forces. He did not mount a horse, but got into his cage or box called the ark. Removing the top, we suppose, he leaned back in dignity, putting on a look of calm confidence, whatever his inward tremor may have been, and altogether resembled one of our American generals in his carriage in a procession. The soldiers were now incited, as is sometimes the custom, to follow

And he said, Nay; but as captain of the host of the Lord am I now come. And Joshua fell on his face to the earth, and did worship, and said unto him, What saith my Lord unto his servant?—Joshua v, 14.

their general into all scenes of danger: "When ye see the ark of the covenant of the Lord your God, and the priests the Levites bearing it, then ye shall remove from your place, and go after it" (Josh. iii, 3). Otherwise God might have been taken by the foe.

Later on the scene which we depict on page 247 took place. The Lord in his ark we suppose had been carried by the priests to some removed point where direct communication with Joshua was impossible, for he seems to have sent that Jewish commander a message by a spiritual being calling himself "captain of the host of the Lord" (Josh. v, 14).

Several miracles had been worked for the invaders before they had arrived at Jericho. Once they were fed with manna. Once the Jordan was parted, à la Red sea, and they passed over without wetting their feet. Perhaps it is in commemoration of this that the most Christian lands at the present day are those in which the inhabitants have the least contact with water. Finally Jericho was surrounded and tight shut up "because of the children of Israel"—as tight as a Freethinker's mouth to-day in lands where Jehovah's children rule. Then the Lord instructed: "And seven priests shall bear before the ark seven trumpets of rams' horns; and the seventh day ye shall compass the city seven times, and the priests shall blow with the trumpets, . . . and the wall of the city shall fall down flat" (Josh. vi, 4). The profuse occurrence of the number seven through this narrative and the rest of the Bible is in itself evidence of the book's superstitious origin. About all of the ancients held the astrological belief that human fortunes are governed by the heavenly bodies, and the number of the best known of these, viz., the sun, moon, and five planets, occurs in all religions of antiquity as a sacred number. It is represented in all sorts of forms; for instance, the candlestick with seven branches in the temple of Jerusalem. The seven inclosures of the temple. The seven doors of the cave of Mithras. The seven stories of the tower of Babylor. The seven gates of Thebes. The flute of seven pipes generally put into the hand of the god Pan. The lyre of seven strings touched by Apollo. The book of "Fate," composed of seven books. The seven prophetic rings of the Brahmins. The seven stones—conse-

And seven priests shall bear before the ark seven trumpets of rams' horns: and the seventh day ye shall compass the city seven times, and the priests shall blow with the trumpets.—Joshua vi, 4.

crated to the seven planets — in Laconia. The division into seven castes adopted by the Egyptians and Indians. The seven idols of the Bonzes. The seven altars of the monument of Mithras. The seven great spirits invoked by the Persians. The seven archangels of the Chaldeans. The seven archangels of the Jews. The seven days in the week. The seven sacraments of the Christians. The seven wicked spirits of the Babylonians. The sprinkling of blood seven times upon the altars of the Egyptians. The seven mortal sins of the Egyptians. The hymn of seven vowels chanted by the Egyptian priests. The seven branches of the Assyrian "Tree of Life." Agni, the Hindoo god, is represented with seven arms. Sura's horse was represented with seven heads. Seven churches are spoken of in the Apocalypse. Balaam builded seven altars, and offered seven bullocks and seven rams. Pharaoh saw seven kine, etc., in his dream. The "Priest of Midian" had seven daughters. Jacob served seven years. Samson was bound with seven green withes, and his marriage feast lasted seven days. The Lord commands Noah to take into the ark clean beasts by sevens,

and fowls also by sevens, and tells him that in seven days he will cause it to rain upon the earth. We are also told that the ark rested in the seventh month, and the seventeenth day of the month, upon the mountains of Ararat. After sending the dove out of the ark the first time, Noah waited seven days before sending it out again. After sending the dove out the second time, "he stayed yet another seven days" ere he again sent forth the dove.

Joshua executed his master's queer plan for taking a city. To save his men's voices for the final shout which was to demolish the walls, he commanded them: "Ye shall not shout, nor make any noise with your voice," such as whistling, cat-calling, mewing, crowing in defiance, calling the enemies duffers or flats, singing Salvation Army hymns, etc., "until the day I bid you shout; then shall ye shout" (vi, 10). At the right moment "the people shouted when the priests blew with the trumpets, and it came to pass that the wall fell down flat, . . . and they took the city" (Josh. vi, 20).

All that were in this city whose only offense was exciting the cupidity of God's pets — all, "both men and women, young and old"—were

So the people shouted when the priests blew with the trumpets, and it came to pass that the wall fell down flat, ... so that the people went up into the city, every man straight before him, and they took the city.—Joshua vi, 20.

put to the sword. "But Joshua had said unto the two men that had spied out the country, Go into the harlot's house, and bring out thence the woman, and all that she hath," that Rahab might be spared as a reward for her treachery.

This page is the most convenient place for introducing some notice of the unauthentic character of this book of Joshua. It is not, as the clergy were accustomed to assert, written by Joshua, but is utterly anonymous. That Joshua did not write it is evident in more passages than we can here notice. One of them is xxix, 29, 30, to have indited which Joshua would have had to describe his own death and funeral. See further xxix, 31, about elders who "overlived Joshua," and xv, 63, where it is said that the children of Judah lived at Jerusalem, though they did not till the time of David.

The book abounds in falsehoods. The conquest of the whole land of Canaan, which here follows in five years after the taking of the city of Jericho, really occupied two and a half centuries. Almost every scriptural narrative compresses whole periods together—as a dramatist often does—attributing to a single man what was really the work of a nation, and forgetting all the secondary circumstances in its desire to glorify its hero alone. Thus the Israelite regarded the deliverance from Egypt, and the whole legislation of his people, as the work of Moses; he looked upon all the psalms as the work of David, and attributed to Solomon alone the fruits of the collective toil of all the proverb-makers. All that the prophets of North Israel had accomplished was put down to Elijah and Elisha; and, in the same way, posterity gradually forgot less conspicuous heroes of every grade to glorify Joshua the son of Nun as the successor of Moses and the man who had led Israel into Canaan. We must think of the Israelites not as quickly and uniformly victorious, but rather as pushing on from time to time, as occasion offered, into the land of the Canaanites, whose power was probably broken by the war with Ramses III. of Egypt. It seems probable that they entered, not only at different times, but from different sides. The main force which bore the brunt of the conflict was "the house of Joseph," under Joshua's command; while other tribes either joined this house on an inferior footing or

But Joshua had said unto the two men that had spied out the country, Go into the harlot's house, and bring out thence the woman, and all that she hath, as ye sware unto her.—Joshua vi, 22.

followed after it and contended for the spoil.
The mountainous districts were the first to
yield. There the Canaanites were conquered,
expelled, slaughtered, or made tributary. But
the invaders found many of the cities too strong
for them, and, indeed, they hardly dared to
show their faces on the plains, for fear of the war
chariots of the Canaanites. Thus the relations
between the ancient inhabitants of the country
and its conquerors were far from being equally
honorable to the latter in all cases, and were
very different in the different districts. Here the
Israelites had effected a definite conquest, and
had rooted out the Canaanites or reduced them
to slavery; but there they had made treaties
with them to regulate their mutual rights and
obligations. In other places, again, they forced
their way amongst the Canaanites but were
soon made tributary by them. In some districts the former inhabitants lived upon good
terms with the invaders, and the two intermar-
ried till they became a single people. Elsewhere there were little Israelite and Canaanite
kingdoms side by side, whose inhabitants lived
in armed independence of each other, frequently

breaking, by marauding expeditions or regular
wars, the peace which existed between them.

Other mistakes are: Amongst the cities that
Joshua is said to have conquered and laid
waste with fire and sword we find Hebron,
the well-known city of Judah, together with all
its dependencies, one of which was Debir
(Josh. x, 36-39; xi, 21; xii, 10). But elsewhere,
in this same book of Joshua, we are told that
Caleb and his brother Othniel conquered these
places (Josh. xv, 13-16); and the book of
Judges confirms this account, adding that the
conquest occurred after the death of Joshua
(Judg. i. 1, 10-13, 20). In like manner we hear
that the king of Jebus, or Jerusalem, fell before
Joshua, who took possession of his land (Josh.
xii, 1, 10); while another account informs us
that this city likewise fell into the hands of the
Israelites after Joshua's death (Judg. i. 1, 8);
but again in the very same chapter, we are told
that the Benjamites have not expelled the
Jebusites "to this day" (verse 21); and it is a
well-known fact that David was the first to
subdue them and to take possession of their
city (2 Sam. v, 6). Again, the honor of having
subdued the princes of North Canaan, who had

And **the young men that were** spies went in, and brought out Rahab, and her father, and her mother, and her brethren, and all **that she had; and they brought out** all her kindred, and left them without the camp of Israel.—Joshua vi. 23.

fixed their headquarters at Hazor, is assigned to Joshua (Josh. xi); but we afterward see that the people of these districts kept the hands of the Israelites full long after Joshua's death. The king of Gezer, too, according to the story, was utterly defeated and his land seized by Joshua (Josh. x, 34; xii, 12); but elsewhere we read that Israel could not expel the Canaanites that dwelt there (Josh. xvi, 10; Judg. i, 29). The fact is that the Israelites themselves were never able to conquer this city at all, and gained possession of it only when the Egyptian king, whose daughter was married to Solomon, took it and gave it to her as a dowry (1 Kings ix, 16).

Our illustration on page 255 treats this event: "And the young men that were spies went in, and brought out Rahab, and her father, and her mother, and her brethren, and all that she had."

The Israelites, if we are to believe the Bible, continued their ravages throughout the land. The priesthood encouraged the masses with promises of Jehovah's help; led forward the ark in which, they had convinced the men, the deity dwelt, and after victory grasped the spoil for which they had made their dupes risk their lives. "All the silver and gold, and vessels of brass and iron, are consecrated unto the Lord: they shall come into the treasury of the Lord." In chapter vii we find that because one poor fellow dared to divert from the priests' spoil into his own tent "a goodly Babylonish garment, and two hundred shekels of silver [a shekel is sixty-two and a half cents], and a wedge of gold," he and his innocent sons, daughters, oxen, asses, and sheep were stoned to death. City after city fell before the infamous Joshua, and in each case "all the souls that were therein he utterly destroyed." "For it was of the Lord," says xii, 20, "to harden their hearts, that they should come against Israel in battle, that he might destroy them utterly." In one case the horses of a numerous enemy who had been overcome were hamstrung and left to die the slow death which follows this infliction. This was by command of God (xi, 6). Who after this can force his hands to hold a Bible instead of dropping it from horror? What a book for our youth! In one encounter, with the Amorites and others, "the Lord cast down great stones from heaven" upon the enemy. Then Joshua, desiring to postpone the

Then spake Joshua to the Lord in the day when the Lord delivered up the Amorites before the children of Israel, and he said in the sight of Israel, Sun, stand thou still upon Gibeon; and thou, Moon, in the valley of Ajalon.—Joshua x, 12.

night which threatened to cut short his pleasure of massacreing the fliers, remarked to the sun, "Sun, stand thou still upon Gibeon; and thou, Moon, in the valley of Ajalon" (x, 12). These civil luminaries at once replied, "Why, certainly," and serenely waited "a whole day" till Joshua's bloodthirstiness was glutted.

There are many stories similar to this to be found among other nations of antiquity. We have, as an example, that which is related of Bacchus in the Orphic hymns, wherein it says that this god-man arrested the course of the sun and the moon. An Indian legend relates that the sun stood still to hear the pious ejaculations of Arjouan after the death of Chrishna. A holy Buddhist by the name of Mâtanga prevented the sun, at his command, from rising, and bisected the moon. Arresting the course of the sun was a common thing among the disciples of Buddha. The Chinese, also, had a legend of the sun standing still, and a tradition was found among the ancient Mexicans to the effect that one of their holy persons commanded the sun to stand still, which command was obeyed.

Had the sun and the moon actually stood still at Joshua's command, the event would have been observed and recorded throughout the world. But the trustworthy annals of no nation mention such a thing.

It will be noticed that Joshua commands the sun to stop, as though that were the moving body. Nowadays one wishing to lengthen a day miraculously would address the earth. Joshua's evident belief that day depends on the revolution of a moving sun about a stationary earth is one of the texts that were appealed to by Christians in persecuting broachers of the modern astronomy. Said Martin Luther: "People gave ear to an upstart astrologer, who strove to show that the earth revolves, not the heavens or the firmament, the sun and the moon. Whoever wishes to appear clever must devise some new system, which of all systems is, of course, the very best. This fool wishes to reverse the entire science of astronomy. But sacred scripture tells us that Joshua commanded the sun to stand still, and not the earth."

And the sun stood still, and the moon stayed, until the people had avenged themselves upon their enemies. Is not this written in the book of Jasher? So the sun stood still in the midst of heaven, and hasted not to go down about a whole day.—Joshua x, 13.

CHAPTER XVI.

THE CAMPAIGN OF DEBORAH AND BARAK AGAINST JABIN AND SISERA.

THE subject upon which we now enter brings us to the book of Judges. This book is totally anonymous, not even making a pretense to a specified author as do the preceding ones. All theologians' conjectures as to its author are not worth the paper on which they are printed. Nevertheless, it contains a larger proportion of truth than its predecessors. The writer followed a number of passably correct traditions. But, say Professors Oort and Hooykaas, "our gratitude to him would be still greater than it is if he had given us all that he found in his authorities unmixed and unaltered. But to an Israelite historian this seems to have been a simple impossibility. The book of Judges, like those of Joshua, Samuel, and Kings, is a prophetic work, and the author makes history subservient to his object of admonishing the people. This tendency of course influenced his representations of the past." Among the other falsehoods of the writer are ones of chronology. This book, as most know, is devoted to the history of Israel under a class of rulers who arose after the deliverers and generals like Moses and Joshua, and preceded the kings. "Judges" is the name given this class, but their functions were not those of that order, for these "judges" were merely heroes who arose here and there from time to time to deliver one or two tribes of Israel from Canaanitish oppression, and had no regular-succession; so when our writer, imagining that they had ruled over all Israel, and uninterruptedly, as the kings in the later days in which he wrote did, assigns them such periods as, with Moses, Joshua, and the first kings, just fill up the time from the conquest of Canaan to the building of Solomon's temple, he invents an artificial chronology which modern researches disprove.

Among these judges was one Deborah, "a prophetess," who held office conjointly with Barak. "And she dwelt under the palm-tree of Deborah between Ramah and Bethel in Mount Ephraim, and the children of Israel came up to her for judgment" (Judges iv, 5).

And Deborah a prophetess, the wife of Lapidoth, she judged Israel at that time. And she dwelt under the palm-tree of Deborah, between Ramah and Bethel in Mount Ephraim; and the children of Israel came up to her for judgment. —Judges iv, 4, 5.

Now, at this time the Israelites had twice fallen from the worship of the one true God—who was he? oh, pshaw, reader, of course you know, Jehovah—and carried their custom to the establishments of rival deities. The true god had sulked, and finally given them into oppression by other nations. They were now in their second period of punishment. Jabin, king of Canaan, was the tyrant under whose yoke they groaned. The subjects of this oppressor actually shoved the Israelites off the macadamized roads of the land and forced them to tramp through the hunters' and shepherds' paths in the mud (Judges v. 6). This used to get them quite riled, and many a night as a harassed Israelite came in with his trousers plastered with mud and his patent leathers spoiled, oaths were sworn, by the whole series of gods available in those days, that flashed blue blazes about till the Canaanites asked what army was coming against them with a search-light. Indeed, so uncivilly were the Israelites treated that "the inhabitants of the villages ceased, they ceased in Israel" (v. 7). At being subjected to such necessities as this, we need not wonder that the

Israelites protested. Forcing one to cease is an injustice which should be resented as promptly and sharply as possible. So the Israelites did exceeding long for a deliverer. They used to get up in the night and howl for one. For some reason they did not apply to Shamgar, then alive (v, 6), who once killed six hundred Philistines with an oxgoad (iii, 31). An oxgoad was an iron-tipped eight-feet pole. We suppose that Shamgar skewered the Philistines all through the middle on it, till he looked like a boy with a stick of spitted frogs. At length a deliverer bounded upon the scene in the person of Deborah, who thus becomes the first female general. She told her co-judge, Barak, that she would "draw" Sisera, Jabin's captain, to the river Kishon, when he should conquer that enemy. How she was to draw him we know not—certainly not by means of any such beauty as appears in our picture. Barak consented on condition that she would accompany the army. "And Deborah arose, and went with Barak" (iv, 9).

On the way Barak must have expressed some forebodings, as General Deborah addressed to

And she said, I will surely go with thee: notwithstanding the journey that thou takest shall not be for thine honour; for the Lord shall sell Sisera into the hand of a woman. And Deborah arose, and went with Barak to Kedesh.—Judges iv. 9.

him several enheartening remarks, such as, "Is not the Lord gone out before thee?" Barak anxiously peered ahead for a few minutes, but as he could catch no glimpse of the garment (Rev. i. 13) which descends to the foot about the individual said to be with the regiment gone to the front, nor descry a gleam of his golden girdle (Rev. i. 13), he was obliged to reply in a dispirited tone that he couldn't see anything of him—"Must be back in the commissary wagons, or with the priests eating burnt offerings." Nervously pulling out his pocket Bible, Revised Edition, to search for encouragement, he found what seemed to him the verse applying most nearly to his case: "They shall walk after the Lord: he shall roar like a lion: when he shall roar, then the children shall tremble from the west" (xi. 10). After this Judge Barak ambled along behind Deb in silence, except for an occasional murmuring "We need thee every hour," pricking his ears hopingly toward every quarter, in expectation each moment of seeing Jehovah appear roaring like a lion and lashing the ground with his tail in fury. At last they arrived at the field of battle, when, to give the Lord his due,

he appeared as per promise. Falling lustily to work, he soon "discomfited Sisera, and all his host." Whereupon "Sisera lighted down off his chariot and fled away on his feet" (iv. 15). Deborah, we suppose, here began to compose that song of victory which occupies chapter v. It is there sung by Deborah and Barak, but its composition is usually attributed to the former. It is a production of high merit (from a poetical viewpoint, as witness some of its finest verses:

Awake, awake, Deborah!
  Awake, awake, utter a song!
Arise, Barak, and lead thy captivity captive,
  Thou son of Abinoam.
They fought against heaven;
  The stars in their courses fought against Sisera.
The river of Kishon swept them away,
  That ancient river, the river Kishon.
O my soul, thou hast trodden down strength.
  Then were the horsehoofs broken by means of the prancings.
The prancings of their mighty ones.
  At her feet he bowed, he fell, he lay down;
At her feet he bowed, he fell:
  Where he bowed, there he fell down dead.
So let all thine enemies perish, O Lord
But let them that love him be as the sun when he goeth forth
  in his might.

Sisera lighted down off his chariot and fled away on his feet.—Judges iv. 15.

But whatever the poetical merit of Deborah's song, when judged by the standard of morals it is most culpable. It contains passages of ferocity revolting in the mouth of a woman, or indeed in that of a man. Gloating over the death of Sisera—which we shall come to later on—Deborah venomously mocks the mother of the fallen warrior:

> The mother of Sisera looks through the window;
> She looks through the lattice lamenting.
> "How long is his chariot stayed?
> How long ere we hear its wheels?"
> Her prudent court ladies reply,
> While she keeps repeating her words:
> "Has he not spoil to divide?
> A slave-girl—nay, two—for each hero,
> And splendid array for Sisera,
> A booty of dyed and glorious garments,
> A cloth of gold for his loved one's neck!"

"We turn," say Oort and Hooykaas, "with a certain feeling of horror from a woman who, herself a mother, could thus mock a mother's grief, and praise the treacherous and cruel act of Jael." This act of Jael, lauded in the song, we have not yet recorded; we will now nar-rate it. There were living at about the bound-ary line between Israel and the Canaanites a people called Kenites. One of these was called Heber, and he had a wife by the name of Jael. "And there was peace between Jabin the king of Hazor and the house of Heber the Kenite" (iv, 17). Trusting to old friendship, Sisera di-rected his flight to the tent of Heber. Jael went out to meet him with effusion of regard and hospitality, and urged him, "Turn in to me, fear not." He thereupon entered her tent, where he supposed himself to have found safety, as the etiquette of Eastern nations forbids search into such a place. "And he said unto her, Give me, I pray thee, a little water to drink; for I am thirsty. And she opened a bottle of milk, and gave him drink, and covered him. Again he said unto her, Stand in the door of the tent, and it shall be, when any man doth come and inquire of thee, and say, Is there any man here? that thou shalt say, No."

Little suspecting a violation of faith and hos-pitality on the part of a friend, and that friend a woman, Sisera allowed slumber to steal over him, and soon lay at the mercy of whomsoever

And Jael went out to meet Sisera, and said unto him, Turn in, my lord, turn in to me; fear not: and when he had turned in unto her into the tent, she covered him with a mantle.—Judges iv. 18.

might entertain evil designs against him, " for he was fast asleep and weary." "Then Jael, Heber's wife, took a nail of the tent, and took a hammer in her hand, and went softly unto him, and smote the nail into his temples, and fastened it into the ground. . . . So he died" (iv, 21). Then when Barak came by in pursuit, Jael called to him to come in, saying, "Come, and I will shew thee the man whom thou seekest." This infamous murderess had slain a friend, in violation too of plighted faith and of the laws of hospitality, simply to curry favor with the victor. If Sisera had overthrown the Israelites and it had been their leader that was flying, she would as readily have betrayed him. Yet Deborah sings of her thus:

> Blessed be Jael, the wife of Heber the Kenite,
>   Blessed be she above all women of the tent!
> When he asked for water, she gave him milk—
>   Gave him rich milk in her creatliest bowl,
> She laid her hand on the tent-peg,

> Her right hand grasped the workman's mallet
> Then she smote Sisera, pierced through his head
>   She crushed it, she pierced it as he slept.

And Deborah, be it remembered, was a prophetess and a woman moved by the Lord, so that the commendations of Jael which she utters are to be regarded as originating with that deity. Jael is one of the Lord's women, one of the holy women of the Bible, whose example our Sunday-school girls suppose we wish them to imitate. The best way to judge the moral character of acts of ancient personages is to suppose them committed by individuals in this land and in the present day. Let some Christian examine his notions of womanliness, let him revolve his conceptions of truth and hospitality in both sexes, let him try to realize the act of Jael in its details, and then honestly say whether he wishes to encourage in his wife or daughter the disposition which a woman must possess to perpetrate such a deed as the Hebrew woman's.

Then Jael, Heber's wife, took a nail of the tent, and took a hammer in her hand, and went softly unto him, and smote the nail into his temples, and fastened it into the ground; (for he was fast asleep, and weary:) so he died.—Judges iv, 21.

CHAPTER XVII.

GENERAL GIDEON.

GIDEON is the next godly exemplar of our series. His history is contained in Judges, and consists of events of the same degree of probability as the preceding from that book. We call the books of Joshua, Judges, Samuel, and Kings historical books; but it is not uninteresting to observe that they were known under quite another title by the Jews who collected the sacred writings. They were called the "Former Prophets," and preceded the works of Isaiah, Jeremiah, Ezekiel, and the twelve minor prophets, which were known as the "Latter Prophets." They were not regarded as histories so much as works of admonition and consolation. This view of their character was certainly the truest, for it was that of the writers of the books themselves, as well as of their first readers. We must, therefore, never forget to take this point of view of the narrators into account, for it always colored their representations very strongly.

At the opening of the veritable narrative of Gideon we find our beloved children of Israel oppressed by a host of horrid Midianites. These rude men "came as grasshoppers for multitude." Against them the Israelites probably tried prayer, that agency which we know has been so efficacious against the grasshoppers of our West, but it was without avail, for "the children of Israel did evil in the sight of the Lord," and that influential citizen refused to lift his finger for them. But at length the hotness of his wrath must have abated to about °60 or °70 Fahrenheit, say temperate or summer heat. for one day while a young man named Gideon "threshed wheat by the winepress," that is, threshed it covertly to hide it from the Midianites, a real live angel appeared to him, and addressed him after this flattering style, "The Lord is with thee, thou mighty man of valor" (Judges vi, 12).

Prior to this the Lord had offered an advance toward making up, for he had "sent a prophet unto the children of Israel, which said unto them, Thus saith the Lord God of Israel, I brought you up from Egypt, and brought you forth out of the house of bondage." You see, his having brought them forth, and led them

And the angel of the Lord appeared unto him, and said unto him, The Lord is with thee, thou mighty man of valor.—Judges vi, 12.

by a pillar of fire, opened the sea for them, wrought uncounted other miracles, and appeared to them the Lord knows how many times, were things so slight as to be easily forgotten, and you will at once perceive how expedient it was in him to keep his people from forgetting them. Jehovah farther urged his fitness for employment by them as a moral and an able-bodied god by reciting that he had robbed for their sake, saying in reference to the Canaanites, 'I drave them out from before you, and gave you their land.' He next told them not to be apprehensive of the other deities who were hanging about that neighborhood, as he was the holder of the championship diamond belt and the knocker-out of them all: "Fear not the gods of the Amorites, in whose land ye dwelt." After these deliverances he fell back into the sulks and abruptly concluded, "But ye have not obeyed my voice."

Now, however, his angel fluttered down to Gideon's side, as we have related, and after giving his wings a few subsiding flaps and pruning his plumage a trifle, observed, "Sure I'll be wid yees, and yees shall smite the Midianites as one man" (vi, 16). Gideon was hugely

tickled; but, shrewdly reflecting that he should make a surer ally of Jehovah by catering to his well-known predilections, he "went in, and made ready a kid, and unleavened cakes of an ephah of flour: the flesh he put in a basket, and he put the broth in a pot, and brought it out unto him under the oak, and presented it" (vi, 19).

"Then the angel of the Lord put forth the end of the staff that was in his hand, and touched the flesh and the unleavened cakes; and there rose up fire out of the rock, and consumed the flesh and the unleavened cakes." Gid watched the Lord devour his luncheon, in this way which he occasionally practiced, and at the conclusion was about to offer a napkin, when seeing that his guest's mode of eating obviated the necessity he drew back and muttering, "So much saved," confined himself to murmuring affably, "Hope you enjoyed it, sir, hope you enjoyed it." Being now left alone with the angel, he hoped for a valuable conversation, but that gentleman gathered his wings preparatory to flight, and, unheeding Gid's solicitation, "Sing, birdie, sing before you fly," "departed out of his sight" (vi, 21). In the

And Gideon went in, and made ready a kid, and unleavened cakes of an ephah of flour: the flesh he put in a basket, and he put the broth in a pot, and brought it out unto him under the oak, and presented it.—Judges vi, 19.

work of art which with careless, regal munificance we give opposite, we are the angelic creature striking a course N. by NE., brandishing his cane at his fellow-denizens of the air that he be not assailed by a king-bird as a crow or by a crow as a hawk, or seized and conveyed to her nest bodily by some enterprising eagless. "And when Gideon perceived that he was an angel of the Lord, Gideon said, Alas, O Lord God! for because I have seen an angel of the Lord face to face." Why Gideon seems to have perceived that he was talking with an angel only at this moment, and what he had supposed himself to be speaking with, is a question of a hardness approaching that of Pharaoh's heart. He may have supposed himself conversing with one of the other supernatural beings besides angels who abounded in those days—perhaps with a witch, which sort of creature we know used to be plentiful at that time, and indeed would be nowadays were it not for the little heed that men give to the teachings of the clergy.

On the night of that day the Lord dropped in on Gideon again, asking for more to eat, and for the dishonoring of his rival deities, in these words: "Take thy father's young bullock, even the second bullock of seven years old, and throw down the altar of Baal that thy father hath, and cut down the grove that is by it: And build an altar unto the Lord thy God upon the top of this rock, in the ordered place, and take the second bullock, and offer a burnt sacrifice with the wood of the grove which thou shalt cut down" (vi, 25, 26). Men who found poor Baal's altar overthrown and his grove cut down very manlily compassionated the unfortunate sufferer of this outrage. Knots gathered at the street corners exclaiming, "Poor god! poor fellow! how he must feel! some people think gods have no rights!" One orator harangued a mob from the work, "The Liberty of Man, Woman, and Gods," till, frenzied, they rushed to Gideon's house and demanded him of his father that they might hang him to a lamp-post or deliver him to the law for cruel and unusual punishment. The father's answer was notable, and we call particular attention to it: "Will ye plead for Baal? will ye save him? he that will plead for him, let him be put to death while it is yet morning: if he be a god, let him plead for himself, be-

Then the angel of the Lord put forth the end of the staff that was in his hand, and touched the flesh and the unleavened cakes; and there rose up fire out of the rock, and consumed the flesh and the unleavened cakes. Then the angel of the Lord departed out of his sight. And when Gideon perceived that he was an angel of the Lord, Gideon said, Alas, O Lord God! for because I have seen an angel of the Lord face to face.—Judges vi. 2

cause one hath cast down his altar" (vi, 31).
This way of viewing such a question we recommend to present-day Christians to be used as to their own God. If that God is wronged by Infidels, let him "plead for himself." Let him defend himself; if he makes no sign, it shows that he is no god.

Gideon, knowing his God's poor reputation for truth and promise-keeping, deemed it advisable to bind him by a second troth, and addressing him thus, "If thou wilt save [Israel] by mine hand, *as thou hast said*," went on to propose a device by which the deity could signify his reaffirmation. The scheme that he recommended was that his invisible friend indicate concurrence by sending dew upon a fleece while the surrounding ground was to be dry (vi, 36, 37).

The Lord could think of no better plan for communication than this, and accordingly adopted it; and so the next morning Gideon " wringed the dew out of the fleece, a bowl full of water." Still hesitating to trust his tricky friend, he solicited a repetition of the promise, endeavoring to soften his demand by the soothing words, " Let not thine anger be hot against me." This time dew was to be on the ground and not on the fleece, and so did it come to pass. This story of a fleece we believe to convey some cloaked reference to the priesthood's fleecing the people, but just what we are unable to say. Gideon now set about mobilizing his forces for war. Lingering apprehensions that the Lord would fail in his promised support might have been detected in his occasional breaking forth into the Hebrew Mololy,

Will yez all be with me when I tackle Paddy Flynn?
(Response: We will!) Will yez all be there when the scrap
   begins?
(Response: Tis!! Let us all be there for the fight is on the
   square,
I'll make a mop of him to-morrow morning,

but beyond these inadvertencies Gid kept a firm and confident front. So many Israelites gathered that the Lord waxed jealous of his honor as a fighter, and came whispering to Gideon, " The people that are with thee are too many for me to give the Midianites into their hands, lest Israel vaunt themselves against me, saying, Mine own hand hath saved me." So he divided them by the comical method of select-

And Gideon said unto God, Let not thine anger be hot against me, and I will speak but this once: Let me prove I pray thee but this once with the fleece; let it now be dry only upon the fleece, and upon all the ground let there be dew.—Judges vi, 39.

ing, when they came to a river, three hundred who lapped the water with their tongues, "as a dog lappeth" (vii, 4 7), perhaps having a preference for currish people. Spying about the enemy's camp Gideon heard a soldier tell a dream to his fellow: "Behold, I dreamed a dream, and, lo, a cake of barley bread tumbled into the host of Midian, and came unto a tent, and smote it that it fell." Anyone wishing further particulars of Gideon's manœuverings and butcheries will find, as the story papers say. "the continuation of this fascinating romance" in the popular work called the Bible, for sale by all dealers.

This man of God "had threescore and ten sons of his body begotten: for he had many wives. And his concubine . . . she also bare him a son" (viii, 30, 31).

The account of Gideon is full of exaggerations. To say nothing of the miracles which form a part of the narrative, it ascribes altogether fabulous numbers to the Midianite army. The two bands of Israelite warriors, which had to march round it in order to throw it into confusion on the night of the surprise, would have had at least a day's journey to accomplish, and would certainly have been unable to hear anything of Gideon's signal. The sound of the trumpets would not have reached a hundredth part of the Midianites, and in the center of the camp the blaze of the torches would have appeared only as a faint spark in the distance. Nor was there food enough in the whole of Canaan for such a host of men and beasts. And as tradition magnified the numbers of the enemy, so it under-estimated the means by which they were defeated, to the glory alike of Gideon's faith and Jehovah's power. Indeed, the desire to make Gideon accomplish everything with the smallest possible number of men leads the tradition to contradict itself. For we are told that after the night on which Gideon had raised a panic in the Midianite army by the aid of his three hundred men, the warriors of the surrounding tribes were called to the pursuit. But when he himself crossed the Jordan and fell upon Zebah and Zalmunna, he was accompanied only by his faithful three hundred. The victory at Raven-rock was won by the Ephraimites alone. What were the warriors of the northern tribes doing all the while?

And when Gideon was come, behold, there was a man that told a dream unto his fellow, and said, Behold, I dreamed a dream, and, lo, a cake of barley bread tumbled into the host of Midian, and came unto a tent, and smote it that it fell, and overturned it, that the tent lay along.—Judges vii, 13.

CHAPTER XVIII.

JEPHTHAH AND HIS HUMAN SACRI-FICE.

JEPHTHAH "was the son of a harlot" (Judg. xi, 1). Kitto's Biblical Cyclopedia says: "After the death of his father he was expelled from his home by the envy of his brothers, who refused him any share of the heritage." This is the way in which theologians, desirous to glorify God's favorites like Jephthah and decry their adversaries, put the fact which is given in scripture thus: "They thrust out Jephthah, and said unto him, Thou shalt not inherit in thy father's house, for thou art the son of a strange woman" (xi, 2). In the text there is not a word about envy. The legitimate offspring merely excluded from inheritance the illegitimate, as is invariably done at the present day. Then "there were gathered vain men to Jephthah" (xi, 9). That is, desperadoes resorted to him. Presently he became chief of a band of brigands or freebooters. As, however, Jephthah, in the words of one commentator, "confined his aggressions to the borders of the

small neighboring nations, who were in some sort regarded as the natural enemies of Israel, even when there was no actual war between them," he is excused by Christians; for crime against those who do not hold the true religion is no crime. At length the Israelites became so in need of a daring military leader that they procured Jephthah for that station. He demanded of the Ammonites their ground for opposing Israel. Their answer was, that the land occupied by the Israelites beyond the Jordan was theirs. It had originally belonged to them, from whom it had been taken by the Amorites, who had been dispossessed by the Israelites; and on this ground they demanded the restitution of their lands. It is thought right in the present comparatively godless governments that stolen property be restored from the hands of a third party to the original owner, but Jephthah, being under godly guidance, decided otherwise, and plunged into war with the plundered and angry nation. "Then the spirit of the Lord came upon Jephthah," and under the influence of this spirit he made the following hell-black vow to God: "If thou shalt without fail deliver the children of Am-

Then it shall be, that whatsoever cometh forth of the door of my house to meet me, when I return in peace from the children of Ammon, shall surely be the Lord's, and I will offer it up for a burnt-offering.—Judges xi, 31.

mon into mine hands, then it shall be, that whatsoever cometh forth of the doors of my house to meet me, when I return in peace from the children of Ammon, shall surely be the Lord's, and I will offer it up for a burnt offering" (xi, 30, 31, King James Version).

"And Jephthah came to Mizpah unto his house, and, behold, his daughter came out to meet him with timbrels and with dances: and she was his only child" (Judges xi, 34). "I have opened my mouth unto the Lord," cried Jephthah in agony, "and I cannot go back!" His daughter, after spending two months in the mountains bewailing her virginity, "returned unto her father, who did with her according to his vow which he had vowed" (xi, 39). To this plain narrative only the more impudent commentators have ventured to offer interpretations palliative or exonerative of Jephthah. The main body of them are forced to deprecate the quibbles of the few and admit that here is a clear case of human sacrifice desired, commanded, and accepted by God, and offered by one who was a deliverer of Israel, and a judge

of it for six years, and is mentioned by Paul as a worker of righteousness through faith (Heb. xi, 32). The chief exculpatory theory of quibbling commentators is that the sacrifice of the girl was commuted to a lifelong confinement and virginity like that of a modern nun. To favor this theory the King James translators did not hesitate to render the passage in verse 39, which correctly is, "And she had known no man," thus: "And she knew no man." The Revised Version has restored the true reading. Other versions have unperverted the "whatsoever" of verse 31 by which excusers sought to convey that an animal sacrifice was promised, to its original "whosoever." "The circumstances of this immolation," says Kitto, "we can never know. It probably took place at some one of the altars beyond the Jordan." And no doubt the hideous scene of murder, disembowelment, and roasting was highly pleasing to the God who enjoined it, and he snuffed a sweet savor and was pleased thereat, but in the name of all that is decent keep the story out of our homes and schools!

And Jephthah came to Mizpah unto his house, and, behold, his daughter came out to meet him with timbrels and with dances. ... And it came to pass, when he saw her that he ... said, Alas, my daughter, thou hast brought me very low, ... opened my mouth unto the Lord, and I cannot go back. — Judges xi. 34, 35.

CHAPTER XIX.

SAMSON THE STRONG.

THE scene opens in the home of a certain Mr. Manoah. You don't know him, I suppose; never heard of him before. Never mind; you will see farther on that an angel of the Lord did know him, and probably you don't care to number among your acquaintance one who associates with persons like that. Mr. Manoah is downtown on business, and Mrs. Manoah is alone. An angel of the Lord appeareth. After pleasantly explaining that he declines the lady's invitation to be seated not out of discourtesy but because of the inconvenient length of his wings, he declares: "Behold now, thou art barren, and bearest not; but thou shalt conceive, and bear a son. . . . And no razor shall come on his head: for the child shall be a Nazarite unto God from the womb: and he shall begin to deliver Israel out of the hand of the Philistines." This sort of announcement to a barren woman by an angel was common among that wonderful people the ancient Jews. The births of Isaac by Sarah (Gen. xvi), of John the Bap-

tist by Elizabeth (Luke i, 1–25), of Mary the mother of Jesus by Anna (Gospel of Mary, Apoc.), were heralded thus, and that of Samuel by Hannah (1 Sam. i, 1–20) came about in a similar manner. When Manoah had got home and was taking his supper his wife started in the midst of the meal and said, "Oh, heavens, I'd almost forgot." Continuing, with a smile over the gratification of her social aspirations, she recounted that she had been honored by a call from one of the very first gentry of the neighborhood, viz., "a man of God," with a countenance "like the countenance of an angel of God" (Judges xiii, 6). It appears from this that she was quite familiar with just how an angel of God looks, which is not surprising, as they were so common in those days. His countenance was, she added, "very terrible." If angels, like men, have their facial expressions molded by the passions working within, we should expect his countenance to be indeed terrible, truculent, and detestable. The angel called again and repeated his words; his host gave him a sacrifice, and "when the flame went up toward heaven from off the altar, the angel of

For it came to pass, when the flame went up toward heaven from off the altar, that the angel of the Lord ascended in the flame of the altar: and Manoah and his wife looked on it, and fell on their faces to the ground.—Judges xiii. 20.

the Lord ascended in the flame" (Judges xiii. 20).

After this surprising ascension, Manoah could not help exclaiming, "We have seen God" (Judges xiii. 22). But his wife, perceiving the harm that such remarks might do their heaven-dwelling friend, as they would involve in self-contradiction his book which says in another place that no man has seen him, placed her finger across his lips and said, "Sh! Sh!" till Manoah caught the suggestion. "And the Lord blessed" Samson. This harmonizes with the account by which he turns out a virtueless common loafer and bully, as we shall see later on. "And the spirit of the Lord began to move him at times in the camp of Dan." Most dwellers in camps are in the habit of being moved by spirit pretty often. Yet we do not know that the spirit which moved him was of the kind contained in a bottle, like that which we refer to camp-dwellers as using. The text seems to say that it was not of that kind, but of a vastly inferior and dangerous brand. As it is not found commonly nowadays we have been unable to examine it, but from its deteriorative effects we presume it to have been

something like what we now call "rotgut," etc. Even a Prohibitionist might have some excuse for suppressing a drink having effects like those imputed to this brand in the Bible.

Samson was to be "a Nazarite unto God from the womb." The Nazarites were a peculiar people, whose chief distinguishing customs were abstinence from wine, avoidance of ceremonial impurity, and the wearing of uncut hair. The last point was the most essential, and it is also the only Nazarite peculiarity mentioned as observed by Samson in his story which follows.

"And Samson went down to Timnath, and saw a woman in Timnath of the daughters of the Philistines. And he came up and told his father and his mother, and said, I have seen a woman in Timnath of the daughters of the Philistines; now, therefore, get her for me to wife" (Judges xiv. 1, 2).

The motive of the young man in this is as well explained in the following from Kitto's Bible Cyclopedia as it would be in our own words: "The Philistines became very naturally the objects of that retributive course of proceedings in which Samson was to be the principal actor, and upon which he could only enter by seeking

And Samson went down to Timnath, and saw a woman in Timnath of the daughters of the Philistines. And he came up and told his father and his mother, and said, I have seen a woman in Timnath of the daughters of the Philistines; now, therefore, get her for me some occasion of exciting hostilities that would bring the two peoples into direct collision. Such an occasion was afforded by his meeting with one of the daughters of the Philistines at Timnath, whom he besought his parents to procure for him in marriage. . . . That he entertained a genuine affection for the woman, notwithstanding the *policy* by which he was prompted, we may doubtless admit; but that he intended, at the same time, to make this alliance subservient to the great purpose of delivering his country from oppression, and that in this he was acting under the secret control of Providence, would seem to be clear from the words immediately following, when, in reference to the objection of his parents to such a union, it is said, that they 'knew not that it was of the Lord that he sought an occasion against the Philistines.' It is here worthy of note, that the Hebrew, instead of '*against* the Philistines,' has '*of* or *from* the Philistines,' clearly implying that the occasion sought should be one that *originated* on the side of the Philistines. This occasion he sought under the immediate prompting of the Most High, who saw fit, in this indirect manner, to bring about the accomplishment

of his designs of retribution on his enemies." Of the moral character of this heaven-directed device — of its underhandness, its involving an innocent girl under pretense of love in the destruction which we shall soon see to follow— we will leave our readers to judge.

One day when Sam was going down courting to Timnath "a young lion roared against him." It is certainly offensive to have a lion roar against one. In public, it is a matter of common manners, a person should meet strangers without passing remarks, and likewise a beast should never be guilty of roaring against one, or at him, or around him, or in any such way as to give him cause to think himself made the object of derisive notice. So we find no fault with Samson that "the spirit of the Lord came mightily upon him, and he rent him as he would have rent a kid." We suppose this means, as he would have rent a kid glove; surely Samson was not in the habit of rending kids with his hands; to do that would be about as wonderful a feat as to rend a lion. "And he had nothing in his hand;" perhaps, after all, he was armed, and struck the lion with a large piece of nothing. It was out of this material, it will be remem-

And he came up and told his father and his mother, and said, I have seen a woman in Timnath of the daughters of the Philistines: now, therefore, get her for me to wife. —Judges xiv, 2.

bered, that God built the universe. When Samson returned from his courting, bees had built and deposited honey in the lion's carcass. "And he took thereof with his hands," his great strength no doubt defending him from stings, "and went on eating, and came to his father and mother, and he gave them, and they did eat but he told them not that he had taken the honey out of the carcass of the lion." Probably he passed it off as market honey bought as a present for them at Timnath, so as to get the credit. Soon he went again to Timnath to his wedding-feast, and must have got pretty well fuddled, for when the guests began that form of amusement common to oriental entertainments, putting riddles, he ridiculously imagined himself able to make one, and blundered out the following rubbish: "Out of the eater came forth meat, and out of the strong came forth sweetness." This was not a riddle at all. It contained no clue by which the keenest mind could guess it, but could be solved only by one who had knowledge of a certain fact in Samson's personal experience—his getting honey from the lion's carcass. Samson put this so-called riddle specially to thirty Philistines

who had been sent in to the feast—as companions, the King James translation says; as guards over Samson, of whom the Philistines were afraid, says an amended version. He wagered with them over their guessing of his riddle "thirty sheets and thirty changes of garments"—better translated, thirty undergarments and thirty robes of state. They learned the secret from his wife, and he had to pay the forfeit. Please note his manner of obtaining the garments to pay them: "And the spirit of the Lord came upon him, and he went down to Ashkelon, and slew thirty men of them, and took their spoil, and gave change of garments unto them which expounded the riddle" (Judges xiv, 19). Thus we have the Lord moving a man who has lost a bet to murder thirty innocent strangers and plunder them for means to discharge the wager. Samson had told the Philistines, "If ye had not plowed with my heifer ye had not found out my riddle," and "his anger was kindled, and he went up to his father's house. But Samson's wife was given to his companion" (xiv, 18-20). Though he had deserted his wife, and she had been given to another, he after a while went down to her father's

Then went Samson down, and his father and his mother, to Timnath, and came to the vineyards of Timnath: and, behold, a young lion roared against him. And the spirit of the Lord came mightily upon him, and he rent him as he would have rent a kid, and he had nothing in his hand; but he told not his father or his mother what he had done. — Judges xiv, 5, 6.

house and impudently claimed her again. The father said, "I verily thought that thou hadst utterly hated her," and offered Samson his younger daughter instead. But Samson refused, as in fact he wanted neither. The whole maneuver was simply an instance of what a pious commentator is obliged to admit was his "vindictive cunning." He was seeking an excuse to injure the Philistines. "And Samson said concerning them, Now shall I be more blameless than the Philistines, though I do them a displeasure." Accordingly he caught three hundred beasts—foxes in old translations, jackals in the best ones—and turning them tail to tail put a firebrand between each couple and let them go into the Philistines' corn, which was altogether burnt up. By "corn" is meant wheat; corn, or maize, was unknown in the Old World before the discovery of America. The practicability of such a scheme as Samson's may be tested by any farmer now. It is indeed beneath comment. The Philistines in revenge burnt up Samson's wife and her father. The Israelites, finding that the quarrelsome bully made too much trouble for them with their neighbors, captured and bound him, but he broke his bonds, and

seizing the jawbone of an ass, laid about so lustily upon the Philistines who had encompassed him that a thousand fell. Through the time of his successors in God's favor, the priests of the Jewish and Roman Catholic and Protestant churches, the jawbone of an ass has continued to slay thousands. Indeed, the death of millions of scientists and outspoken men may be charged to this instrument, wielded beneath the cowls or tonsures or black hats of ecclesiastics. But the weapon is diminishing in efficacy.

After this feat Samson seems to have degenerated into a common bruiser and adopted the habits of a professional pet of the prize-ring. So swollen with pride did he become that he openly frequented the country of the enemy, where he used to hang about barrooms, meet John L. Sullivan and his other brothers of the craft, spin stories of his prowess, get into fights, and, we suppose, become beastly drunk. One time when he was painting red the hostile city of Gaza he "saw there a harlot, and went in unto her" (Judges xvi, 1). The Gazites closed the city gates, and, thinking that they had him fast, made preparations to kill him in the

And after a time he returned to take her, and he turned aside to see the carcass of the lion: and, behold, there was a swarm of bees and honey in the carcass of the lion. And he took thereof in his hands, and went on eating, and came to his father and mother, and he gave them, and they did eat; but he told not them that he had taken the honey out of the carcass of the lion.—Judges xiv. 8, 9.

morning. But the Lord, to show his admiration of Samson's general course, or perhaps to evince his special approval of the particular occupation which his favorite was then engaged in, filled him with the marvelous strength with which he had before been visited, and Sam made a brilliant escape after the manner shown on page 299. Our hero—oh, no, bah, we mean God's hero—next devoted himself to a harlot named Delilah. She often besought him to tell her the secret of his strength, which he at last did, whereupon she cut off the locks in which resided his miraculous power while he slept, and called in the Philistines, who easily subdued him and put out his eyes. At this uncivil act Samson remarked:

> Light, the prime work of God, to me's extinct,
> And all her various objects of delight
> Annulled,   .   .   .
> O dark, dark, dark, amid the blaze of noon!

He next had the temerity to enter upon an anti-design argument just like any Infidel, finding fault with the handiwork of his creator in this strain:

> Why was the sight
> To such a tender ball as th' eye confined,

So obvious and so easy to be quenched!
And not, as feeling, through all parts diffused,
That she might look at will through every pore?

To be sure, we find these extracts not in Judges but in Milton's poem about Samson written some score of centuries later, but the Bible is put together in any way, so we might just as well say that Samson spoke them as not. The Christians prove a future life by the beautiful little argument, *There ought to be*; if Samson did not say the above he ought to have done it, so let it go.

The Philistines "bound him in fetters of brass; and he did grind in the prison-house." One commentator says that he was made to do the work of grinder-general for the whole prison. Here he long tugged and sweat, ever and anon grumbling forth such sentiments as the following: "I find more bitter than death the woman whose heart is snares and nets, and her hands as bands." This maxim appears in a later part of the Bible as an utterance of Solomon, but it has suited the convenience of our tale to assign it to Samson, and we shall not change. We have a right to compose this Bible of ours

And Samson went and caught three hundred foxes, and took firebrands, and turned tail to tail, and put a firebrand in the midst between two tails. And when he had set the brands on fire, he let them go into the standing corn of the Philistines, and burnt up both the shocks and also the standing corn, with the vineyards and olives.—Judges xv, 4, 5.

on the same principles upon which the former one was put together.

Milton represents Manoah as visiting the captive, and the following sentiments as being uttered by the pair in regard to their God and Dagon the god of Samson's oppressors:

This only hope relieves me, that the strife
With me hath end; all the contest is now
Twixt God and Dagon; Dagon hath presumed,
Me overthrown, to enter lists with God . . .
The God of Abraham, be sure,
Will not connive, or linger, thus provoked,
But will arise, and His great name assert:
Dagon must stoop, and shall ere long receive
Such a discomfit, as shall quite despoil him
Of all these boasted trophies won on me,
    . . . For God,
Nothing more certain, will not long defer
To vindicate the glory of His name
Against all competition, nor will long
Endure it, doubtful whether God be lord,
Or Dagon.

This is quite right. We do not blame Jehovah, if he really had the best wind, reach, and all hitting and staying qualities, among the gods of the countryside, for coming forward and beating the others and raising his name "against all competition." A fair field and let the best man

—we mean, God—win, has ever been our motto. And how unpleasant it must have been for Jehovah, if he really was the better god, to have the public remain "doubtful whether God be lord, or Dagon." But as Jehovah's enemies had by stratagem disabled his champion for the time, that deity had to sit in sullen silence, revolving dark schemes of revenge on Dagon, till Samson's hair could grow again. That the Philistines neglected to keep it cut is so incredible that we should not believe it did we find it outside of the inspired lids. At last they held a feast, and "when their hearts were merry" they said, "Call for Samson, that he may make us sport. And . . . he made them sport" (xvi. 25). First he gave his favorite imitation of how to hold two hundred and ninety-nine foxes while catching the three-hundredth, his famous firebrand-and-tail-tying trick, and his world-renowned lion-tearing act. Next he exhausted his stock of jolly yarns such as that about his sitting up in bed while at harlots' houses in Gaza to try cases brought clear from Israel for him to judge (" He judged Israel twenty years." says Judges xv. 20. and xvi. 31). After this the company grew more

And Samson said, With the jawbone of an ass, heaps upon heaps, with the jaw of an ass have I slain a thousand men.—Judges xv, 16.

rude, and set him at such games as catching with his mouth a cherry at one end of a revolving stick that had at the other end a candle which came along and burnt his nose. This made Sam mad, and when, taking further advantage of his blindness, they played on him some monkey-shines by which bags of flour were emptied into his mouth, nose, ears, and hair, and down his neck, he grew still madder. Grabbing two pillars of the temple he threw the building down, and there perished himself and three thousand men and women—innocent women—and perhaps the god Dagon too, for his name has since become quite insignificant before Jehovah's.

The whole story of Samson is simply a solar myth. Among all ancient peoples we find indications of the worship of Nature and of the various heavenly bodies—first of the moon and then of the sun. And since the ancients were in the habit of throwing their religious thoughts and emotions into the form of stories or myths, we meet almost everywhere with "solar myths," or stories in which the sun appears as a person. His rising and setting, his fostering power in the spring, his consuming heat in the summer, and his failing strength in the autumn are described as the birth, the conflicts, the triumph, the defeat, and the death of a hero. Feasts were held in many countries at various seasons of the year in honor of the sun, or rather of the solar deity or sun-god. After the longest day, for instance, there was a time of lamentation, because the days began to grow shorter, and a day of rejoicing after the shortest, because they then began to lengthen again.

Many ancient solar myths have come down to us, but never in the original forms. When they were at last put into writing, it was by men who no longer retained the old simplicity of faith in them, and who, therefore, dissected and endeavored to explain them. Thus the sun-god became a king, a priest, a hero, or a hunter, at the pleasure of the writer or the people.

Sun-worship was by no means unknown to the Israelites, and was still more prevalent among the Canaanites. There were two places in the country, one in Dan (Josh. xv, 10; 1 Sam. vi, 9 ff.; 1 Kings iv, 9) and the other in Naphtali (Josh. xix, 38, and Judges i. 33), called Beth-shemesh or Ir-shemesh, that is, "house of the sun" or "city of the sun," and the deity

And Samson lay till midnight, and arose at midnight, and took the doors of the gate of the city, and the two posts, and went away with them, bar and all, and put them upon his shoulders, and carried them up to the top of a hill that is before Hebron.—Judges xvi, 3.

worshiped under the names of Baal and Molech was really no other than the sun. The myths that were circulated amongst these people show that they were zealous worshipers of the sun. These myths are still preserved, but, as in all other cases, they are so much altered as to be hardly recognizable. The writer who has preserved them for us lived at a time when the worship of the sun had long ago died out. He transforms the sun-god into an Israelite hero who chastises the hereditary enemies of his nation terribly, but at last is conquered by them.

The legends of Samson have a solar myth at the bottom of them, as we may see by the very name of the hero himself, which signifies "sun-god." In some of the features of the story the original meaning may still be traced quite clearly, but in others the myth can no longer be recognized. The exploits of some Danite hero, such as Shamgar, have been woven into it; the whole has been remodeled after the ideas of the prophets of later ages, and finally it has been fitted into the framework of the period of the judges, as conceived by the writer.

Samson was remarkable for his long hair. The meaning of this trait in the original myth is easy to guess, and appears also from representations of the sun-god amongst other peoples. These long hairs are the rays of the sun.

The myth that lies at the foundation of this story is a description of the sun's course during the six winter months. The god is gradually encompassed by his enemies, mist and darkness. At first he easily maintains his freedom, and gives glorious proofs of his strength; but the fetters grow stronger and stronger, until at last he is robbed of his crown of rays, and loses all his power and glory. Such is the sun in winter. But he has not lost his splendor for ever. Gradually his strength returns, at last he reappears; and though he still seems to allow himself to be mocked, yet the power of avenging himself has returned, and in the end he triumphs over his enemies once more. This final victory is represented by the scene in the temple of Dagon. The death of the sun-god, and his burial at the very place from which he began his course (Judges xvi. 31), are features common to all solar myths. They are explained by the belief that the sun lived and ruled for one year, after which he descended to the nether world and was succeeded by the next year's sun.

And she made him sleep on her knees; and she called for a man, and she caused him to shave off the seven locks of his head; and she began to afflict him, and his strength went from him. And she said, The Philistines be upon thee, Samson. And he awoke out of his sleep, and said, I will go out, as at other times before, and shake myself. And he wist not that the Lord was departed from him.—Judges xvi. 19, 20.

To understand some features of this story borrowed from the solar myth that lies at the foundation, we must remember the path which the sun appears to pursue in the heavens as the year goes by. In consequence of the earth's motion around the sun, the sun itself appears to us to be constantly changing its position in the heavens, as we see by its relation to the various constellations. In the twelve months of the year the sun rises and sets with twelve different constellations, which are called the signs of the Zodiac. They are, the Ram, the Bull, the Twins, the Crab, the Lion, the Virgin, the Scales, the Scorpion, the Archer, the He-goat, Aquarius (or man with the watering-pot), and the Fishes. Now, although it is tolerably certain that the Israelites' knowledge of the zodiac dates from before the invasion of Canaan, it is nevertheless highly improbable that the old myth described the passage of the sun through all the twelve signs. At any rate there are no clear traces in our story of any of them except the Lion. Samson rends a lion—that is to say, the sun passes through the constellation of that name. This also gives us the clew to the riddle and its answer. As given in the story it is utterly unintelligible. And bees do not build in putrefying carrion. Probably the riddle originally ran, "How can the sweet food, honey, proceed from a strong and ravenous lion?" and the answer, "When the sun passes through the Lion, the bees make their combs, and when he leaves it the honey is ready."

If we treat the fox or jackal story as the language of mythology we shall see that it has a very intelligible meaning. In the reddish-brown jackals, with torches between their tails, we easily recognize the lurid thunder-clouds, from the projecting points of which the lightning flashes seem to dart.

And the myth of Indra comes in most appropriately to explain the meaning of Samson's exploits with the ass's jaw-bone. This is in fact nothing but a symbol of the jagged thunder-clouds from which the lightning shoots. It has this meaning in the mythology of more than one nation.

And Samson said, Let me die with the Philistines. And he bowed himself with all his might; and the house fell upon the lords, and upon all the people that were therein: so the dead which he slew at his death were more than they which he slew in his life.—Judges xvi, 30.

CHAPTER XX.

RUTH AND BOAZ.

"Any credentials?" asks St. Peter of a newly arrived soul. Said N. A. soul answers confidently, "Oh, yes; I spent my life getting up stories about Atheists struck dumb, profane men struck by lightning, etc., to be telegraphed by the press associations. Highly moral work, sir." St. Peter replies cordially: "Come in, then. The place across the way claims a larger population than we have, and I can make you useful in the census department." In our present chapter we arrive at a book which is the work of just such a pious fabricator as that in the anecdote, only this effort of holy mendacity is written not to traduce God's enemies but to glorify his friends. Its design seems to be to fill up a gap in David's genealogy, and to do this with respectable and commendable characters. The characters thus invented and inserted are exceptionally worthy for those times, but how much so judged by present standards the reader will see. David being the "man after God's heart," we suppose that a lie for the

glory of David ranks in heavenly estimation next to a lie for the glory of God. Christian authorities are mainly in favor of ascribing the book to Samuel. We with the same warrant might attribute it to Beelzebub or Gargantua; there is as much authority for one as for the other.

A Jewish gentleman with his wife Naomi and two sons emigrated to the land of Moab. Successfully passing an examination to see that they were not paupers or Chinamen, they settled down, took out their knitting, and stayed awhile. When some years had winged their flight, behold, the father and sons had died, and Naomi was left with two daughters-in-law, Moabitish women whom her sons had married. We premised that the writer of this tale aimed to give his heroes and heroesses as exalted moral characters as possible, and now we see him the very first thing ascribing to one a virtue truly sublime—we might almost say supernatural—devotion to a mother-in-law. For when Naomi set forth to return to Israel, and one daughter-in-law, Orpah, decided to forego her society and remain, the other, Ruth, "clave unto her" and

Then said Boaz unto Ruth, Hearest thou not, my daughter? Go not to glean in another field, neither go from hence, but abide here fast by my maidens.—Ruth ii, 8.

decided that she would follow and never leave her. When "Naomi saw that she was steadfastly minded to go with her, then she left speaking unto her." Many persons would be glad to have their mothers-in-law do the same by them. When the pair reached the land of Naomi's birth, her old friends cried, "Is this Naomi?" She replied, "Call me not Naomi [which means loveliness], call me Mara [bitterness]." We shall leave those names for the selection of those possessing mothers-in-law. Ruth, going to glean wheat after reapers, went into the field of Boaz, a wealthy old kinsman of Naomi's. The text says that she took his field by chance; further events lead one to suppose that she did so with design. Presently Boaz strolled by and said to the reapers, "The Lord be with you." They were obliged to answer him, "The Lord bless thee" (ii, 4), but it was with a sulky grace, as they know by experience with these pious old fellows that a blessing was expected to take the place of part of the wages that they deserved. Boaz soon took notice of Ruth, though why he should have been especially attracted to her among the other gleaners we do not see, unless because of

some meretricious behavior on her part. The pair grew very thick in conversation, Boaz saying among other things, "Have I not charged the young men that they shall not touch thee?" We suppose that the young men were not charged to refrain from touching the other damsels. He bestowed on her many other favors, for which she said thanks, adding, "Your kindness is too great, for I am less than one of your servants" (Ruth ii, 13, in an amended version). Indeed, she was soon to become less than one of his servants, for as his wife she would hold a position which in those times was about on a level with that of a slave. These flatteries tickled the old man. Ruth that night went home well laden, as Boaz had commanded his reapers to "let fall also some of the handfuls of purpose for her," so that she had gleaned that day, in what hours had not been occupied in flirting, "an ephah of barley" —that is, three pecks and five pints. Naomi now gave Ruth these directions: "Behold, he winnoweth barley to-night in the threshing-floor. Wash thyself therefore, and anoint thee, and put thy raiment upon thee, and get thee down to the floor; but make not thyself known unto

And it came to pass, at midnight, that the man was afraid, and turned himself; and, behold, a woman lay at his feet. And he said, Who art thou? And she answered, I am Ruth thy handmaid; spread therefore thy skirt over thy handmaid; for thou art a near kinsman.—Ruth iii, 8, 9.

the man until he shall have done eating and drinking. And it shall be, when he lieth down, that thou shalt mark the place where he shall lie, and thou shalt go in, and uncover his feet, and lay thee down, and he will tell thee what thou shalt do." As Paul avers that "all scripture is profitable . . . for instruction," there can be no doubt that this is, and accordingly fathers and mothers will wisely issue these directions to their daughters whenever there are sleeping in the neighborhood any wealthy men whom it would be advantageous for those maidens to marry. Be sure to have your daughter bathe and perfume herself, and wait till the man has done drinking. When Boaz had imbibed "till his heart was merry"—that is, till he was half drunk—Ruth "came softly and lay by him," and at the right moment aroused him and said, "I am Ruth thine handmaid; spread therefore thy skirt over thy handmaid; for thou art a near kinsman." The old codger was delighted to find that he had prevailed in at least one instance over the young gallants who had so often outcourted him, and blessed her, saying, "Inasmuch as

thou followedest not young men, whether poor or rich" (iii. 10). "Tarry this night," he said. In the morning he directed, "Let it not be known that a woman came into the floor." He then gave Ruth six measures of barley for having stayed with him that night, and she returned to Naomi, who sagely said: "The man will not be in rest, till he have finished the thing this day" (iii. 18). By a law (Deut. xxv, 5-10) it was the duty of a brother-in-law of a widow, whether he was already married or not to take her to wife and raise up seed in his brother's name, "and the very common practice of polygamy," say Oort and Hooykaas, "made it comparatively easy to do so." A nearer kinsman than Boaz offered to take Ruth's possessions, but on learning that the widow would accompany them declined, perhaps having too many wives already. Had he accepted, the passage between Boaz and Ruth that night would have taken still darker hues. Boaz accordingly took the conquering charmer, giving his shoe to the deferring kinsman, as we see in the picture, which was the custom in sealing bargains.

And Boaz said unto the elders, and unto all the people, Ye are witnesses this day that I have bought all that was Elimelech's, and all that was Chilion's and Mahlon's, of the hand of Naomi. Moreover, Ruth the Moabitess, the wife of Mahlon, have I purchased to be my wife, to raise up the name of the dead upon his inheritance, that the dead be not cut off from among his brethren, and from the gate of his place: ye are witnesses this day.—Ruth iv, 9, 10.

CHAPTER XXI.

UNSTABLE AS WATER, GOD SHALL NOT EXCEL.

BESIDES the self-contradiction over which the pair of distinguished theologians in our picture are at odds, there are others in the Bible upon the same subject. Notwithstanding Jehovah's boast in Mal. iii, 6, "For I am the Lord, I change not," this sorry old deity has been perpetually vacillating, revoking, and repenting. A notable change of purpose is found on comparing Gen. vi, 7, and viii, 20-22. On these two texts Oort and Hooykaas are forced to remark: "The story inspires us with no great respect. The writer actually repels us. For how does he make his god think and act with regard to man? Yahweh repents that he has made mankind. He is deeply grieved because there is nothing but evil in man (Gen. vi, 1-8). Noah alone is an exception to the rule. So all created things, to which life has been given, are destroyed,

except the men and beasts secured within the ark. But after the flood, when Yahweh smelt Noah's sacrifice, half pleased by the offering, half vexed to think of the futility of what he had just done, he said, 'I will never destroy the earth again for the guilt of men, for they are bad from their very birth; so what is the use of destroying them' (Gen. viii, 21, 22)? . . . In this story the whole conduct of Yahweh is unworthy. We should be offended by such behavior in a man. To destroy his work because it had not turned out particularly well, and then to say dryly that he really need not have done so, for after all the result will never be any better,—such conduct would not speak very well for the character of a man, and yet it is ascribed by this writer to his god! Surely, a writer who can make such representations can have no very exalted conception of his god." For other instances of the Lord's repenting see Ex. xxxii, 14; 2 Sam. xxiv, 16; 1 Chron. xxi, 15; Judges ii, 18; Jere. xxvi, 19.

A DISAGREEMENT—WHICH IS RIGHT, THE MONKEY OR THE PARROT?

CHAPTER XXII.

DAVID, GOD'S FAVORITE.

A BOY who in punishment for fighting had been condemned to learn a passage of scripture, chose the following: "Blessed be the Lord, my strength, which teacheth my hands to war, and my fingers to fight." These are words that have heretofore been attributed to David, the peculiar favorite of God. These are the sentiments, and the hideous series of crimes to be recorded in this chapter are the deeds, of that father of Israel who, according to the inspired scripture in 2 Sam. xxii. 22, 23, "kept the ways of the Lord" and did not "depart from his statutes." "I have pursued mine enemies," gloatingly chants this bloodthirsty savage, in a "psalm of thanksgiving" which forms a fit opening to our detailed record of his acts—"I have pursued mine enemies and destroyed them: and turned not again until I had consumed them. And I have consumed them, and wounded them, that they could not arise: yea, they are fallen under my feet. . . . Thou hast also given me the necks of mine enemies, that I might destroy them that hate me. They looked, but there was none to save: even unto the Lord, but he answered them not. Then did I beat them as small as the dust of the earth: I did stamp them as the mire of the street, and did spread them abroad. . . . A people which I know not shall serve me. Strangers shall submit themselves unto me: as soon as they hear, they shall be obedient unto me. Strangers shall fade away, and they shall be afraid out of their close places. It is God that . . . bringeth down the people under me" (2 Sam. xxii, 38-48).

Some of the most easily classifiable and mentionable crimes of the detestable author of the above, may be preliminarily catalogued as follows: Usurpation of the throne; conversion of a constitutional to a despotic monarchy; extermination of the deposed king's kindred (2 Sam. xxi, 8, 9); countless robberies of the lands of innocent nations; butcheries of all the men among these peoples, including captives; wholesale murders of women and children; massacre of all the men, women, and children of three nations to hide a previous lie (1 Sam. xxvii, 11); torture of a captured people (2 Sam.

And he sent and brought him in. Now he was ruddy, and withal of a beautiful countenance, and goodly to look to. And the Lord said, Arise, anoint him: for this is he. Then Samuel took the horn of oil, and anointed him in the midst of his brethren: and the spirit of the Lord came upon David from that day forward. So Samuel rose up, and went to Ramah.—1 Sam. xvi, 12, 13.

xii, 31); hamstringing sixteen hundred or more horses (2 Sam. viii, 4); supplanting his legitimate successor with the son of a stolen female favorite; deception by treacherous promises (2 Sam. xix, 23, and 1 Kings ii, 8, 9); lying (1 Sam. xxi, 1-9; xxvii, 8-12); perjury (1 Sam. xxiv, 21, 22, and 2 Sam. xxi, 6, 9; 2 Sam. xix, 23, and 1 Kings ii, 8, 9); destruction of Uriah to hide consequences of adultery with his wife, this captain's death involving that of faithful soldiers; freebooting; blackmail; life-imprisonment of ten innocent women; indecent exposure; rape, seduction, or whatever means were necessary to dishonor such females as Abishag; adultery; concubinage; polygamy. To these add connivance with the priesthood to fasten their yoke of imposture more firmly on the people's shoulders, and add too such other accessory crimes as were involved in the accomplishment of the above, and we have the record of the man who is the ideal of our Sunday-schools, and of whom it is written, "The Lord God of hosts was with him" (1 Sam. v, 10).

The drama in which this favorite Christian personage will enact the leading part will now be brought on, and in the presentation no expense will be spared as to scenery, costume, or any other detail. The drama will be an extended one—lasting say till 11:30 o'clock—and the audience will be regaled with the introduction of an interesting assortment of minor characters, varying in nature from the most shining virtue in a few to shocking shades of vice in the many. Judge of the attractions of these *dramatis personæ* from the following partial list—Samuel the Subtle Priest; Saul the Fallen Hero; Jonathan the Ideal Friend; Michal the Wife or No Wife; Joab the Generalissimo; Nabal the Deceived Husband; Abigail the Intriguing Spouse; Uriah the Virtuous Victim; Bathsheba the Ravished Wife; Shimei the Rebuker; Absalom the Dude; Adonijah the Dispossessed Prince; Solomon the Mother's Darling; Abishag the Fair, with a host of others. The elements of the grotesque and the supernatural will not be neglected, but will be supplied by Goliath, with Four Other Giants, one of them Twelve-Fingered and Twelve-Toed, and by the thrilling part of the Witch of Endor. A Bear and a Lion, too, we expect to create no small delight among the audience. Priests, soldiers, concubines, peasants, etc., by a full

And it came to pass when the evil spirit from God was upon Saul, that David took a harp, and played with his hand: So Saul was refreshed, and was well, and the evil spirit departed from him. — 1 Sam. xvi, 23.

company. And last, but not least, we have the pleasure to announce the veteran actor, whose impersonations under the several characters of El Shaddai, Yahweh Jareh, Jahveh, etc., have never failed to delight and have won a fame bounded only by the limits of this world—GOD. This celebrated performer needs no praise of ours. Though he has been cast in all the foregoing dramas of this series, yet we believe our audience to be so far from tiring of his skilled characterizations that they will extend a warm reception to the reappearance of their old favorite of whom age cannot wither nor custom stale the infinite variety. Besides employing the costumes with which our patrons are already familiar, he will also appear in the course of this play as images, and later on as high winds. N.B.—Do not miss the gorgeous chariot scene. In Act 4 GOD is brought on the stage in the Ark. We claim this scene never to have been surpassed in magnificence on the boards of this or any other place of amusement.

Let us first ask seriousness for a moment, and matter-of-fact attention to the books whence this story is drawn. The history of David, together with that of Samuel and Saul, the two chief characters connected with him, is contained in the two books called after Samuel himself. The Greek and the old Latin translations called them the first and second books of Kings, while the two books that go by these names with us were called the third and fourth of Kings. These are the names still used in the translation adopted by the Roman Catholic church, the Vulgate, and are preserved as second titles in our own "authorized version." The degree of reliance to be placed on the different sections of Samuel varies greatly. There is no book in the Bible which shows so clearly that its contents are not all derived from the same source. Some of the elements of these books are ancient traditions, which not only give us a fairly accurate account of real events, but faithfully reproduce the religious ideas of ancient Israel. Others, on the contrary, are simply inventions, which teach us more about the narrators' views and opinions than about the past history of their people. As long as we have to follow the book of Samuel we shall meet with the same evidence of composite authorship with which the examination of the book of Genesis has made us familiar. Two

[*] And the Philistine said, I defy the armies of Israel this day; give me a man, that we may fight together. When Saul and all Israel heard those words of the Philistine, they were dismayed and greatly afraid.—1 Sam. xvii, 10, 11.

conflicting traditions relating to the same subject are constantly placed side by side in perfect simplicity, and apparently with no idea that the one contradicts the other. The clergy, anxious to produce authors for all the writings on which their bread and butter depends, have been in the custom of teaching that the first twenty-four chapters of 1 Samuel were written by Samuel, and the remainder of this book and 2 Samuel by Nathan and Gad. This doctrine was founded on the text of 1 Chron. xxix. 29: "Now the acts of David the king, first and last, behold, they are written in the book of Samuel the seer, and in the book of Nathan the prophet, and in the book of Gad the seer." But this theory must go the way of all the rest of the preachers' notions. Even in the part ascribed to Samuel there are undeniable evidences of an intermingling of two partially contradictory narratives. First a passage from one is taken and then a passage from the other, and when the incidents of the first are not contravened they are unnecessarily told over again. In 1 Sam. x, 1, Samuel anoints Saul king by personal choice, whereas in x, 20-25, he has him chosen by lot. Two ac-

counts are given of the people's reason in demanding a king, one (1 Sam. viii, 5) being the profligacy of Saul's sons, and the other (xii, 12, 13) a menaced invasion of the Ammonites. The origin of the saying, "Is Saul also among the prophets?" is described in 1 Sam. x, 11, but in xix, 24, another reason and occasion are assigned for its national currency. David is introduced to Saul in two different manners (1 Sam. xvi and xvii), and by the insertion of a statement that Saul had forgotten the youth the discrepancy is attempted to be concealed. The Roman Catholic version of the scriptures coolly cuts out twenty-five verses to remedy this fault, and still leaves the narrative unsatisfactory. The circumstances of the final outburst of Saul's hatred, which drove David into exile, are in a sad mess. The narrative of 1 Sam. xx, which is the principal account of this matter, should precede xix, 11-24, yet this would leave contradiction. In xx David is still at court and Jonathan is unaware that his friend is in any danger, while the preceding verses represent the former as already a fugitive. Chapters xxiv and xxvi give irreconcilable accounts of the sparing of Saul's life by David. Besides

And David said unto Saul, Thy servant kept his father's sheep, and there came a lion and a bear, and took a lamb out of the flock; And I went out after him, and smote him, and delivered it out of his mouth: and when he arose against me, I caught him by his beard, and smote him, and slew him.—1 Sam. xvii, 34, 35.

direct contradictions, there are interpolations, late alterations, gaps, and no end of other entanglements in this work of God. Every now and then a brief list of names or events from some foreign source is stuck into the middle of the narrative, which it interrupts and harms —for instance 2 Sam. iii, 2–5. Other inconsistencies, contradictions, anachronisms, and interpolations will be noticed as we proceed.

We may remark upon a source of the poetic materials of 1 and 2 Samuel. These were drawn from one or more ancient collections of Hebrew poetry. Such collections abounded among all Eastern peoples, and often contained their earliest history, though altered by poetic and other exaggeration so as to be of little trustworthiness. 2 Sam. i, 18, gives an extract from "the Song of the Bow" in the perished Book of Jasher. The one which occupies verses 19–27 of the same chapter is from the anthology entitled "The Book of the Upright."

That 1 and 2 Samuel were projected in furtherance of the interests of the priesthood appears throughout. The fragments of which they are composed were doubtless written

originally by priests for the glory of God—that is, themselves—afterward bunglingly collated by like hands, and through successive ages interpolated and altered as ecclesiastical occasions gave necessity. As Rev. John Eadie, Professor of Biblical Literature, ingenuously remarks, "the theocratic element of the government is not overlooked. It is distinctly brought to view in the early chapters concerning Eli and his house, and the fortunes of the ark; in the passages which describe the change of the constitution; in the blessing which rested on the house of Obed-Edom; in the curse which fell on the Bethshemites, and Uzza, and Saul, for intrusive interference with holy things. The book shows clearly that God was a jealous God; that obedience to him secured felicity; that the nation sinned in seeking another king; that Saul's special iniquity was his impious oblivion of his station as only Jehovah's vicegerent, for he contemned the prophets and slew the priesthood; and that David owed his prosperity to his careful culture of the sacred principle of the Hebrew administration."

The credibility of these books is curiously grounded by Kitto's Cyclopedia on the follow-

So David prevailed over the Philistine with a sling and with a stone, and smote the Philistine, and slew him; but there was no sword in the hand of David.—1 Sam. xvii, 50.

ing proofs: "The authenticity of the history found in the books of Samuel rests on sufficient grounds. Portions of them are quoted in the New Testament (2 Sam. viii, 14, in Heb. i, 5; 1 Sam. xiii, 14, in Acts xiii. 22). References to them occur in other sections of scripture, especially in the Psalms, to which they often afford historic illustration." This we are to believe demonstrates beyond a doubt the truth of every word of these writings, including both of two conflicting statements of an event, and all.

Of the three chief figures in our narrative, Samuel and Saul and David, the first two were on the scene of action, and had performed many of their leading tricks, before David's appearance. The tricks were in those two time-honored lines of imposture, priestcraft and kingcraft. We will begin with Samuel. At about the period of his youth there had been no prophetic deliverance for a long time. Whether this was through the priests' fear of some sharp-eyed observer and investigator of a skeptical turn who chanced to be about just then, we cannot say. If there had been, the priests at length got rid of him through some

of those methods well known to their profession; or perhaps they thought it safer to put at the front as a figurehead a young boy; for at any rate the lad Samuel now came forward and announced himself to be in the pleasing and profitable habit of receiving communications from God. Whether he was prompted in this by the priests, or like Joan of Arc plunged into the lucrative but dangerous prophetic profession unbacked and on his own account, scripture sayeth not; but at all events he succeeded. What a clerical writer awesomely styles "the Lord's first and fearful communication, the doom of Eli's apostate house," was followed by events said to bear out the verity of that communication. "Other revelations," continues our reverend author, "speedily followed this; the frequency of God's messages to the young prophet established his fame; and the exact fulfillment of them secured his reputation." We will say that if the Lord here fulfilled the prophecies which he had had made by his oracle, it was about the only time that he did so in his whole career.

But in spite of these evidences that Jehovah undeniably existed, and possessed talents of no

And Michal, Saul's daughter, loved David: and they told Saul and the thing pleased him.—1 Sam. xviii, 20.

inferior order; and in spite, too, of his having been showing himself and doing wondrous things for generations, the Jews, before long, very queerly turned from him to serve other gods who our preachers say were utterly destitute of power. These ill choosers long persisted in their inexplicable course, and returned to the right worship only after the most earnest adjurations from Samuel — "Put away the strange gods and Ashtaroth . . . and prepare your hearts unto the Lord, and serve him only." So at length "the children of Israel did put away Baalim and Ashtaroth." Whether these deities objected to being put away—whether they received the news with the dignity of Marius in the cell, or became unbalanced like Lear—whether they took a calm farewell of the assembled nation as Napoleon of his army at Fontainebleau, or furiously flung out to the wine-shops to drown the memory of their wrongs—these things we know not. Whether they were put out by a dispossess warrant, or hustled away by a policeman, or excommunicated, or boycotted, or starved out, or set upon with dogs, or ruled out of order and put out by the sergeant-at-arms, or ejected

with the help of the new favorite Jehovah, we know not. To tell the truth, in this age so painfully barren of intercourse with gods we are able to satisfy not a hundredth part of our curiosity concerning the ways of those undeniably interesting creatures. However, these particular gods were put out, or off, or somewhither or other, and Israel "served the Lord only"—in consequence of which the Lord's priests who were now "served only" soon waxed fat.

Presently the Israelites became oppressed by the Philistines. This was the result, we are inclined to believe, of stinginess on their part in provisioning their supernatural military ally, for when "Samuel took a sucking lamb and offered it for a burnt offering *wholly* unto the Lord, . . . the Lord heard him, . . . and thundered with a great thunder on that day upon the Philistines, and discomfited them" (1 Sam. vii, 9, 10).

By the time that Samuel had reigned over the people for a long while they must have penetrated some of his priestly tricks, for they made bold to come forward and ask for a change of government, requesting nothing less than the

But Jonathan, Saul's son, delighted much in David: and Jonathan told David, saying, Saul my father seeketh to kill thee. Now, therefore, I pray thee, take heed to thyself until the morning, and abide in a secret place, and hide thyself.—1 Sam. xix, 2.

substitution of kings for the prophets, or judges, or prophet-judges, who had previously ruled them—or in other words, the supplanting of a theocracy by a monarchy. Samuel, as we should expect, fumed and chafed in rage at this demand, and fulminated against these radicals all the epithets and denunciations with which the pope now belabors Italy. A Christian commentator on the incident, who plainly shows his sympathy with Samuel, brings against this move, among other reproaches, the charge that it was "an infringement on the rights of the divine head of the theocracy," i. e., God. Of course, looked at from this point of view, the action perhaps might successfully be impeached. It is repugnant to the feelings of every right-minded man to violate anyone's "rights." If, as is represented by this writer, the *rights* of Jehovah were here invaded by force, we can do no less than treat the act with grave disapproval. The overriding of rights becomes additionally reprehensible when perpetrated against the feeble and helpless; that the headstrong Jews chose for their injuries one who has no earthly arm for defense and has ever been unable to resent wrongs except at rare intervals, and by

odd, imperfect, and uncertain means, must be admitted to redound to their disadvantage. Yet their now-rejected friend had not been altogether puny and powerless—not uniformly so—certainly not despicably so; we have no wish to represent him thus. To the contrary, he had at times displayed sufficient prowess, we should say, to have won on the people's estimation a hold of not inconsiderable enduringness. His helplessness was exhibited only on occasions. Only a page or two back we generously gave notice to his gallant feat of coming forward at a very ticklish moment and scaring the enemy with thunder. At times impotent, it is true, he yet on other occasions displayed a prowess that had at least made him eagerly sought for as a military ally, and the cases wherein with his aid the Jews were not able to win the day (1 Sam. iv, 1-11; Judges i, 14) are outnumbered by those wherein the opposite was the result. His fighting value certainly exceeded that of any one man; we believe that we can reckon it as equivalent to that of almost any dozen men without overestimation; and we think that the doughty deeds which he had performed by the side of the Jewish warriors might have produced

And when Abigail saw David, she hasted and lighted off the ass, and fell before David on her face, and bowed herself to the ground. — 1 Sam. xxv. 23.

in their hearts a fellow-feeling that would have dictated resistance of any infringement of their comrade's rights by the rude and fickle populace. But nevertheless the ungrateful action was taken, and for some days the deposed spiritual ruler and his vicegerent Samuel could have been seen stalking over the mountains arm in arm with the sulky dignity of two would-be second-term presidents after a defeat. At every café which they would enter the Israelite *Secularist* lying about on the reading-tables would stare them in the face with a great rooster and a Cock-a-doodle-do! or on the front page of their own Gilgal *Mail and Express* or Beersheba *Christian Statesman* would be a like bird with his head ignominiously placed where his toes should be; while as they passed gangs of boys the vociferation of their names after the inquiry, "Who's—who's—who's in the soup?" nearly drove them mad. Perhaps the most pitiful mark of their sufferings was the sinking of Jehovah into such a state of despondency that he could reply to Samuel's repinings only by the repeated grumbling, "They have not rejected thee, but they have rejected me, that I should not reign over them" (1 Sam. viii, 7).

But we must hasten on to overtake Saul and David. Our delay over the foregoing affair at any rate fixes firmly in our minds the considerable event of the change of government and establishment of a line of kings in Israel. After further unsuccessful endeavors to deter the populace from their design by representations of the abuses which they would have to suffer from kings (1 Sam. viii, 10–22), the dethroned pair proceeded to the selection of one Saul, "and there was not among the children of Israel a goodlier person than he: from his shoulders and upward he was higher than any of the people" (1 Sam. ix, 2). Samuel now delivered an address expounding to the people a new code of duties for them which had been agreed upon by him and his new partner in despotism and imposture, Saul; and, not content with this, wrote it all down in a book and gave it to them. Wishing, however, as all priests do, to keep the church above the state, he could not forbear including even Saul in his threats of destruction against any who should neglect Jehovah and his ministry. Saul prudently said nothing to this at the time, and for a long while acted as the pliant tool of the priesthood which Samuel had

And Abigail hasted, and arose, and rode upon an ass, with five damsels of hers that went after her; and she went after the messengers of David, and became his wife.—1 Sam. xxv, 42.

desired. He gratified the pride and added to the receipts of the regular and state-indorsed priesthood by suppressing their rivals, both the class of fortune-tellers and legerdemainists (1 Sam. xxviii, 3), and the still more dangerous persons and tribes who were "heathen," "idolators," worshipers of Baals and other "strange gods." But presently he slackened in devotion to the ecclesiastical interests. In the words of Rev. Robt. Lee, D.D., of Edinburgh, "Saul could not understand his proper position, as only the servant of Jehovah speaking through his ministers, or confine himself to it." This lamentable disposition, not to recognize that heads of governments, and indeed all persons, are properly but servants of God's ministers, is even more general at present than in Saul's day. It is safer now. As for poor Saul, it caused his destruction. Once he dared to offer sacrifice himself, to the excitement of the fierce jealousy of the monopolizers of that rite (1 Sam. xiii, 8–14); and then as there gradually asserted itself in his heart a pity for the heathen whom the priests wanted completely exterminated that their worship and profits alone might have place, he spared a captive king whose death Samuel bloodthirstily demanded (1 Sam. xv). Priestly and Godly flesh and blood could stand such goings-on no longer, and Samuel and the Lord prepared to select a new king. Samuel, on being directed to go down to one Jesse, from whose sons the king was to be selected, objected, "How can I go? If Saul hear it, he will kill me!" The Lord paused. and exclaiming, "Bless me, that's so; I'd clean forgotten that," scratched his head and puckered his brows for some time without hitting on any means of preventing Saul from the deed. Finally he was compelled to employ deception, and instructed Samuel to lie to the people about the object of his visit, taking a heifer with him and saying that he had come down only to offer sacrifice (1 Sam. xvi, 2). This dishonesty on God's part disgusts even Professors Oort and Hooykaas, who, good old Dutchmen soothed with their pipes (we suppose) into pleasant and lenient moods, always endeavor to put on everything as good a face as possible. They cannot forbear remarking: "Remember that this Jahweh instructs Samuel to invent a false pretext for going to Bethlehem, in order to make it safe to do so. Is this dishonesty worthy of God?" To have

SUBSCRIBE FOR THE TRUTH SEEKER
BELL'S HAND BOOK

had so many proofs already of the want of any fine perception in such matters on the part of the Israelite historians, that this trait does not at all surprise us." One of those "proofs already" of unsensitiveness to moral distinctions, these Dutch worthies refer us to as follows: "We can see from the way in which he [the Bible writer] tells us about him [Jacob] that he had no very high standard of honesty; for he evidently took a certain delight in Jacob's cunning. He speaks of the patriarch's tricks with the same kind of pleasure that many of us too feel in hearing of ingenious plots and cleverly executed knaveries. But the one thing that is worst of all, and that really does need some explanation, is that the wealth obtained by Jacob, in consequence of all this cheating, is called a blessing of Yahweh. How is it possible? That a man may grow rich by dishonest means is but too true; but if any one who had done so were to say that he had become possessed of his wealth by the blessing of God, we should consider him a hypocrite. And yet this writer, who represents Jacob as a cheat, and condemns his conduct, acknowledges at the same moment that these knaveries enabled him,

by the blessing of his god, to obtain the right of the first-born son, his father's blessing, and the greatest wealth." But to return. Samuel went down, lied as bid, and anointed David Jesse's son. But as Jehovah and Samuel continued in fear of Saul, they were obliged to keep the matter secret. Presently "an evil spirit from the Lord" troubled Saul (1 Sam. xvi, 14). We don't know much about these evil spirits from the Lord, and consequently shall have to pass the incident over without saying much upon it. Perhaps these evil spirits of the Lord are what get into our parsons and other religious cranks nowadays and make them so disagreeably cantankerous. We cannot join in the line of conjecture which the artist by putting a certain object in Saul's hand evidently desires to open up; as our readers will testify, we endeavor to keep our treatment of the narrative on the high plane of dignity which the solemn and important character of the theme demands. At the suggestion of a servant who had heard of young David's skill at music, Saul sent for that youth, whose playing proved too powerful for the Lord's endeavor to possess Saul with evil spirits, and these creatures speedily unten-

And Saul disguised himself, and put on other raiment, and he went, and two men went with him, and they came to the woman by night: and he said, I pray thee, divine unto me by the familiar spirit, and bring me him up whom I shall name unto thee.—1 Sam. xxviii. 8

ntal zeal of themselves and skurried off.
Thus Jehovah for the time being was compelled
to put up with a defeat.

Next we are horrified by seeing a great rude
giant coming up at the head of the naughty
Philistines to butcher our old friends the Israelites. This giant was named Goliath. His
height was six ells and a span (nearly ten feet).
His breastplate alone weighed five thousand
shekels (three-quarters of a hundredweight).
He came up and blackguarded the trembling
Israelites daily for "forty days." This forty
was a sacred number with the Jews. It occurs
throughout the Bible with disproportionate
and unnatural frequency. When the scripture-
writers wanted to assign a number to something
which they knew nothing about, and felt weary
of using their other chief sacred number seven,
they stuck in "forty." At this dread conjuncture young David happened along. "It
shall be," the men told him, "that the man
who killeth him [Goliath] the king will enrich
him with great riches, and will give him his
daughter, and make his father's house free in
Israel" (1 Sam. xvii. 25). The young shepherd
thereupon launched into scurrility against the
giant, professing him detestation of him and
ability to kill him. "This uncircumcised Philistine," was a favorite term of abuse for Goliath
with him. In these degenerate times we frown
down the use of religious distinctions as reproaches, but from this holy example it is clear
that we should at once begin contemptuously
referring to Jews as "circumcised" in all our
mentions of them; they should call us "uncircumcised dogs;" Catholics and Protestants and
all should bring their sectarian differences into
every-day employment in epithets of derision,
and doubtless the resulting broils and wars
would count nobly to the glory of God. Then
David, to substantiate his claims to prowess,
told the bigotry-pigheaded story which we have
on page 319. It may be remarked that the race
of bears, at least, have profited by the incident
to keep their beards well barbered down ever
since, so that three manly—or twenty—orna-
ments are now very far from affording a utiliz-
able hold in a scuffle. The details of the fight
between David and Goliath are already so
familiar—indeed, painfully (familiar—to all of
us reformed Sunday-school scholars that we
will here skip them and devote our space to

And he said unto her, What form is he of? And she said, An old man cometh up; and he is covered up with a mantle. And Saul perceived that it was Samuel, and he stooped with his face to the ground, and bowed himself.—1 Sam. xxviii, 14.

some serious remarks on the incredible character of the narrative. The story cannot be accepted as a correct account of the way in which David and Saul became known to each other. We have seen already that it contradicts the story that precedes it (see page 318), and a few small inaccuracies show that its author lived after the time of David. For instance, he says that Goliath's head was carried to Jerusalem (1 Sam. xvii, 54), whereas that city was still in the hands of the Canaanites at the time. Elsewhere in the book of Samuel (2 Sam. xxi, 19) the honor of having slain Goliath is attributed to another man. The passage referred to runs (after an amended version): " When there was war again with the Philistines, at Gezer, Elhanan, the son of Jair, the Bethlehemite, slew Goliath of Gath, the shaft of whose spear was like a weaver's beam." There cannot be the smallest doubt that the Goliath mentioned here is the same as the Goliath of our story. Now, he cannot have been slain both by David and by Elhanan; and since popular legends are always prone to heap upon a single favorite the achievements of a number of less celebrated heroes, it is far more likely that the credit of Elhanan's exploit should

have been given to David than that anything which David had really done should have been attributed to a warrior otherwise unknown. The writer of the book of Chronicles noticed the contradiction, and tried to remove it; for we can hardly suppose his version of the affair to be due to a mere slip of the pen. He says (1 Chron. xi, 5), " And Elhanan, the son of Jair, slew Lachmi [N.B. 'Beth-hallachmi' is the Hebrew for ' the Bethlehemite'], the brother of Goliath, the Gittite, the shaft of whose spear was like a weaver's beam." This is an example of the way in which the Israelites of the third century before Christ were prepared to pervert a text rather than admit that two passages of the holy scripture contained contradictory accounts. Similar motives urged our own translators to imitate the Chronicler; and in the " Authorized Version" the passage in the book of Samuel itself is given thus (2 Sam. xxi, 19) : " Elhanan, the son of Jaareoregim, a Bethlehemite, slew *the brother of* Goliath the Gittite." though the Hebrew says nothing of the kind. This is but a specimen of the dangers into which we are brought by the conviction that there can be no contradictions in the Bible.

And David took him more concubines and wives out of Jerusalem.—2 Sam. v, 13.

In reading 2 Sam. xvi we are thrown into a
high excitement by reading of four other giants
who menaced Israel, but were nobly overcome.
However, according to our preceding remarks
on the falsification of the Goliath story, one of
these four was not an "other" giant, but Goliath
himself.

We now find Saul becoming intensely jealous
of David, who appears to have associated himself with the priesthood and won over the major
portion of that powerful body by promises of
greater favors, should they make him king, than
they obtained under Saul. When we find David's
military exploits at this time noised about
as surpassing those of Saul, who was a powerful
and sagacious warrior, we may suspect the
agency of the priests. In their ascription of
superior military ability to David, we may believe there to be as little truth as there is in
their present celebration of most of the fathers
of this republic and total silence as to Thomas
Paine. Under the influence of a very natural
resentment of David's attempts to undermine
the legitimate monarch, Saul one day cast his
javelin at that young intriguer, who narrowly
escaped. That Saul did so twice is still believed

by old-fashioned Christians who have not
learned that chapters xviii and xix are dupli-
cate accounts of one occurrence. Advanced
and informed Christians, who know this, and
consequently hold the true belief, will some day
be in the cheerful position of sitting on heaven's
battlements and passing remarks on the mis-
takers as they writhe below. Merab, Saul's
elder daughter, who had been promised to the
slayer of Goliath, was given to another man.
Then learning that Michal his younger daughter
loved David, Saul planned to make that young
man's desire of her his undoing. "And Saul
said, I will give him her, that she may be a snare
to him. . . . And Saul commanded his servants, saying, Commune with David secretly,
and say, Behold, the king hath delight in thee,
and all his servants love thee : now therefore
be the king's son-in-law. . . . The king de-
sireth not any dowry but a hundred foreskins
of the Philistines." By this device "Saul
thought to make David fall by the hand of the
Philistines." This treacherous scheme of one
who had in his anointing as king received the
spirit and grace of the Lord, speaks poorly for
the moral virtues of that afflatus. However, his

And David danced before the Lord with all his might; and David was girded with a linen ephod.   2 Sam. vi, 14.

enemy was so much more vile that there need be no hesitation in choosing Saul between the two. David with his men went forth and, finding the business to his native tastes, slew of the Philistines twice the number required, and took their foreskins, and brought this elegant dowry to Saul, who, disappointed, was obliged to give him Michal his daughter. Verse 14 of the chapter (xviii) which recounts this says that "David behaved himself wisely in all his ways; and the Lord was with him." Accordingly, any one of us contemplating marriage will behave himself wisely to enter some neighboring state, or Mexico or Canada, and murder two hundred men, cut off their foreskins, and bring the neat but not gaudy collection to his prospective father-in-law and bride. Should these overnice persons disdain the offering, or should the unrighteous laws of what Christians lament as our "godless government" make trouble for the offerer, he will be comforted by knowing that "the Lord was with him." Soon we find Saul swearing, "As the Lord liveth, he [David] shall not be slain" (1 Sam. xix. 6). About four verses thereafter we find him attempting David's life. The oaths of those who by

regal consecration had become as part of God himself evidently were not always to be depended on; thus differing from the oaths of Christians nowadays, not one of which persons, as we all are aware, is ever known to perjure himself.

Next Saul sent soldiers to the house of the would-be usurper, to wait during the night and kill him as he came forth in the morning. Michal let David down through a window and he escaped, and then rigging up a god in clothes to look like her husband she prepared to pass it off as his veritable person (1 Sam. xix. 12-17). The usual version says that she thus utilized an *image*. The word in the original is *teraphim*. This means not *image* in general, as the Bible translators would have us conceive, but image of a god, idol—or a deity or god himself. The *teraphim*, in the words of Dr. Bialloblotsky of Göttingen, were "tutelar household gods, by whom families expected, for worship bestowed, to be rewarded with domestic prosperity such as plenty of food, health, and various necessaries of domestic life." The translators, unwilling that we should learn of idols being worshiped in this people of Jehovah's, or of Jehovah him-

And it came to pass in an eveningtide, that David arose from off his bed, and walked upon the roof of the king's house: and from the roof he saw a woman washing herself; and the woman was very beautiful to look upon.—2 Sam. xi, 2.

self being worshiped there (as was sometimes the case) in the form of an idol, have misrepresented for the glory of God by rendering *teraphim* images. First Michal took this handy god for home consumption and laid him in the bed. At this of course the deity beamed with gratification, and upon the fair arms of Michal next bolstering up his head with a pillow of goat's hair and tucking a cloth snugly around him he softly purred his thanks and cast at his sweet attendress the languishing glances of half a dozen preachers. However, at the arrival of Saul's messengers, and Michal's admonitions, "Now, now, lie still—you must play sick—ah! there's a good boy!" he assumed an immovable attitude and a dolorous facial expression, and continued as quiet as a mouse till after some time an exceptionally inquisitive soldier pulled down the clothes and to his great shame exposed his godly form to all onlookers. Saul angrily reproached Michal, saying, "Why hast thou deceived me so, and sent away mine enemy, that he is escaped" (1 Sam. xix, 17)? To this she was forced to reply with a fabrication, to the effect that David had threatened to kill her did she not aid him. The treatment which this

faithful wife received in return **we shall see** when we reach 2 Sam. vi, 20-23.

Let us solace ourselves for being obliged to contemplate such a throng of unlovely personages, by dwelling for a moment on the beautiful character of Jonathan, Saul's son. This young man becomes smitten with an irresistible affection for David at that young warrior's feat of overcoming Goliath. He feels no envy, no jealousy—nought ignoble finds place within the youth's generous breast. He takes the stranger to his arms and enters upon that course of attached comradeship which has become an ideal and caused the linked names of David and Jonathan to be mentioned along with that famous couple of paganism, Damon and Pythias. "Then Jonathan and David made a covenant because he loved him as his own soul. And Jonathan stripped himself of the robe that was upon him, and gave it to David, and his garments, even to his sword, and to his bow, and his girdle" (1 Sam. xviii, 3, 4). That is, the two made a reciprocal exchange of garments —though scripture inadvertently fails to mention the giving of David's attire to Jonathan.

And David sent messengers and took her.—2 Sam. xi, 4.

This pledge of friendship was not uncommon in ancient nations.

David, being driven from the neighborhood of Saul, fled to Nob. Here he met Abimelech the priest, who suspected from his visitor's unprovided and unattended condition that something was wrong, and inquired, "Why art thou alone, and no man with thee?" David at this critical conjuncture no doubt had recourse to the Lord who moved within him, and was by him directed to use the means so common with that adviser, viz., falsehood (1 Kings xxii, 20 23; Ezek. xiv, 9; 1 Sam. xvi, 1, 2); for we find David replying with this lie, "The king hath commanded me a business, and hath said unto me, Let no man know anything of the business whereabout I have commanded thee" (1 Sam. xxi, 2).

Chapter xxiv of 1 Samuel tells us that while Saul was hunting David the latter stole behind him and unobserved cut off the skirt of his robe. How likely it is that such a thing could happen the reader may judge. Chapter xxvi gives a totally different account of the adventure. The difficulty of choosing the true account, or of believing both, we also shoulder off on the reader.

Presently David in one of his blackmailing negotiations attempted to make one Nabal the victim of his pious rapacity. He represented, "Now thy shepherds which were with us, we hurt them not, neither was there aught missing unto them," and for having refrained from stealing he requested a tribute. Nabal very sensibly refused, saying, "Shall I then take my bread, and my water, and my flesh that I have killed for my shearers, and give it unto men whom I know not whence they be?" David departed in high rage, swearing that he would not leave of Nabal's men by the morning light "any that —— against the wall" (1 Sam. xxv, 22). Thanks to the scripture so profitable for instruction, we now know that it is commendable to garnish our discourse with oaths of the class of the above. But Abigail, Nabal's wife, took it into her false head to play a perfidious trick on her husband. She took of Nabal's possessions "two hundred loaves, and two bottles of wine, and five sheep ready dressed, and five measures of parched corn, and a hundred clusters of raisins, and two hundred cakes of figs,"

THE YOUNG LADIES
BIBLE CLASS
ARE
DISCUSSING
DAVID and BATHSHEBA,
(II. SAM. XI. 4 & 5.)
Remember
THE LORD
was with
DAVID
IN ALL
THAT
HE
DID

"AH THERE!"

and, overtaking David, presented them to him, while, ogling this stranger, she ran down her husband with the following pun: "Let not my lord, I pray thee, regard this man of Belial, even Nabal; for as his name is [Nabal means fool], so is he; Nabal is his name, and folly is with him." By her further language it would seem that the Lord must have informed her of his intentions concerning David, for she asked, Remember me "when the Lord shall have done to my lord according to all the good that he hath spoken concerning thee, and shall have appointed thee ruler over Israel." Probably the Lord had been in the habit of dropping in at Abigail's farmhouse while on his peregrinations, and in some late chat had informed her of his intention of patronizing the young man David, who had always treated him in a friendly and respectful manner. Doubtless the huge store of loaves, sheep, raisins, figs, and other goodies at the comfortable place had had for the deity an attraction not easily to be resisted. We may imagine him as having spent many pleasant times there with Nabal's wife. Perhaps Nabal was something of a fool after all.

Abigail concluded by repeating, "When the

Lord shall have dealt well with my lord, then remember thine handmaid." What she meant by the Lord dealing well with her husband was that the Lord was to kill him. Had God found it good in his eyes to kill a man that he might give the widow to his favorite? Or did Abigail intend to poison Nabal? At all events, David parted from her after repeating his elegant phrase about "any that —— against the wall," and in a few days "Nabal's heart died within him, and he became as a stone. . . . And the Lord smote Nabal, that he died." And David married the witty Abigail that she might enliven the royal presence daily with her brilliant puns. "David also took Ahinoam of Jezreel; and they were also both of them his wives." (1 Sam. xxv, 43).

David and his robber band were now dwelling in the land of the Philistines. Among his other ravages upon unoffending peoples, he and his men on one occasion "went up and invaded the Geshurites, and the Gezrites, and the Amalekites." These nations "were of old the inhabitants of the land" (1 Sam. xxvii, 8), but their titles to peaceful possession were given no regard by David. To prevent the deed becoming

And it came to pass in the morning, that David wrote a letter to Joab, and sent it by the hand of Uriah.   And he wrote in the letter, saying, Set ye Uriah in the fore-front of the hottest battle, and retire ye from him, that he may be smitten, and die.—2 Sam. xi, 11, 14, 15.

known to the Philistine king Acnish David 'left neither man nor woman alive." He told the king that he had been making war not on these peoples but on his own countrymen the Israelites. Achish, who had feared that the Israelitish refugee would in some battle turn against him and take the part of his old countrymen to reinstate himself in their graces, was deceived by the lie and thereafter trusted David, who flourished on the deception.

Saul continued to be as uneasy at the machinations of David as we are to-day at those of all the underworking pious rogues like him. And when to this discomfort there was added the imminent peril in which an invasion of the Philistines that now took place put him, he "inquired of the Lord" for counsel. But "the Lord answered him not, neither by dreams, nor by Urim, nor by prophets" (I Sam. xxviii, 6). "Then said Saul unto his servants, Seek me a woman that hath a familiar spirit, that I may go to her, and inquire of her. And his servants said to him, Behold there is a woman that hath a familiar spirit at Endor." Saul repaired in disguise and by night to the eerie and dismal dwelling-place of this lady so peculiarly attended. At her appearance, wild and eldritch, he started, exclaiming (we believe),

Live you, or are you aught
That man may question? I' the name of truth,
Are ye fantastical, or that indeed
Which outwardly ye show?

The dame assured him that she was all right despite her unpromising exterior, that her bark was worse than her bite, that all is not gold that glitters, that roughest barks hide stanchest woods, that many a ragged coat covers an honest heart, that a woman's a woman for a' that, etc., whereupon he took heart, sat down, and stroked the fiendlike black cat (all witches have devilish-looking black cats, as our readers must have observed in their consultations of those persons). He then requested, "Divine unto me by the familiar spirit, and bring me him up whom I shall name unto thee" (xxviii, 8), his design being to summon the spirit of Samuel, who had lately died. The crone, however, was apprehensive of a secret design against her, and replied, "Behold, thou knowest what Saul hath done, how he hath cut off those that have familiar spirits,

And it came to pass, when Joab observed the city, that he assigned Uriah **unto a place where he knew** that valiant men were. And the men of the city went out and fought with Joab: and there fell some of **the people of the servants** of David; and Uriah the Hittite died also.—2 Sam. xi, 16, 17.

and the wizards, out of the land: wherefore then layest thou a snare for my life, to cause me to die" (9)? Saul then swore that she should be safe, in these words, "As the Lord liveth, there shall no punishment happen to thee for this thing" (10). The beldame long hesitated over accepting this oath. She repeated Saul's words, "As the Lord liveth," in dubious tones, stole glances at her private Old Testament, King James translation, where in 1 Sam. iv she read of much discomfiture of Jehovah, and muttered, "Hm! 'Israel smitten?' 'The ark of God taken?' Baal and the other gods victorious? Jehovah in their hands ever since? Not a word heard from him? Very doubtful if he's alive now. That swearing 'As the Lord liveth' doesn't amount to much." But at last yielding, she set about the usual blood-curdling ceremonies necessary to spirit-evocations, chanting as she did so:

Thrice the brinded cat hath mew'd.
Thrice; and once the hedge-pig whin'd.
Harpier cries;—'Tis time, 'tis time.
Round about the cauldron go:
In the poison'd entrails throw.
Toad, that under coldest stone,
Days and nights hast thirty-one
Swelter'd venom sleeping got,
Boil thou first i' the charmed pot!
Double, double toil and trouble;
Fire, burn; and, cauldron, bubble.
Fillet of a fenny snake,
In the cauldron boil and bake;
Eye of newt, and toe of frog,
Wool of bat, and tongue of dog,
Adder's fork and blind-worm's sting,
Lizard's leg and owlet's wing,
For a charm of powerful trouble,
Like a hell-broth boil and bubble.
Double, double toil and trouble;
Fire burn; and, cauldron, bubble.
Scale of dragon, tooth of wolf;
Witch's mummy; maw and gulf
Of the ravin'd salt-sea shark;
Root of hemlock, digg'd i' the dark;
Liver of blaspheming Jew;
Gall of goat, and slips of yew,
Silver'd in the moon's eclipse;
Nose of Turk, and Tartar's lips;
Finger of birth-strangled babe,
Ditch-deliver'd by a drab,
Make the gruel thick and slab;
Add thereto a tiger's chaudron,
For the ingredients of our cauldron.
Double, double toil and trouble;
Fire, burn; and, cauldron, bubble.
Cool it with a baboon's blood,
Then the charm is firm and good.

And David's anger was greatly kindled against the man, &c.   And Nathan said, Thou art the man.—2 Sam. xii. 3–7.

SONG.

Black spirits and white,
Red spirits and gray;
Mingle, mingle, mingle,
You that mingle may.

Pour in sow's blood, that hath eaten
Her nine farrow; grease, that's sweaten
From the murderer's gibbet, throw
Into the flame. Come, high, or low;
Thyself, and office, deftly show.

At the proper moment our old friend Samuel arose and groaned, "Hamlet, I am thy father's ghost," or something of that sort. Upon Saul's questioning him he said that that king had offended the Lord by not being sufficiently bloodthirsty for that deity's purposes (see 1 Sam. xxviii, 18) and that the kingdom was therefore given from his hand into David's. As if this was not enough, the vengeful old codger announced, "To-morrow shalt thou and thy sons be with me." Considering who the speaker was, this was truly dreadful tidings. Think what it would be if some pious old rogue like Samuel should appear to one of us enemies of the Lord like Saul and declare that we should on the next day begin an eternity in his company.

Fancy an everlasting life with John Wesley, Calvin, or Jonathan Edwards! Saul appears to have realized the horrible nature of this fate, for on hearing of it he at once dropped to the ground. As the scripture takes pains to make clear, he "fell straightway all along"—that is, not curled up, or upcoiled, or intervolved, or fancifully curved, or tied into a bow-knot, or in any shape having a touch of grace or attractiveness, but just straight out, right along, as limp as a dishrag or as we should lie at the announcement of a never-ending *tête-à-tête* with Talmage. The ill-boding specter with his encircling fumes and phantasmagoria having vanished, Saul's attendant exclaimed:

The earth hath bubbles, as the water has,
And these are of them:—Whither are they vanished?

Saul quavered in reply:

Into the air; and what seemed corporal melted
As breath into the wind.—Would they had staid!

The attendant, still dazed and uncertain, returned:

Were such things here, as we do speak about?
Or have we eaten of the insane root
That takes the reason prisoner?

And Nathan departed unto his house.   And the Lord struck the child that Uriah's wife bare unto David, and it was very sick.—2 Sam. xii. 15.

That is, the preceding conversation takes place between two persons somewhere who have seen a witch and a vision, and whether in the Bible or in some play or where the dickens it is we don't care a fig. By this time the fastening of our attention on scripture, and the ways in which it was made, and the methods of commentators in commenting it, has just about destroyed the regard for truth and the honest principle with which we began this book, and now that we have found it convenient to use the above we will swear on a stack of Bibles that it is in scripture, and all we need to make it so is to get a train of followers powerful enough to put it there or make people believe it is there even if it isn't.

The brave and independent but fiery-tempered Saul did indeed perish soon, with his sons, as the witch of Endor had predicted. In a battle with Philistines Saul's three sons, including the admirable Jonathan, were slain. The king, at his armor-bearer's refusing to slay him, put an end to himself with his own sword, and the armor-bearer in grief imitated his example.

At Saul's death Ishbosheth (properly Ishbaal, a son of his who had not perished, became king over ten of the twelve tribes of Israel. David desired to win over Abner, Ishbosheth's relative and general. Casting about for a suitable pretext for calling Abner to his city of Hebron that he might bargain with him, David hit upon the device of sending for his former wife Michal that Abner might come as her escort. Michal at David's flight from Saul had been given to another man, who loved her exceedingly, and "went with her along weeping behind her to Bahurim." But his or Michal's wishes were not heeded by the scheming David. Abner deserted to David and Ishbosheth was overthrown and murdered. An additional motive of David in reclaiming Michal was, it is supposed, that his title to the throne might be confirmed, in the eyes of those who had felt attachment to Saul, by his possessing as a wife that unfortunate king's daughter.

David now reigned sole king. He soon began wars in all directions, on hostile and peaceful peoples alike. The record of his atrocities is too long to be transcribed here. We will mention only the form in which the Lord fought for his side in one of his early battles. Having inquired of that ally whether it would be ad-

And he brought forth the people that were therein, and put them under saws, and under harrows of iron, and made them pass through the brick-kiln: and thus did he unto all the cities of the children of Ammon. So David and all the people returned unto Jerusalem. 2 Sam. xii. 31.

visable to give battle, David received the reply: "Let it be, when thou hearest the sound of a going in the tops of the mulberry trees, that then thou shalt bestir thyself: for then shalt the Lord go out before thee, and smite the host of the Philistines" (2 Sam. v. 24). David went forth as appointed, and the Lord being with him in the form of a wind, he enjoyed a victory.

King David at about this time took it into his head to send for the ark. This traveling menagerie was at the time at Kirjath-jearim, where it had arrived after the following thrilling adventures. Many years previously it had been captured by the Philistines (1 Sam. iv), who, regardless of the piteous cries of its occupant and even of his threats to jump out while going at full speed and kill himself if they didn't stop running off with him, whirled the cage and the caged off to their own wicked land of Ashdod. "The more the merrier!" cried the priest who kept the idols of that region, and Jehovah in his Saratoga trunk was set up right beside Dagon in the great idol-house. But the next morning Dagon had fallen on his face before the ark. At least, so say the Israelitish priests who wrote the book of Samuel. Of course the Philistine

priests wrote just the opposite. But we will follow the Israelitish story. Dagon, who was indeed one of the largest and fiercest gods of the "heathen," must have felt much shame at having been thus knocked out in the first round; however, he took his corner again and was sponged down, etc., by his backers, and at the next call of "Time!"—i. e., the next night— toed the scratch as game as ever, but owing to some cause, perhaps to Jehovah's unfairly dodging back into his ark at necessary moments, the Philistine Pet soon grew groggy and at length went down altogether. Jehovah now probably made the foul of jumping on a prostrate antagonist, for in the morning Dagon's backers found the poor fellow with his head and hands broken clear off. Jehovah, it is said, followed up this brisk opening by smiting the Ashdodites with ulcers, till they sadly concluded that they had taken a white elephant on their hands when they had picked up Jehovah, and packed him off to Gath. Here the old gentleman, who must have been in a very bad humor—perhaps dyspeptic—caused disease on every hand. We have remarked in our own time that diseases ravage most those nations that have most to do

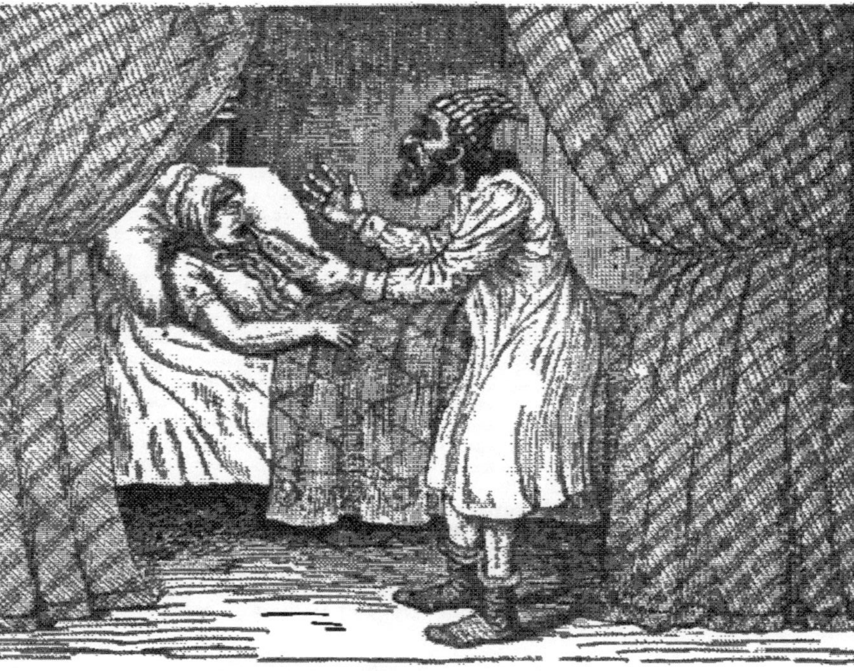

And David comforted Bathsheba his wife.—2 Sam. xii. 24.

with Jehovah. The men of Gath shifted him off on Ekron. This seems very unwise. One would think that they would have put the offender to death. But perhaps there were laws against deicide. In Ekron the cantankerous deity produced diseases, and ulcers on those not killed by the diseases, and innumerable mice that destroyed the harvest. The " priests and diviners" advised the people, if the crabbed old fellow would not behave better, to let him go back to his friends, who might get him into a better humor. To propitiate him before he left, they presented him with golden models of the ulcers and the mice. As God never changes, no doubt it would be judicious, when he plagues us with the grip and grasshoppers, to offer to him golden models of the inflamed surfaces of that disease and like images of those over-familiar insects. To make sure that home-sickness was the thing that was vexing their cross-grained guest, the Ekronites placed him on a cart drawn by two milch cows whose calves were confined near by. Their suspicions were confirmed by the cows, moved by mystic influ-ence, forsaking their calves and tearing off toward Israel like mad. Indeed, at such a pace did they go that Jehovah got terribly jounced, and waxed angrier than ever, but all to no avail, for on they scuttled and on the cart rattled ; the ark, having no one to attend to its " This side up with care," finally turning upside down and imprisoning its shrieking occupant, till the equipage reached a harvest-field of Beth-shemesh. The reapers at seeing this runaway circus, with museum attachments of models of ulcers and mice, come flying down the hill, gathered, stopped the concern, admired the pro-prietor, and offered sacrifices made—somewhat ungratefully—of the cows who had brought it to them. But so terribly worked up was the Lord over his rough experience that he "smote the men of Beth-shemesh, because they had looked into the ark of the Lord, even he smote of the people fifty thousand and threescore and ten men." The survivors bundled the plaguy ark off to Kirjath-jearim, where the Lord be-haved himself better, and continued a good many years. Hither now came David and thirty thousand men, and put the ark on " a new cart," and started off with it, when, lo, at Uzzah putting his hand on it to steady it, " for the oxen shook it," the Lord struck him dead.

HOW TO SELL B'BLES—A SUGGESTION TO THE AMERICAN BIBLE SOCIETY.

"And David was displeased, because the Lord had made a breach upon Uzzah. . . . And David was afraid of the Lord that day, and said, How shall the ark of the Lord come to me? So David would not remove the ark of the Lord unto him into the city of David: but David carried it aside into the house of Obed-edom the Gittite" (2 Sam. vi, 8–10). The Gittite gentleman not trying to look into the ark, the Lord grew pleasant (i. e., the Gittite not trying to pry into the priests' imposture, the priests grew pleasant); and so David at last took courage and brought the affair to his capital. "And David danced before the Lord with all his might; and David was girded with a linen ephod." As some of the higher cancan steps began to be taken by David, his scanty apparel rendered the scene unseemly, and Michal, who had "looked through a window" and "despised him in her heart," when he was through rebuked him thus: "How glorious was the king of Israel to-day, who uncovered himself to-day in the eyes of the handmaids of his servants, as one of the vain fellows shamelessly uncovereth himself!" David, who perhaps had been drinking, informed her that he would be still viler if he wanted to (2 Sam. vi, 22); while the Lord, taking a hand in, cursed Michal with perpetual barrenness for her very just action. However, God was foiled in this design, for Michal had five children (2 Sam. xxi, 8).

We find ourselves so near the limit of our space that we must fain be content with brief mention of the remaining personages of our over-true tale, devoid of any further pokings of fun at sacred things—for which necessity we shall doubtless be devoutly thankful when at that stage which we know makes cowards of all Infidels, viz., the deathbed.

David spied the wife of his captain Uriah bathing; sent men who forced her to his couch; failed to induce the brave and faithful Uriah to leave posts of danger for home that he might seem to beget the child whom David had really generated; and finally directed his corrupt tool Joab to put the captain in a situation of peril that he might be slain. Uriah was slain, and David wedded his widow. The priest Nathan, in one solitary instance opposing David (probably because of personal piques), told the king of a man with many sheep who had taken his

But the king took the two sons of Rizpah . . . and the five sons of Michal. . . . And he delivered them into the hands of the Gibeonites, and they hanged them in the hill before the Lord. . . . And Rizpah . . . suffered neither the birds of the air to rest on them by day, nor the beasts of the field by night.—2 Sam. xxi. 8–10.

neighbor's one ewe lamb. David was wroth at
this wrong-doer, whereupon Nathan cried,
"Thou art the man!" and reproached him, a
man with many wives, for taking the wife of a
man who had but one. The Lord took Nathan's
view, but in administering vengeance in his
usual blunderheaded manner struck and killed,
not David, but the child of him and Bathsheba.

David's son Amnon, being of his father's disposition, ravished his half-sister Tamar, and
then refused to marry her. (Marriage between
persons of half-blood was proper under God's
rule; Sarah was Abraham's half-sister.) Their
brother Absalom plotted revenge, and killed
Amnon two years thereafter.

Absalom was a prince of extraordinary beauty
and address. He wore his hair long, and at its
yearly cutting a quantity weighing six and a half
pounds was shorn off. In a quarrel with his
father he ravished ten of David's concubines on
a housetop in sight of all the people, which
helpless and unoffending women were in consequence shut up for life by that king. Escaping
horseback from soldiers pursuing him for head-
ing a rebellion, he was caught by the hair on a
tree-limb, and overtaken and dispatched.

Shimei, a member of the house of Saul who
still entertained resentment for the underminer
of his family, flung stones at David. That king
dissembled his anger, but dying ordered Shimei's destruction (1 Kings ii, 8, 9).

On the pretense that a famine in Gibeon was
sent by God as a punishment for not avenging
wrongs done by Saul on the Gibeonites, David
and the priests hanged seven of Saul's sons,
whom they feared as rivals of David's line (2
Sam. xxi, 1-11).

When David became "old and stricken in
years," they "covered him with clothes, but he
gat no heat" (1 Kings i, 1). So Abishag a Shu-
nammite, who was "very fair," was ravished from
her home to lie in his bosom and cherish him.

The dying darkey exhorted to forgive a foe
said, "Yes, sah, if I dies I forgib that nigga,
but if I gots well that nigga must take car'!"
David was worse, for on his deathbed he ordered
the execution of Joab, whom he had ever used
for vile designs but feared, and of Shimei, as
has been told. And Adonijah, the rightful heir
to the throne, was supplanted at David's dying
command by Solomon, the son of Bathsheba,
who used her influence over the king to this end.

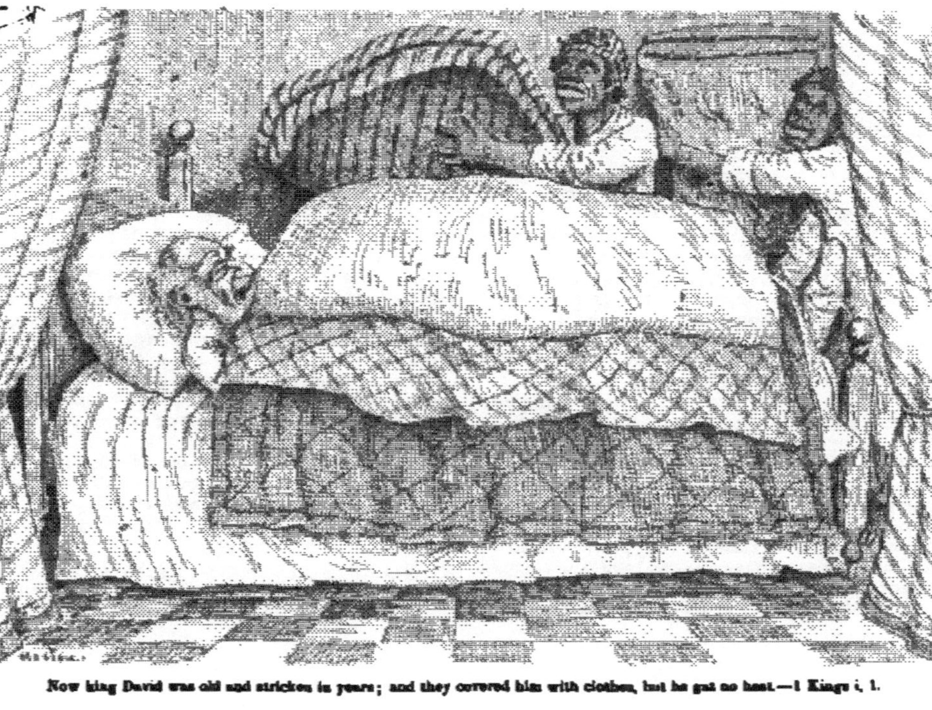

Now king David was old and stricken in years; and they covered him with clothes, but he gat no heat.—1 Kings i. 1.

CHAPTER XXIII.

SOME STORIES FROM THE BOOK OF KINGS.

One day a prophet of Jehovah, incensed that King Jeroboam had taken his custom from him and his master to the shops of the other gods across the way, rushed into one of the aforesaid shops and cried, "O altar, altar, thus saith the Lord; Behold a child shall be born unto the house of David, Josiah by name; and upon thee shall he offer the priests of the high places that burn incense upon thee, and men's bones shall be burnt upon thee" (1 Kings xiii, 2). This grim announcement that Jehovah was hankering for more of his old dish, human sacrifice, the prophet offered to give immediate proof of, saying, "This is the sign which the Lord hath spoken; Behold, the altar shall be rent, and the ashes that are upon it shall be poured out" (verse 3). The altar obediently gaped; and King Jeroboam's hand which he had stretched forth against the man of God was withered, and restored only at said M. of G.'s intercession. The M. of G. now, we suppose, passed the hat, and collected enough pennies for one legerdemain performance, for he refused the king's request to do more funny things and bundled off for home. The Lord, perhaps being aware of a liability to get fuddled on the part of his servant, had forbidden him to stop to eat or drink. He disobeyed; a lion slew him, and then this beast and a mule waited decorously and peacefully till men came, who buried him in this foreign land.

The cities of Samaria, spoken of in the tale, were at that time—Jeroboam's reign—so far from being at the head of the kingdom that they were not even in existence.

Oort and Hooykaas make this guess at the origin of the legend: "Our story was evidently attached to a certain grave in Bethel, known as the grave of the man of God from Judah. Why had not the prophet whose bones lay there been allowed to rest in his own family sepulcher? The legend answered that he owed his fate to his disobedience, and then wove around this central thought the motley garment which now clothes it."

And when he was gone a lion met him by the way, and slew him; and his carcase was cast in the way, and the ass stood by it, the lion also stood by the carcase.—1 Kings xiii, 24.

The texts opposite are irreconcilably contradictory.

Other self-contradictions contained in God's one attempt in the literary profession, are as follows. This same Asa is said in one place to have had war with Baasha all his days, and in another to have begun this war only in the thirty-fifth year of his reign. Thus: "In the third year of Asa, king of Judah, began Baasha . . . to reign over all Israel, . . . twenty and four years. . . . And there was war between Asa [king of Judah] and Baasha king of Israel all their days" (1 Kings xv, 83, 32). On the other hand "there was no more war until the five and thirtieth year of the reign of Asa. . . . At that time Hanani the seer came to Asa, king of Judah, and said unto him, Because thou hast relied on the king of Syria, and not relied on the Lord, . . . therefore from henceforth thou shalt have wars" (2 Chron. xv, 19; xvi, 7, 9). Another event about which we are given two accounts is the death of this Baasha. In one place we learn that he died in the twenty-sixth year of Asa, but our chances of salvation—consequent on right belief—are just halved when we meet elsewhere the statement that he was alive in Asa's thirty-sixth year. Thus: "Baasha slept with his fathers, . . . and Elah, his son, reigned in his stead. . . . In the twenty and sixth year of Asa, king of Judah, began Elah, the son of Baasha, to reign over Israel" (1 Kings xvi, 6, 8). But "in the sixth and thirtieth year of the reign of Asa, Baasha king of Israel came up against Judah" (2 Chron. xvi, 1).

To give good measure, we will throw in a few more self-contradictions from Kings and Chronicles. They are so abundant in the inspired book as to be very cheap and enable us to do so at little cost. Compare:—1 Kings iv, 26, and 2 Chron. ix, 25. 1 Kings v, 16, and 2 Chron. 11, 18. 1 Kings vii, 13, 14, and 2 Chron. ii, 14. 1 Kings vii, 15, and 2 Chron. iii, 15. 1 Kings vii, 23, 26, and 2 Chron. iv, 2, 5.

SEARCH THE SCRIPTURES.

CHAPTER XXIV.

ADVENTURES OF THE PROPHETS.

No reader will complain of any falling off in the interest of our narrative when he finds us opening this chapter with a conflict between two gods. He must have learned already in the course of our history that these beings were creatures of uncommon strength and prowess, excelling in these qualities certainly the run of men, and perhaps even our very greatest athletes and the giants of old. So when he hears that two of these individuals had been brawling and raising street rows all over the land for some time, and were now approaching a close and conclusive encounter, he will know that he is to meet a tale that will be no small potatoes. To add to the interest that every sporting man, and indeed every other, must feel in these happenings, the two gods who are pitted against each other are none less than Jehovah and Baal, well known as among the very gamest of their species.

Jehovah one day sent one of his adherents to King Ahab, the chief backer of his rival Baal, to issue this challenge or threat: "As the Lord God of Israel liveth, before whom I stand, there shall not be dew nor rain these years, but according to my word" (1 Kings xvii, 1). When Elijah—which was the name of this adherent of Jehovah—uttered this menace, King Ahab, who had read in histories of the French Revolution Marie Antoinette's saying when told that the people had no bread, "Then let them eat cake," put off the threat with a joke modeled on that remark, "Well, 'Lije, if we don't get water I s'pose we'll have to fall back on beer." Elijah replied only with the venomous look of a deacon sent to threaten law to a Freethinker working on Sunday, and departed. "And the word of the Lord came unto him" (1 Kings xvii, 2). How this word came is not stated. Perhaps it walked up to him like "the voice of the Lord God walking in the garden in the cool of the day" (Gen. iii, 8). Or maybe this word, or voice, as there was occasion for promptness, came hurrying up horseback or assback, or drove up in a chariot or an ox-cart. But let voices and words choose whatever form of traveling they will, we must go on with our story. This word directed Elijah as follows: "Get thee hence, and turn thee east-

And the ravens brought him bread and flesh in the morning, and bread and flesh in the evening: and he drank of the brook.—} Kings xvii, 6.

ward, and hide thyself by the brook Cherith, that is before Jordan. And it shall be, that thou shalt drink of the brook; and I have commanded the ravens to feed thee there" (1 Kings xvii, 3, 4). The man of God, who had grown dainty in his tastes during a long subsistence on the yellow-legged chickens of his parishioners' wives, felt like murmuring some doubts of the satisfactory capacity of ravens in the catering business, but perforce repressed his discontent, and betook himself to a cave in the appointed locality. Here, he found, God had conveyed a company of trained ravens, who, with troupes of performing dogs, educated cats, fortune-telling white mice, etc., had once constituted an animal circus exhibited to the natives and winning many shekels. With a little trouble he was able to send these creatures on foraging expeditions and subsist on their inbringings. "The ravens brought him," says xvii, 6, "bread and flesh in the morning"—and, we suppose, flesh and bread "in the evening," thus affording him quite a variety.

"I 'clar ter goodness," cried Deacon Mokeby in his neighbor's melon patch at night, "I 'clar ter goodness ef I an't tempted to backslide.

Here I've prayed fo' four nights, right erlong, for dis ter be er dark night, an' dar's dat moon comin' up as big as life." Alas, it now becomes our duty to chronicle a similar disappointment which betided our prophet who had trusted to his Lord. The Lord's means gave out! "And it came to pass after a while, that the brook dried up, because there had been no rain in the land" (xvii, 7). Poor Elijah now began to regret that he had not looked out for himself instead of depending on Jehovah. A modern preacher one morning announced, "I have forgotten my notes and shall have to trust to Providence, but this evening I will come better prepared," and then wondered what his congregation laughed at. Elijah was feeling very much like expressing similar sentiments in earnest, and things had come to a dreadful crisis, when on a sudden who should come knocking at the door but his old friend the Word, or Voice? "Saved! saved!" cried Elijah and the ravens melodramatically, and in rushed the noble Word and grasped their hands—we mean, Elijah's hands—in hearty friendship. After relating the news of the day to the secluded man of God and handing him for perusal some war extras giving

And as he lay and slept under a juniper-tree, behold, then an angel touched him, and said unto him, Arise and eat. And he looked, and, behold, there was a cake baken on the coals, and a cruse of water at his head. And he did eat and drink, and laid him down again —1 Kings xix, 5, 6.

full particulars of the conflict between the infuriated gods which was desolating the land, the Word issued this instruction: "Arise, get thee to Zarephath, which belongeth to Zidon, and dwell there: behold, I have commanded a widow woman there to sustain thee" (xvii, 9). At this the prophet's face fell disappointedly, and he exclaimed in disgust, "Pshaw, pshaw, is that the best von can get up? That trick's as old as the hills! Why, isn't that the way I and the rest of the prophets have been living all our lives—on the widows and wives till they couldn't keep us any longer?—and that's why I'm here!" The Voice in some resentment returned that Elijah must put up with what was supplied him—that the Lord was no Delmonico—that there was no use putting on frills and wanting gilt-edged fare when half the land was starving and those not famishing were being trodden out of existence under the ramps and sallies of the belligerent gods. Besides, added the Voice, there was more in this than Elijah supposed— let him just go to the widow's and ask for food and something would happen that would surprise and please him. Elijah consented, and set off.

We may pause to amuse ourselves with some remarks of the learned pious on the foregoing. One reverend thinks it noticeable that when the Brook & Raven Purveying Co. broke down in their contract to nourish Elijah, "we do not find him taking one step for his own preservation, till the God whom he served said," etc. "Encouraged by past experience of his Heavenly father's care of him, the prophet still waited patiently till he said," etc. This behavior of Elijah's scarcely needed remark; it is the custom of his kind never to lift a finger in their own support but to throw the burden of their maintenance entirely on others—widows or else. Then, the ravens have been the subject of vast conjecture. Some commentators, availing themselves of the fact that *orebim*, which we translate *ravens*, means in Ezek. xxvii, 27, *merchants*, have tried to explain away the miraculous character of God's preservation of his servant at Cherith. Others again have thought that the original signifies *Arabians*, as in 2 Chron. xxi, 16; Neh. iv, 7; where the like word is used; or possibly the inhabitants of the city of Arabah, near Bethshan (Josh. xv, 6, and xviii, 18, etc.). But against these undoers of the miracle Kitto's

And he said, Go forth, and stand upon the mount before the Lord. And, behold, the Lord passed by, and a great and strong wind rent the mountains, and brake in pieces the rocks, before the Lord; but the Lord was not in the wind; and after the wind an earthquake; but the Lord was not in the earthquake; and after the earthquake a fire; but the Lord was not in the fire; and after the fire a still small voice. And it was so, when Elijah heard it, that he wrapped his face in his mantle and went out, and stood in the entering in of the cave. And, behold, there came a voice unto him and said, What doest thou here, Elijah?—1 Kings xix, 11, 12, 13.

Biblical Cyclopedia takes a stand thus: "In the face of such opinions as these, we still believe that ravens and not men were the instruments which God, on this occasion, employed to carry needful food to his exiled and persecuted servant; and in this he would give us a manifest proof of His sovereignty over all creatures." This remark we are willing to treat with some consideration. Certainly if God has sovereignty over ravens the same as over other creatures, and this has been denied—as it seems from the above language—then it is right that he should demonstrate that he is no half-way God but has dominion over those birds as well as over the rest of the animal kingdom. The Cyclopedia continues to exercise its devout brains thus: "But it has been inquired, how could these birds obtain food of a proper kind, and of a sufficient quantity, to supply the daily wants of the prophet? The answer to this inquiry, is very simple. We cannot tell. It is enough for us to know that God engaged to make a provision for him, and that he failed not to fulfill his engagement." If not "enough," it at any rate is worth learning, that when God had "engaged to make a provision for" Elijah "he

374

failed not to fulfill his engagement." Nothing is more highly regarded in these days than commercial probity. One rumor of a failure of a merchant to meet his engagements sometimes works great harm; and as there have already been more reports of that nature against Jehovah than could be wished, we think that if in this case he really furnished goods as per sample, date, and other stipulations, the fact should be put beyond doubt.

We do not see any further brilliant theories of that very sensible and useful class, the commentators, that we care to copy, except perhaps one regarding Elijah himself. On his origin and nature there has been much speculation. Most writers wonder at the silence of scripture on his parentage and birth. He is introduced, thinks Rev. J. Doran, LL.D., Secretary of the Church Missionary Society, "as if he had dropped out of that cloudy chariot which, after his work was done on earth, conveyed him to heaven." Some rabbis have deemed him to be *Phineas*, the grandson of Aaron; and these have had to wrangle fiercely with others who thought him an *angel* who for the purpose of reforming King Ahab put on the form of man. But then,

And Elijah took his mantle, and wrapped it together, and smote the waters, and they were divided hither and thither; so that they two went over on dry ground.—2 Kings 2, 8.

all priests and prophets are angels, for did not the Scotch clergy so inform us, and make us say yes to it too, when in the zenith of their power? Did not Durham write: "Ministers are called Angels, because they are God's Messengers, intrusted by him with a high and heavenly employment; and it is a title that should put Ministers in mind of their duty, to o God's will on earth as the angels do it in eaven; . . . and it should put people in mind of their duty, to take this word off Ministers' hands, as from Angels. . . . Therefore are Angels called Ministers; and Ministers, Angels." And as for one of the clergy, he is nothing less than Christ himself—we refer to Mr. Pecci, a gentleman of Rome. So we see no need of all this argument to show that Elijah was, as all our ministers are, a thoroughly angelic creature.

Elijah found the widow designated to possess but a scanty bit of oil and meal, but he encouraged her to use that for him, saying, "Thus saith the Lord God of Israel, The barrel of meal shall not waste, neither shall the cruse of oil fail, until the day that the Lord sendeth rain upon the earth" (1 Kings xvii, 14).

So they ate "many days," and "the barrel of meal wasted not, neither did the cruse of oil fail." This was accomplished by Elijah by means of false bottoms which he had inserted in the receptacles of the meal and the oil, through which he supplied them continuously from a store of those commodities that the Lord had had secreted for him in the neighborhood. He had learned this trick from Chaldean and Egyptian priests, who used it among the many legerdemain contrivances with which they fooled the masses. Some, to be sure, suppose this story of the widow's mite being returned to her manifold because given to the clergy, to have been got up by that class to incite imitation.

Elijah's next maneuver to gain the fame of a miracle-worker was to slip a narcotic in the dish of the widow's son, who therefrom became as dead. The widow blamed Elijah for this supposed death, though believing it to have been brought about in a far different way. "What have I to do with thee, O thou man of God!" she cried; "art thou come unto me to call my sin to remembrance, and slay my son?" What she meant by her words about calling

And it came to pass, as they still went on, and talked, that, behold, there appeared a chariot of fire, and horses of fire, and parted them both asunder; and Elijah went up by a whirlwind into heaven.—2 Kings ii, 11.

her "sin to remembrance," is thus explained by commentators: "The presence of so holy a man might well bring Yahweh's wrath upon a sinful mortal whose unrighteousness was now forced upon his attention." That is, God would not have become aware of the widow's unrighteousness only that in his glances at his prophet he finally chanced to find her in his line of vision, and discovered her unworthiness. This information comes as very timely instruction to Infidels. If those hardened creatures *will* go on in their blasphemous courses, they will at least, if they have any prudence, be as quiet in so doing as possible, and thereby they may escape divine detection. They will find it advisable, we should say, to exhibit their Freethought books and papers only at night and in a close room and to but one or two friends. Their irreverent remarks should be made in low tones, with a careful avoidance of those loud and obstreperous notes which might easily catch the ear of God if he should chance to be passing. And they should eschew all special places of God's attention, such as churches, the neighborhood of holy men, etc.—not forgetting barber-shops

and the vicinity of sparrows, where the deity is always hanging around counting and so on.

When the operation of the narcotic on the widow's son was about over, Elijah pretended to restore him to life miraculously.

Another pretended miracle brought about by the same sort of means was the ignition of a sacrificial pile by fire supposed to be sent from heaven, but really produced by chemicals. Baal and his priests had just failed to do this trick, and when Jehovah's champion succeeded he raised a cry against the defeated god and incited the people, "Take the prophets of Baal; let not one of them escape." So the people seized Baal's priests and "Elijah brought them down to the brook Kishon, and slew them there" (1 Kings xviii, 40). The Baalists, however, regained the upper hand and drove the bloodthirsty trickster to the deserts and caves. Here he was fed by an angelic Diddy, depicted on page 371, and held another conversation with the Voice, as on page 373. Father, forgive the artist for putting the frog in the picture—he knows not what he does.

After some further adventures the wily man of God, first having taken out a heavy insur-

And he went up from thence unto Beth-el:" and as he was going up by the way, there came forth little children out of the city, and mocked him, and said unto him, Go up, thou bald head; go up, thou bald head. And he turned back, and looked on them, and cursed them in the name of the Lord. And there came forth two she bears out of the wood, and tare forty and two children of them.—1 Kings ii. 23. 24.

ance policy, went off into the country with Elisha and never returned. Elisha had been instructed to say that his friend had been taken to heaven in a fiery chariot, and he told this yarn accordingly, but of course Elijah had merely gone off to Canada, whence he sent for his family when they had got the insurance money, and lived in affluence to a respected and pious old age. He had turned his mantle over to Elisha, and this gentleman now filled his place as chief prophet, fanatic, and bigot to the Jewish people.

One day Elisha was mocked by some children, who cried, "Go up, thou baldhead!" meaning up to heaven like Elijah. In our benighted ignorance of true morals some of us might favor a milder way of dealing with such children than putting them to death. But Elisha kindly furnished us with an example to follow in these cases, by cursing the thoughtless young offenders. And, triumphantly writes a pious commentator, "the inhabitants of Beth-el were to know, from bitter experience, that to dishonor God's prophets was to dishonor himself; for . . . God, who never wants for instruments to accomplish his purposes, caused two she-bears to emerge from a neighboring wood, and destroy the young delinquents."

Elisha got so into the habit of working miracles that he did not give up that custom at death, but when lying in his grave in the seemingly unpowerful shape of a few bones performed the great feat to be seen on page 381.

And Elisha died, and they buried him. And the bands of the Moabites invaded the land at the coming in of the year. And it came to pass, as they were burying a man, that, behold, they spied a band of men; and they cast the man into the sepulchre of Elisha: and when the man was let down, and touched the bones of Elisha, he revived and stood up on his feet.—2 Kings xiii, 20, 21.

CHAPTER XXV.

JONAH THE TRUTHFUL SAILOR

Among all the stories to be found in our collection of wonderful tales, probably none has oftener been referred to than the one giving an account of Jonah and the whale. Fishermen, like sailors, have from time immemorial been noted as great story-tellers. Their yarns and adventures have been so incredible that they have passed into a proverb. To such extent has it been thought that fishermen's and sailors' stories are extremely apocryphal, that where an incredible tale or impossible yarn has been spun that nobody could believe, it has, by common consent, been denominated "fishy," or a "fish story." Among this large class of stories, that of Jonah and the whale stands preëminent, the fishiest of all. Yet we are still required to believe it, and it is still, Sunday after Sunday, preached from the pulpit, because it is bound up in the holy book which we are repeatedly assured contains the truth, the whole truth, and nothing but the truth

Our hero is first introduced to us as a

prophet. We are told that the word of the Lord came unto Jonah, saying, "Arise, go to Nineveh, that great city, and cry out against it." This was one of the very few cases where the God of the Jews seemed to take the slightest interest in the people of heathen nations; the Jews appearing to occupy all his time and attention. He was not only wholly indifferent as to the good of the nations that were not Jews, but he seemed ever to be plotting against them, venting his spite upon them and continually aiding his special people to slaughter them. But in this case the wickedness of Nineveh troubled him greatly, and he made an unusual effort to reclaim it.

Jonah seemed to be a disobedient prophet, much like the ungoverned children in this age of the world who when told to do a certain thing do directly the opposite. Thus Jonah instead of going to Nineveh started for Tarshish where he could get away from the presence of the Lord. Where in the world Tarshish is, or was, no geographer has been able to determine, but wherever it was, God seems not to have visited it, for by going there Jonah was to escape his presence. The prophet proceeded to Joppa,

Now the word of the Lord came unto Jonah, saying, Arise, go to Nineveh. But Jonah arose up to flee unto Tarshish, and he found a ship going to Tarshish; so he paid the fare thereof and went down into it.—Jonah i, 1–3.

where he took passage on a boat in the Joppa
and Tarshish line, and paid his fare like a man.
In this particular we place him ahead of the
prophets and priests of our own time; when
they travel by boat or by rail they either want
to go at half-price or be deadheaded through.
Jonah was no deadhead.

He was destined, however, to have an unpleasant voyage, for the Lord sent a great wind
and brought on a mighty tempest so that the
ship was in danger of being wrecked, and the
sailors became alarmed.

Jonah "went down into the side of the ship"
and went fast asleep while all this commotion
and terror prevailed around him. He must
have been a man of remarkable equanimity of
mind. It proves, at all events, that his conscience, for trying to get away from the presence of the Lord, did not trouble him severely.
The captain of the vessel, however, in his great
fear, hunted around and found Jonah and
waked him up, and asked him what he meant,
sleeping at such a time, and said that he ought
to be awake, crying to God to save them from
destruction. After the sailors had been some
time engaged in throwing overboard such

freight and luggage as would lighten the vessel,
they concluded to cast lots to see which man
among them had caused this terrible storm—
as though a man could cause it, and as though
casting lots would indicate with any certainty
which man it was. As well might we now try
murderers, thieves, incendiaries, perjurers, and
adulterers by drawing straws, throwing dice,
playing cards, or flipping pennies. It would be
merely gambling to ascertain whether a man
was guilty or not.

Of course the lot fell upon our poor Jonah;
the story could not have otherwise run in the
right channel and the grand *denouement* could
not have been as desired by the writer.

When the court which tried Jonah and found
him guilty inquired of him what punishment
should be executed upon him, he answered:
"Take me up and cast me into the sea." They
cast him into the sea and it immediately became very calm. He was the oil cast upon the
troubled waters, and his being thrown into the
surging billows seems to have had a very paci-
fying effect upon God, and he calmed the winds
and stilled the waters at once.

A big fish, which providentially happened to

And they said every one to his fellow, Come and let us cast lots, that we may know for whose cause this evil is upon us. So they cast lots and the lot fell upon Jonah.—Jonah i, 7.

be on the spot, " took the stranger in " out of the wet, where he could finish his nap at his leisure. As Jonah had such a happy faculty of adapting himself to surrounding circumstances, it may be supposed that his new berth was just to his taste. It was *snug* at all events.

The book of Jonah does not inform us what kind of a fish it was that took charge of the prophet; but Jesus afterward said that it was a whale; and the original story says that God prepared the fish for the purpose. If it was a whale, he must have *prepared* him, for the naturalists inform us that the true whale can not take anything into its mouth and swallow it larger than four inches through. God must have "prepared" the mouth and throat of that particular whale pretty extensively by stretching it and enlarging it, to enable him to swallow a man at a gulp. A shark could soon dispatch a prophet, but would chew him up pretty badly first, and it is to be feared that in such a case, even with God's help, the man would not be of much use three days afterward.

It may be imagined that though Jonah landed safely in the stomach of the fish, it would be difficult for him to find air enough there to sustain him for three days. If the fish had kept his mouth and throat constantly open, so as to let air in, it would not have answered, for the water would also have rushed in and drowned the poor prophet at last. How he obtained air to breathe, and to enable him to keep up a three days' cry to God, is not satisfactorily explained. A rubber hose extending from the fish's stomach to the open air above the surface of the water, after the plan of a diving-bell, would have been very convenient, but we have no right to suppose that God provided such an apparatus.

Notwithstanding the extreme improbability of this fish story, it is amusing to see how easy it is for our Christian friends to believe it. It does not stagger them at all. If the book had said that Jonah had swallowed the whale, or half a dozen of them, for that matter, they could easily swallow it, Jonah, whales, and all.

Fishes have astonishing digestive powers, and whatever is taken into their stomachs is usually digested in a short time. Under this state of things it is a marvel how Jonah could have for three days escaped the strong digestive functions of that big fish. He must have

Now the Lord had prepared a great fish to swallow up Jonah.—Jonah i, 12

been tough, or the Lord must have "prepared" the fish's stomach, as he had previously "prepared" its mouth and gullet. Fish, also, are a hungry, voracious race, and as this big fish did not digest Jonah, and had no room for any other food for three days, he must naturally have become very hungry. And Jonah, too, poor fellow, getting nothing to eat for over three days, must have become quite hungry also. Probably God "prepared" Jonah so that the fish could not digest him, and "prepared" the fish so that he should not become too hungry, and "prepared" Jonah's stomach likewise and for the same purpose. This was, by the way, considerable of an enterprise, the Lord took upon himself on that occasion. There were several points to which he had to direct his attention. As an experiment or an adventure, it was probably quite amusing to him.

We are glad to be informed that after God had punished Jonah until he was satisfied, for the disobedience indulged in, he just spoke to the fish, and his words immediately acted as an emetic, and caused the fish to throw up Jonah on dry land, as good as ever. This experience

was of much value to the prophet and he proceeded without delay to do the missionary work allotted to him. He went to the exceeding great city of Nineveh which was three days' journey across, and cried out, "Yet in forty days and Nineveh shall be overthrown." His prophecy seems to have had a marvelous effect, and the king issued orders that neither man nor beast should eat or drink anything, and that they should all be covered with sackcloth.

A few points to wonder at arise in connection with this subject:

Why should the Ninevites, who worshiped Baal, and who had never heard of Jehovah, become so greatly frightened when Jonah visited them, that they should so readily abandon their own God and accept Jonah's? It was certainly the most effectual missionary work ever accomplished. Nowadays it takes several missionaries, several thousands of dollars, and sometimes a year's time, to convert a single heathen, and he often doesn't stay converted; but here this one man Jonah converted a large, populous city in a short time.

Why should the beasts also be covered with

And Jonah was in the belly of the fish three days and three nights.—Jonah i, 17.

sackcloth? Had they offended God, that they should repent before him?

How could life be sustained if the people and the beasts were forbidden to eat or drink? What harm could there be in horses and asses taking food?

Many such questions will arise in the minds of the skeptical and those of little faith, but your true believer takes it all in without a question or a doubt. "Blessed are they who believe all they are told, they shall always be easily imposed upon."

The Ninevites quit their evil ways, and God changed his mind about destroying them. But this course of God's made Jonah very angry. After he had prophesied that the city should be destroyed, he wanted the destruction to come without failure or postponement on account of the weather, or any other reason, and rather than that the people should not be destroyed he preferred to die himself. He retired from the city and made a booth on the east side, where he could see if God would do what he had agreed to do.

The Lord seemed to take a little pity on Jonah and caused a gourd to grow up in a single night so as to shade the disappointed prophet, but even in this he changed his mind again, for as soon as he found that Jonah was exceedingly glad of the gourd, he "prepared" a worm to eat it and to make it wither and die.

The finale of this fish story is well known. Nineveh was not destroyed.

What became of Jonah we are not told. Our opinion is that after that adventure he kept away from the water. If another fish got him and swallowed him, we have no account that it vomited him up, and it is more than probable that his body, or portions of it, became, like this story, fish, fishy.

The principal use made by our Christian friends of this remarkable fish story, is, that it was a grand symbol of a prototype of the death, burial, and resurrection of the savior. The quotation from Matthew (xii, 40) is well remembered, where Jesus says, "For as Jonas was three days and three nights in the whale's belly; so shall the son of man be three days and three nights in the heart of the earth." But here again is a slight discrepancy—Jesus, according to the record, was not three days and three nights in the heart of the earth. He

And the Lord spake unto the fish, and it vomited out Jonah upon the dry land.—Jonah ii, 10.

was placed in the tomb on Friday night, and Sunday morning he was up bright and early, in good time for breakfast—only one day and two nights, the most that can be made of it. Thus his own words were proved untrue. It is barely possible, however, that he found the heart of the earth so uncomfortably hot, that he did not wish to stay there his time out. Scientists assure us that the center of the earth is hotter than any furnace that can be conceived of. If this is so—and it seems very probable—it would not be a very comfortable place for a God to stay in for three days and nights.

That the story of Jonah is an allegory, and that it, as well as that of Saktideva, Hercules, and the rest, are simply different versions of the same myth, the significance of which is the alternate swallowing up and casting forth of day, or the sun, by night, is now believed by many scholars. The day, or the sun, is swallowed up by night, to be set free again at dawn, and from time to time suffers a like but shorter durance in the maw of the eclipse and the storm-cloud.

Professor Goldzhier says:

"The most prominent mythical characteristic of the story of Jonah is his celebrated abode in the sea in the belly of a whale. This trait is eminently solar. . . . As on occasion of the storm the storm-dragon or the storm-serpent swallows the sun, so when he sets, he (Jonah, as a personification of the sun) is swallowed by a mighty fish, waiting for him at the bottom of the sea. Then, when he appears again on the horizon, he is spit out on the shore by the sea-monster."

The sun was called Jona, as appears from Gruter's inscriptions, and other sources.

In the Vedas—the four sacred books of the Hindoos—when day and night, sun and darkness, are opposed to each other, the one is designated red, the other black.

The red sun being swallowed up by the dark earth at night—as it apparently is when it sets in the west—to be cast forth again at day, is also illustrated in like manner. Jonah, Hercules, and others personify the sun, and a huge fish represents the earth. The earth represented as a huge fish is one of the most prominent ideas of the Polynesian mythology.

At other times, instead of a fish, we have a

So Jonah arose, and went unto Nineveh, according to the word of the Lord.—Jonah iii. 3.

great raving wolf, who comes to devour its victim and extinguish the sunlight. The wolf is particularly distinguished in ancient Scandinavian mythology, being employed as an emblem of the destroying power, which attempts to destroy the sun. This is illustrated in the story of Little *Red* Riding-Hood (the sun) who is devoured by the great black wolf (night) and afterward comes out unhurt.

The story of Little Red Riding-Hood is mutilated in the English version. The original story was that the little maid, in her shining red cloak, was swallowed by the great black wolf, and that she came out safe and sound when the hunters cut open the sleeping beast.

In regard to these heroes remaining three days and three nights in the bowels of the fish, they represent the sun at the winter solstice. From December 22d to the 25th—that is, for three days and three nights—the sun remains in the lowest regions, in the bowels of the earth, in the belly of the fish; it is then cast forth and renews its career.

Thus, we see that the story of Jonah being swallowed by a big fish, meant originally the sun swallowed up by night, and that it is identical with the well-known nursery-tale. How such legends are transformed from intelligible into unintelligible myths is very clearly illustrated by Prof. Max Müller, who, in speaking of "the comparison of the different forms of Aryan Religion and Mythology," in India, Persia, Greece, Italy, and Germany, says:

"In each of these nations there was a tendency to change the original conception of divine powers: to misunderstand the many names given to these powers, and to misinterpret the praises addressed to them. In this manner some of the divine names were changed into half-divine, half-human heroes, and at last the myths which were true and intelligible as told originally of the sun, or the dawn, or the storms, were turned into legends or fables too marvelous to be believed of common mortals. This process can be watched in India, in Greece, and in Germany. The same story, or nearly the same, is told of gods, of heroes, and of men. The divine myth became an heroic legend, and the heroic legend fades away into a nursery tale. Our nursery tales have well been called the modern patois of the ancient sacred mythology of the Aryan race."

And the Lord God prepared a gourd, and made it to come up over Jonah. . . . But God prepared a worm, . . . and it smote the gourd that it withered. . . . And the sun beat upon the head of Jonah, that he fainted and wished himself to die, and said, It is better for me to die than to live — Jonah iv, 6ff. — — The book of Jonah leaves its hero under this withered gourd talking to God. History saith not what became of him, and neither can we.